THE BENEFIT OF HINDSIGHT

The Benefit Of Hindsight

A Simon Serrailler Case

Susan Hill

Chatto & Windus
LONDON

1 3 5 7 9 10 8 6 4 2

Chatto & Windus, an imprint of Vintage,
20 Vauxhall Bridge Road,
London SW1V 2SA

Chatto & Windus is part of the Penguin Random House group of companies
whose addresses can be found at global.penguinrandomhouse.com.

Penguin
Random House
UK

First published in the United Kingdom by Chatto & Windus in 2019

penguin.co.uk/vintage

'Morning Has Broken' by Eleanor Farjeon © The Miss E Farjeon Will Trust
from *The Children's Bells*, published by Oxford University Press by kind
permission of David Higham Associates

A CIP catalogue record for this book is available from the British Library

HB ISBN 9781784742782
TPB ISBN 9781784742799

Typeset in 11/14 pt Palatino LT Std
by Integra Software Services Pvt. Ltd, Pondicherry

Printed and bound in Great Britain by Clays Ltd, Elcograf S.p.A.

Penguin Random House is committed to a sustainable future for
our business, our readers and our planet. This book is made
from Forest Stewardship Council® certified paper.

FSC
www.fsc.org

MIX
Paper from
responsible sources
FSC® C018179

For
Dedda and Bratto,
Book Rearrangers Par Excellence

One

Carrie wanted to stay out longer. She had nothing else to do but she did not want to go home. She had come out of the newsagent's in a churn of anxiety about what she had found out, what was happening, and until she had processed it in her head, she could not walk into the house and face Colin.

There were cafes on either side, new and smart, old and comfortable, but all full. Someone bumped into her, someone else almost tripped her up. A man sat in a doorway on a piece of old matting, with a dog and a mug of coppers, and spat on the pavement. Her hair was damp from the drizzle, as were the sleeves of her coat and the handles of her tote bag.

She felt a surge of panic, and the need to move, to get away, though it was herself she really wanted to get away from. She went down the side street towards the cathedral, past the great west door and into the new visitors' centre which had opened just before Christmas, to equal choruses of delight and disapproval. It was cool and beautiful there, a calm place, like the ancient cathedral itself, and there were only a few people in the refectory. Carrie got her pot of tea and a cheese scone, and went to the far end of the cafe, beside a glass wall through which she could see the tiled space beyond. She closed her eyes. She did not come to the cathedral to pray, she had no particular belief, though sometimes she spoke aloud to someone, someone who might be listening, and if there was no one and she was only talking to herself, it still helped.

Perhaps she would not have to tell him, she thought, spreading butter on her scone, perhaps he would work it out for himself. No. Colin was incapable of working anything out except the figures he saw on his computer screen from early morning until late at night, the white electronic arrows moving up and down.

A woman came into the refectory, took a tray, gave her order, the sort of woman who usually came in here, a volunteer who manned the shop, or sat behind the new glass counter giving out information and leaflets, or arranged the flowers. No, not flowers, Carrie remembered that the flower arrangers came in as a group, three or four of them, clattering their trays and talking cheerily. A lot of the people who helped out in the cathedral and this visitors' centre were cheery.

She pushed some crumbs around her plate with her forefinger, and pressed them together to form a ball.

Then the swing doors opened again and there was bumping and shuffling and voices. Two young women with pushchairs. They came down the aisle towards her, and settled down at a table with a lot of fuss and chat and coat removing and chair scraping. The refectory was noisy because all the surfaces were hard. No one had thought of that. Every cup and saucer clattered, cutlery clashed, the sudden noise of the coffee machine muffled speech.

She came here for peace and quiet, a place where she could be safely herself, and sooner or later people and their racket always drove her away.

One woman had gone to the counter, the other sat with the children. A baby was on her lap, its arms jerking up and down like the arms of a string puppet, not yet within its control. Carrie did not want to look at it. She looked at it.

And then she saw the other child. It had not been taken out of its pushchair and it was turned slightly to face Carrie. She did not know how old it might be, only that it was not a baby. Children like that could be any age.

Children like that. It was still but not asleep. Its lolling head was too large and it wore a bib into which it was dribbling. Its eyes did not focus. Its face was the colour of dough.

2

The woman was bringing over the tray of drinks and as she set it down on their table she looked at the child and her face broke into a smile and seemed to blaze up at the sight, as if she had been bathed in sunshine. The look was joyous, a look of delight. But most of all, a look of love, unconcealed, all-absorbing.

The child saw nothing, only moved its head a little, as it dribbled and its eyes rolled up and round and up again.

Carrie left, almost knocking over her chair, startling the baby on the lap. But the child in the buggy was not startled. It seemed to be unaware of every sound, every movement around it, every person.

Outside she leaned on a pillar and felt her heart race and lurch and her mind spin and nausea rise up in her, like a creature springing out of water deep down, and she retched, but nothing came out of her mouth except an ugly sound, so that a man walking past flinched slightly, before quickening his step. She took in gulps of air which tasted of rain.

Somehow she had to find her car and drive home and, eventually, talk to Colin, tell Colin, make Colin angry or shocked or miserable. Frightened, perhaps, as she was. Her fear was deep-rooted and powerful. It was absolute, certain, real, the fear of her worst nightmares and waking terror. A fear that was growing inside her.

She had plenty of time to think about what she was going to say. She made shepherd's pie with three vegetables, peeling, chopping, mashing, making gravy, process after process which was soothing. She baked apples, stuffing the cores with brown sugar, raisins and ginger, which took more preparation, so that she would be even calmer. But of course it was no help at all, she did everything slowly, mechanically, and all the time the lines she had to speak were being rehearsed in her head, over and over again, and with them came the questions – what would he say, how would he react, would he be silent or angry, shocked or irritated, or perhaps even disbelieving? No, there would be no reason for that. Why would she lie to him about this of all things?

3

The scene in the cathedral refectory played itself out again too. The two young women. The baby with jerking hands. The one in the pushchair. The way it had been and would be forever, and yet still, the mother had given the child such a look of blazing love. So that could happen? It was possible, was it?

But Carrie could not believe it.

The table was laid and the supper ready when, as he always did, apparently knowing the moment by some sixth sense, Colin came out of his office, where the monitors would sit by themselves, scrolling through their eternal rows of figures, their flashing panels of red or green, occasionally remaining calm for moments, before going into a dance of non-stop manic moves and then a brief panic. She had sometimes gone in and glanced at the three screens and felt panic in turn. It was infectious and yet she did not understand any of it, did not have any idea what the frenzy meant.

'Good?'

'Very good.' Did he know that he rubbed his hands together, like a man in a cartoon about greed? Was it greed, or just satisfaction with his job, a day's decent results? She never knew. The money came in, was stored away somewhere, in more rows of numbers, moved out again, increased, decreased. How much money?

He went into the cloakroom to wash his hands, which was the signal for her to start carrying supper into the dining room.

'Careful, Carrie, it isn't properly on the table mat.'

She shifted the hot dish a millimetre. Colin reset his knife and fork exactly parallel to one another.

'Profitable day?'

'Very. The markets have been going crazy, all over the place.'

'So that's a good thing? I never understand it.'

'You don't have to. It just means I can dip in and out making quick profits and locking them in, making more, locking them in too.'

When she had met him he had been about to leave the City hedge fund he worked for and set up on his own. They had moved out of London and were renting this house until they found one he thought was worth buying. She would have been happy to stay here. She liked it, the house, the garden, the park beyond which belonged to a large estate. But he said it was not an investment. It was pointless, bad financial management, to rent for any length of time.

He ate neatly, taking small mouthfuls. Carrie ate nothing, though she pretended to, even putting food into her mouth, but she could not swallow it because her mouth was already full, of the thing she had to tell him.

'Sorry . . .' She went into the kitchen to get rid of it.

'No bones in shepherd's pie,' Colin said.

Back in the dining room, she sat down again. He had taken four carrots and they were arranged on his plate in order of size, though to her eye there was little difference between them. He was hesitating. Which end should he begin to eat from? Once he had decided, he was committed.

'I'm having a baby,' Carrie said, and the words seemed to blurt out of their own accord. She had not meant to tell him just then.

There was a long and terrible silence while he stared down at his plate and she sat very still and the nausea rose again, filling her mouth.

'The worst is that you didn't tell me and now it's too late.'

Colin had paced round the room like a zoo animal, sat down again without looking at her, paced again, sat down again. Gone into his office to check his screens and come out, shaking his head.

'I can't focus, I can't concentrate, this is all I can think about. Why didn't you tell me when you first found out? We could have done something.'

'I was frightened of what your reaction would be.'

'And now?'

'It was unavoidable.'

'We said we would never have children, I couldn't cope with children and you certainly could not.'

'Why "certainly"? Why do you say that?'

'Because of the way you are with all of this. Because of . . . Listen, when do you have to see a doctor or go to a hospital or something?'

'I don't know. I don't think I can. I'm afraid of what I'll find out. You know that.'

'That's in your head. It isn't fact.'

'It is.'

He paced round the room again. Round and round.

'What are you going to do?'

'Nothing.'

'Yes you are, you're going to have a baby.'

'That. Yes.'

'Dear God, after all we said. You should have been more careful. Why weren't you more careful?'

'You could have had the vasectomy.'

'I trusted you.'

'This is not only me. It's you. It's both of us. I'm not taking all the blame.'

'You have a neurosis, a phobia, whatever, about having a deformed child . . . handicapped – I don't know what one is supposed to call it these days. I simply do not want any child. It isn't going to have problems, it will be fit and healthy and living in the house, and I can't face that.'

'Why? If you believe it will be fit and healthy.'

'Because it will intrude on my life . . . I need to think about this. I need to go away to think about it.'

'Why go away? Why can't you think here?'

'I won't be able to work.'

'Take a break from work.'

He stared at her.

She got up and started to clear away the dishes.

'Leave that. Sit down. We have to decide what to do.'

'Nothing. There's nothing we can do. It's too late for . . . to get rid of it. Far too late.'

'Are you sure about that?'

'I don't think . . . I couldn't do that. Kill a child.'

'But at the beginning . . .'

'This isn't the beginning.'

'No.'

'When will it be born?'

'I'm not sure.'

'All right.' He stood up. 'I'll help you clear the table. I can't go back to work now.'

He came round to her. Put out both his hands. Carrie took them. 'If this is what happens, it happens.'

'I won't be able to cope with a child who isn't right.'

'That's all the nonsense in your head. Forget that.'

'I can't.'

'You can and you will.' His eyes did not flicker away from her face. She had always believed him, believed him when he said she should marry him, that they would work perfectly together, that it was the right thing for her, no one else would ever have married her, plain and awkward as she thought herself to be, she had been amazingly, miraculously lucky really. But she could not believe him about this because it was simply not a question of belief, but of knowledge. She knew the baby had something gravely wrong with it, so that nothing he said to try and reassure her, convince her, could possibly make any difference.

She followed him, with the loaded tray he was carrying, into the kitchen.

Fact was fact.

Two

Tim's train was forty minutes late, which meant that he was not home until well after nine o'clock.

'Sorry, sorry . . .' He shook his raincoat off at the front door and put his wet boots on a wodge of newspaper.

'OK, but there's only so long you can keep liver and bacon before it curls at the edges and goes leathery.'

He went into the kitchen where Ade was putting plates into the warming oven.

'Bloody railways.' Tim gave him a hug and went to the wine cooler.

'No,' Ade said, 'I've opened a bottle of red. It's ready.'

'What can I do then?'

'Sit down. How was the day?'

'Good actually. Boring in parts – the paper about . . . well, you don't want to know, just before eating, but it went on and on and bloody on, and if that's how the guy teaches med students he's putting them off for life. The charisma of a mollusc. But Tiedemanns was brilliant. Worth going just for him. This looks amazing.'

'Just the usual, but thankfully not charred to a cinder. Cheers. Many there?'

'The lecture theatre was packed and people were standing. All to hear Tiedemanns of course. If you knew half of what he has done in his lifetime . . . makes you humble.'

'You've no need to be humble. You've pioneered procedures, you've transformed the surgical aspect—'

Tim spooned creamed potato onto his plate, shaking his head. 'I'm not putting myself down. I'm proud of what I do and have done – and I've got lucky once or twice. But beside Tiedemanns – he's a god, Ade.'

'Making me jealous.'

Tim's sudden, loud laugh made Ade wince, as always.

'Remind me to show you his photo in the conference brochure. This mash is great. What about you today?'

'Bloody models. The girls were great, but the boys –' He made a two-fingered gesture. 'It was only a mid-level fashion mag, I mean not *Vogue* or anything, God knows why they wanted me, but that's fine, I'm cool with that so long as they pay my going rate. I am not cool with boys who act like they're Naomi Campbell only more so. And it was pissing down. But done and dusted and I'm going to Tanzania on Wednesday.'

'Fashion again?'

Ade shook his head. 'Travel. Upcountry – wild animals. Make a change from mad models. Been too much of that lately.'

'I can't remember if you've been before.'

'Not Tanzania. Botswana. But Africa's Africa and I love it.' He smiled across the table and reached out for Tim's hand. 'Wish you could come.'

'I know. Helluva a week though. One day at a conference and my list has been set back too much, though Max is fine – nearly as good a surgeon as me now. Anyway, I don't regret the day, just to hear—'

'Tiedemanns. I got you.'

'How long are you going to Tanzania for?'

The doorbell rang before Ade could reply. They lived in what had once been a farmhouse on the outskirts of Lafferton. The address was Up Starly but the house was almost a mile away from the village, with a view over meadows to the river and a garden, Tim's province, which they had extended by buying another acre when the farm next door had come up for sale. The house was everything Tim had ever wanted or dreamed of – a boy from a Birmingham terrace without a blade of grass or a green tree to be seen, who had fallen in love with the country when he had been fostered for the fifth or sixth time, by a couple who had lived on a farm. They had been efficient, brisk, kind enough, but never loving. They had taught him to work hard and to be polite and thoughtful. He had liked them, even become fond of them, but had fallen in love with the farm, the land and the animals, the whole way of life. He had also been clever and they had not only encouraged but pushed him to do well. 'You don't want to get stuck like us. It's what we are, what we do, but you can do better for yourself, Timothy. You owe it to take every chance sent your way.' Owe it to whom? Them? The parents he had barely met? The other foster families? The social workers? But in the end he had understood that they meant he owed it to himself.

He had gone to medical school and left the farm – and the Nowells had died within a year of one another not long after, so that the nearest he had known to home was gone. He had been left with a passionate ambition, not only to qualify and do well as a doctor, but to earn enough to buy somewhere for himself among fields and trees and birds and creatures. When he had met Ade, who had come to photograph hospital staff for a colour supplement, they had found not only that they wanted to be together but that both longed to live as deep in the country as was consistent with work.

The house they had found, after months of searching and several disappointments, was Ash Farm. Three years and a lot of work later, and it was exactly as they wanted it. They were not rich but both owned some pictures and small sculptures, which combined more easily into a collection than they had expected, given that Ade's taste was for the very modern, and for classic photographic prints, Tim's for rare English porcelain and art nouveau. Their furniture was a mixture of well-designed traditional and Ikea; Tim's baby grand piano and harpsichord were unmatched by anything of Ade's, but he was a serious birdwatcher, with a valuable collection of rare ornithological books. The rugs were another blend, of Habitat and good-quality Persian. Looking around now, Tim felt the familiar sense of deep satisfaction, and of being completely settled.

Ade answered the door. It was pouring with rain and a chill wind blew into the wide hall. The outside light came on, but for moment Ade thought nobody was there. Then a young woman appeared, coat up over her head.

'Hello?'

'I'm so so sorry to bother you but you're the only house, we've walked what feels like miles and your light was on. I'm Beth, this is Ryan . . .'

Ryan was huddled into himself, thin, spectacled, and rain was running off his hair and down his face. He had no coat, only a jacket.

'Our car packed in just as we came out of the last village, I've spent half an hour in the pouring rain trying to get it started but I need to get the AA and my bloody phone's out of battery.'

'And I forgot mine, it's at home on the hall table. Do you think we could just come into the porch and use your phone to ring them? We'll pay for the call, obviously.'

'For heaven's sake – just come in, please. I'm Ade. Take your wet things off . . . the phone is in the kitchen.'

'Who is it?' Tim came to the doorway.

'This is Beth and Ryan . . . sorry, didn't get your last names.'
'Brown.'

'This is so kind of you, it won't take a minute, and then we'll just go back to the car and wait for the AA.'

'No, no, I'll drive you down to it. But listen, come and have a coffee or a drink? Ryan, there's the phone – have you got a number?'

'Yeah, the AA card's in my wallet somewhere. Thanks a lot, thank you.'

'If your lights hadn't been on I think I'd have cried.'

'What can I get you? Sit down, sit down.'

'It's lovely and warm in here. And dry!'

'Where have you come from? Look, please sit and have something.'

'Honestly, don't trouble yourself. As soon as he's sorted the AA we'll be out of here.'

Ryan was talking on the phone now, giving the location and details of the car and what had happened. Tim had gone into his office. Ade made a pot of coffee, put milk on to warm . . . Ade, always sociable.

11

'So, what do you do, Beth?' She had thick dark brown hair, fringed over her forehead, and brilliant blue eyes. It was a striking combination, and although her features were unremarkable, her looks drew attention. Those of her husband did not. Odd how that happened.

'I'm a classroom assistant. Ryan teaches PE. This is a lovely kitchen! Lovely house – I'm envious! Have you lived here long?'

'Nearly three years.'

'It's beautiful. Wish we could afford something like it. What do you do?'

'I'm a photographer – mainly fashion – you know, *Vogue*, *Harper's* – and international travel mags. So I get about. Tim's a doctor.'

'Right. How lovely.'

'Shortbread? I did make it actually, though I'm not much of a baker. Go on, help yourself.'

Ryan had come back to the table. 'Right, they'll be about half an hour – they've actually got a van ten miles away just finishing off another job.'

'Thank goodness for that. So, we can get out of your hair . . . this shortbread's fab – you should definitely make it more often.'

'Ryan – have some?'

'No, you're all right thanks. I'll just go and check if it's still raining.'

'I wonder . . . do you think I could use your loo?' Beth asked.

'Sure – second door on your left off the hall. The light's outside.'

'Such a beautiful place,' she said, returning to the kitchen. 'I love that statue – sculpture, what is it, the one on the hall table?'

'Isn't it charming? I was so lucky with that – got it in a Sotheby's auction when there were some big continental pieces up for sale so no one was taking much notice of it. She's actually a Henry Moore maquette.'

'Just beautiful. Listen, thank you, we should go so we don't miss the AA man.'

'You mustn't do that – I'll take you down to your car.'

'Here's Ryan . . . you're soaked again, Ry. Maybe we'd better let you take us . . . thanks again so much, you've been amazing.'

'What was the matter with you?' Ade said when he got back.

'Nothing. I just wish you wouldn't become bosom buddies with every waif and stray, that's all.'

'You are so bloody STUFFY.'

Three

Half an hour before the end of the film, Fern Monroe and Kelly Jones exchanged glances and, as one, edged their way along the row and escaped from the cinema.

'That was pants.'

'Total. Honestly, you ought to be able to get your money back.'

'What are we going to do now?'

Fern looked at her watch. 'Half eight. Half past EIGHT?'

They had both found themselves recently single, and over tea in the police station canteen one day, had said more or less in the same breath, 'I'm done with men.'

Talking on, they had discovered that they both liked films, football and wine, among many other things. That night had been the start of several trips to the cinema, the next weekend had seen them both in the stands watching Bevham United. They were not alike in all respects but, for now, they enjoyed one another's company. Kelly was a sergeant, Fern a DC. They rarely worked together and almost never talked shop but tonight, settled in the wine bar with glasses of a warming Shiraz which had spicy notes, Fern said, 'How's uniform? You snowed under at the moment?'

'Lot of bad drugs around at the moment so we've had some nasty things happening – kids having to be practically brought back from the dead by A&E. Not saying any drugs are OK but some of these we're seeing are a whole different ball game – ten times stronger, often spliced with dangerous additives. Otherwise, it's the usual – some break-ins, domestics, your usual Friday and Saturday nights, traffic offences. You?'

Fern shook her head. 'Been dead, so it's going back over old records, catching up, clearing out. I'm bored to sobs with it.'

'Don't say that.'

'Kelly, I didn't fight and sweat my way into CID to bring in a duster and polish the desks.'

'Something'll blow up. Always does.'

'Maybe now the boss is back he'll be a magnet for some really offbeat cases we can get our teeth into. If not, it'll be seeing year ones across the zebra.'

'Don't know why you expect Serrailler to attract interesting crimes.'

'Come on, look at his track record.'

'You obviously have.'

'Yes, well.'

'Fern!'

She did not flicker, or rise to the bait.

'OK . . . You want another?'

'No, I've got the car.'

'We're not going home yet – when I've finished this I'm having a virgin mojito. Anyway, what's he really like to work with? I know about his arm and all that obviously.'

'He was bloody lucky.'

Kelly raised an eyebrow.

'No, I realise, of course, losing your arm isn't great, but he very nearly died.'

'Is he gay?'

'Absolutely not. I do know that much.'

'How?'

'Oh, just word around.'

'Has he been married?'

'Not sure. Don't think so.'

'I know he's said to have played the field a bit . . . lots of girlfriends, never settled on one. Makes you wonder what's wrong with him. I bet he is actually gay, just doesn't make it known.'

'There's nothing gay about him.'

Kelly rolled her eyes, and looked over to the passing waitress to order more drinks.

'You hungry? They do good tapas.'

'Yes, OK . . . keep things going.'

'Thing is, Fern, and don't take this the wrong way – and you might not agree with me and I'm not in any way getting at disability—'

'It's only one arm for heaven's sake.'

'Yes. But still . . .'

'They wouldn't have had him back in the force if they'd thought it would make any difference – uniform, yes, maybe, I don't know, but CID, no probs.'

'It's not that. I . . . Oh, never mind. Probably me being weird.'

'Go on.'

'No. Forget it.'

Their waitress came by with the drinks, quickly followed by their tapas, preoccupying them for several minutes while they were set down, arranged, identified, tasted, given marks out of ten.

'I know what you were going to say.'

Kelly shook her head. 'You don't. These little things in pastry shells are something else – you had one?'

'Not yet so don't eat them all. You were going to say you couldn't fancy a man with . . . one arm. A prosthesis.'

Kelly filled her mouth to avoid having to answer. She did not meet Fern's eye.

'Right. Then just say so. I don't feel the same – wouldn't bother me. The person's still the person.'

Kelly nodded.

'And as such, he's a great boss. And don't look at me like that.'

Four

'Ade . . . look at this.'

The address on the envelope was typed 'To Ade and Tim'. Tim took the sheet of paper.

Dear Ade and Tim,

We still can't thank you enough for so kindly and trustingly welcoming us into your home after our car broke down that terrible wet night, and for letting us dry out, use your phone, giving us drinks etc. If it hadn't been for you we don't know where we'd have been – with a long, wet walk ahead, that's for sure. We have been racking our brains to think of a way of saying thank you and then Beth remembered you had some CDs of opera on your table and the idea struck. There is an opera company coming to the Apollo Theatre in Bevham and so we have got two tickets for you and are enclosing. Sorry, we don't know much about it so hope it's one you like and that you're not already booked to go. Fingers crossed and thank you both again SOOOOO much. Have a great evening.

With best wishes from
Beth and Ryan

'Oh my God, how sweet is that?'

'And I was supposed to be checking out the ENO tour and I forgot. Which night is it?'

Ade checked the tickets. 'Thursday. Do not tell me you're operating late.'

'Do not tell me you're on a shoot in Buenos Aires.'

'Nope.'

'Me neither.' They high-fived as Tim dashed out of the door.

'We'll have dinner, yes? It's not the longest Britten, we should be fine to eat after.'

'Will you book somewhere?' Tim shouted through the open car window as he roared off.

Ade had a quiet couple of days ahead. He was going to do some serious tidying up before Sheila, their daily help, arrived to shoo him out of the way, then book the best dinner venue.

He went into the sitting room, humming an aria from *A Midsummer Night's Dream*.

Five

'Is Sam asleep?'

'Sounds like it.'

'Are you saying I snore?' Sam sat upright in the back of the car.

'As if.'

'Where are we?'

'Outskirts of Lafferton.'

'OK, just drop me at the end of Palmerston Road, I'll walk down to the flat.'

'Don't worry, Sambo, we won't expect to be asked in for coffee.'

'Place is spotless.'

'You mean you vacuum the floor?'

'Eat my dinner off it.'

Kieron took the dual carriageway. It was nearly midnight and quiet.

'Great match though.'

'Ronan says T20 isn't real cricket.' Ronan, junior doctor, one of Sam's flatmates.

'He has a point,' Simon said, 'it isn't – but if you accept it for what it is and don't make comparisons it's a fantastic game.'

'Thought we weren't going to do it, though, that last couple of overs.'

'Never in doubt.'

'Bloody hell, what's that place lit up like what Ma would have called a gin palace?'

On their right, set back and high up, the house they were looking at was illuminated front and back, inside and out. It blazed with security lights, fairy lights, water-fountain lights, steps lit up, some of them changing from silver to white to ice blue and back.

Kieron slowed. 'I can't have been this way after dark for a while – I've never seen it lit up like that.'

'Declan McDermid's place,' Sam said casually. 'He was in the hospital last month, handing over some new cardiac equipment.'

'I haven't met him but I'm always reading about him and hearing about him and seeing his face on the local news. You know anything more about him, Simon?'

'Mainly what I've been told by the media, like you.'

'How did he make his money?'

'He's some sort of importer-exporter and he has a few factories. I think,' offered Sam.

'A few factories! What do they make?'

'Not a clue. OK, left turn and drop me on the corner. Thanks a lot . . . thanks for a great day, Si.'

'Thank your stepfather, he got the tickets.'

Sam scrambled out, hitched on his small rucksack and went down his street without looking back.

Kieron laughed. 'He's all right. He loves that job. Have you been introduced to Rosie?'

'Who's Rosie?'

'Ah, you've been away. A lot happens in a couple of months.'

Serrailler had been in Barbados advising their police on a gang of criminals coming in from the UK, and updating their tactics. It had been very hot, he had swum in the bright blue seas twice a day, eaten more fish than in the past decade and felt in danger of relaxing too deeply. It had been a time out of time, he had needed it to refresh and escape some overhanging shadows.

But it was good to be back.

'Wonder why he has his house lit up like that at midnight,' Simon said. 'Draws attention.'

'Maybe that's what he wants.'

'I'll check him out.'

'Why? It may be a waste of electricity but so long as he pays the bill it isn't a crime and you've better things to do.'

They were ten minutes from the farmhouse. Simon was staying there while his flat was being rewired, work that should have been finished before his return. His sister and Kieron were always welcoming but he felt that he imposed on them too much and he also longed for his own quiet, private space. In Barbados, he had lived in an apartment provided by the police, right on a road, noisy inside and out. Sometimes he had slept on a mat on the beach, in spite of their warnings.

'So, what's been going on in our sleepy corner?'

'Petty crime wave that takes up too much time and some serious drug stuff.'

'Related?'

'Almost certainly.' He turned into the drive. 'Ah . . . she's out on a call.'

Cat's job as a partner in a private GP practice meant that when she was on duty she was back to night and weekend calls.

'You fed up with it?'

'No, it's fine. She doesn't often go out at night to be fair. Come on, I need a beer.'

It was a soft, quiet night, warm for late spring. They took their drinks onto the terrace.

'God, I couldn't live in a place like that,' Simon said, after downing half his beer.

'Barbados?'

'All very cool for holidays. And rich. There's a British doc out there who makes a good income from Botoxing the wives of millionaires. But it isn't real.'

Kieron finished his beer and stood up. 'Another?'

'Why not? Sunday tomorrow.'

The lights of Cat's car washed across the hedge.

'On second thoughts, I think I'll just go to bed,' Simon said. 'Leave you with your wife.'

'Don't be ridiculous. Since when were you ever intruding on us?'

'Since too often. Night, Chief.'

Kieron threw the empty beer can at his back but it fell far short.

Six

At six thirty Ade and Tim left the house. The driver in a car waiting in the lay-by a hundred yards away watched them until they were well out of sight, then sent a text message. *Gone.* He waited until seven before sending the second message. *All clear. Go?*

The reply pinged back. *Go.*

Headlights appeared round the corner behind him, and then a large white van turned into the driveway of Ash Farm. He flashed a couple of times then followed the van.

It took forty minutes, working quickly, for the two men to disable the alarm, get into the house and pick out what they wanted. They took some carefully selected small items of furniture, and then pictures, silver, china in the locked cabinet, small sculptures, two rugs, lamps, three clocks, a case of miniatures, books. They worked from a list and a roughly sketched map.

They did not trouble with anything else. They were not in the small-fry business of taking laptops and televisions.

A large and heavy Chinese vase which stood beside the front door was lifted as they went. They had read about Chinese vases like that. The door was closed and the bulb on the outside light sensor smashed. Two minutes later the van and car had gone.

Ade and Tim turned into their drive well after midnight.

'Bloody outside light's gone.'

'Odd – I put in a new bulb last week.'

'Tim, the door isn't locked.'

'Of course it is, I locked it as we went out, you saw me.'

'Well, it isn't locked now . . . Oh Christ.'

'What?'

They stood in the hall. Ade walked slowly into the sitting room, then the dining room, the kitchen, the study, switching on lights as he went.

He looked at Tim, who sat down on the edge of the sofa. Looked round the half-empty room. Looked at the spaces on the walls. The empty dresser. Bare floorboards where the Persian rugs had been. Stared round. Realised. It had been the easiest thing in the world for them, he thought.

But there was no point in saying it. It was only much later that Tim spoke, after the police had been and taken statements, almost three o'clock, when they were drinking whisky, sitting in the kitchen because it was the only room which was more or less untouched.

'I never want to see or hear the *Dream* again.'

In a unit on an industrial estate twenty miles away, the two men unloaded the last items. The younger man – brown hair and eyes, glasses, nondescript features – walked round the items slowly, a small smile on his face. Most of the large building was in darkness. It was also damp and cold.

'That's the lot,' he said at last, stopping to run his fingers over a small grandfather clock. 'Let's cover it up and get out of here.'

The haul from Ade and Tim's house was covered in tarpaulin and anchored down with metal bars.

'Good work, Jake,' the other man said, walking over to an unmemorable red Ford saloon. Which was exactly the way he needed it to be.

Seven

Quite often now Carrie went down to the far end of the garden where there was an old wooden bench from which she could just hear the sound of the river slipping through the reeds and green undergrowth. It soothed her. So did the birdsong. She knew that Colin sometimes watched her from his office window, which was on this side, but he never came to sit with her, though once or twice he had brought her tea when he was pausing briefly to make his own. He would listen to the sounds she mentioned, nod, pat her on the shoulder, or touch her arm, but then go back.

He had stopped asking her anything about her pregnancy or mentioning the baby. It was as though it did not exist, something that he could not engage with, perhaps he even felt it was her business alone. But she knew that would not be true. Theirs was a strangely separate relationship but she still knew him, knew that inside himself he would be processing both what it was and what it would be, how it would affect their future. His future. What she did not know, and she changed her mind every day about it, was whether he believed that there was something wrong with the baby or thought she was mad. He had said once that she was mad – or, as he had put it, mentally unstable.

'Did you think that when you married me?'

But he had just shrugged. She had never really known why he had married her, though she knew why she had married him – for love, and yes, yes, it was love, as well as for security and because he had asked her and her mother had told her that nobody would ever do that. But her mother had believed nothing of anyone. Life was against you and always would be. That was where it all came from, Carrie knew, but the knowledge didn't help.

'Tea.'

Colin came cautiously down the garden with the tray, which held two cups.

'Is everything all right?'

'It can run by itself for five minutes. I've set everything to "hold" except steel, which is on "buy".'

'I thought I read somewhere that steel was . . . I don't know what the term is, but in a bad way somehow.'

'You did. That's why it's a "buy".'

'I'll never understand it.'

'You don't have to. That's my job.'

'So what's mine?'

He set down his cup. He was not handsome but Carrie found that reassuring. She had never been afraid that Colin would leave her for someone else, or even be unfaithful. It had never crossed her mind. They were alike, both plain-looking, self-contained people. Was that why he had wanted to marry her?

'No children,' he had said. 'I hope you won't mind.'

She had always assumed, like everyone else, that being married meant having children and the idea of not doing so was surprising and had caught her unawares. She had said, 'No, of course not,' but then had to think about it, what exactly it meant, how her married future would be. She had been working as a receptionist in the clinic to which he had gone for a series of appointments to assess his worsening sight. He had talked to her, and as he had waited to be seen, looked at her closely – perhaps studied her would have been a better description. Carrie had become aware of it and kept her head down, embarrassed and uncertain what to make of him. When she had typed up his notes, she had not done so automatically, reading and yet not reading, simply copying, but had followed their meaning and seen what treatment was proposed. After five months, his sight had deteriorated to the point where the only options were a difficult operation or blindness and she realised that she was worried about the outcome of the first and the possibility of the second. She had found out that he was a hedge fund trader, and had only a vague idea of what that meant, though she knew it would involve studying a screen every day. Would he be unable to do that?

Once, while stationary at a traffic light on her way home, she had been thinking about Colin Pegwell's possible future with such concentration that it took a few seconds for her to notice the angry hooting of drivers behind her. It had shaken her, just as her overwhelming feeling of joy and relief had shaken her when she heard that his operation had been a complete success, that his sight was to be no worse than that of anyone who had to wear rather strong glasses.

The thing that had troubled her most was his age. She had been typing up his notes and was startled to find that he was forty-seven. She was twenty-six.

But it had not mattered. They had found one another, become engaged, then married and been so for two years and not once had the age gap been referred to, let alone caused any problem. It had worked out. Colin had left his firm, she had left her job, and for a few months they had travelled. It had been the best time of all, Carrie saw now, because of everything they had seen and everywhere they had enjoyed together, because they were away from their old, familiar and perhaps dull lives, and most of all from their families.

Back home, they had moved and Colin had set up on his own. He had worked even longer hours and made even more money and everything had changed.

A moorhen climbed out of the river, pushed its way through the undergrowth and was dabbing about on the grass. Moorhens. They nested so unwisely, lost their young to predators, nested again and perhaps eventually reared a brood. Why did they not learn from experience?

She had assumed that she would feel unwell in pregnancy, having heard about it from other women, but apart from an aversion to certain smells, particularly that of onions, there had been little to complain about. Only the slow, inevitable thickening of her body.

Colin did not look at it. He was never in the room when she undressed or went to and from a bath. She existed for him, but she, as a woman having a baby, did not.

And as a woman having an abnormal, damaged, sick baby, without the possibility of living a fragment of an acceptable life, she did not touch upon his consciousness at all.

She put a hand across her stomach and felt the usual movement. So little separated it from her and from the world she was seeing and in which she was breathing – a mere inch of membrane. But, invisible and unknowable, it was in some other place, and in a quite different form of existence.

She had decided that she would not think ahead, or try to picture how her, their, life would be, even as far ahead as the following day, let alone the future. It was unimaginable anyway, she would not torment herself with it.

She would go along and along and at some point it would happen and then she would deal with it.

The sun went in. The moorhen bustled back to the stream. Carrie drank her cold tea.

Eight

DC Bilaval Sandhu and DC Karen Rhodes had walked into the elegant but comfortable house and through to the sitting room, trying not to ogle.

Sandhu mouthed 'pink pound' to Karen behind Ade's back but she ignored him. True though, she thought. If you have two people in highly paid jobs, with no children, your income goes way further – not to mention the fact that your gorgeous house and its contents stay unsullied and things remain where you last left them.

Except, of course, in the case of a carefully targeted and successful burglary.

'What can I get you? Coffee, tea, something cold?'

They glanced at one another. Karen would have killed for a strong coffee.

'No thanks.'

Typical. Ade looked at Karen. 'No reason why you shouldn't accept, is there, just because your partner doesn't want anything?'

'No. And thank you, I'd love a coffee – a splash of milk, no sugar if that's OK.'

Ade smiled. Nice smile, she thought. Good-looking. Great cashmere sweater. She had had cashmere once, before a husband and three sons. Who of course were worth everything, far more than a beautiful home and pale blue cashmere. All the same . . .

'Tim may be back later if traffic is good from the airport but the chances are that he won't so we should start without him.' Ade had brought china mugs of coffee for Karen and himself. No biscuits.

'What does Mr . . .'

'Letts – Timothy Letts. He's a doctor.'

Sandhu was checking details in his notebook. 'So you're Adrian Holland.'

'I am.'

'Do you have a full list of everything that was taken?'

'I sent it over to the police as an email attachment – the insurance company also have it.'

'Well insured, are you?'

'Yes. I used to think too well but I've changed my mind. Unsurprisingly.'

'So you won't be out of pocket.'

Karen jumped in. 'I'm sure it isn't only the monetary value of what you lost. Money doesn't make up for sentimental value.'

Ade turned a charming smile onto her, ignoring DC Sandhu. 'You are so right. Of course we get the money less the excess and so on – that really isn't the point. It's knowing we were conned – that leaves a very nasty taste because you're tempted to say that you'll never do a good deed for any stranger in future – which isn't how it should be. We feel stupid – though I honestly don't think we were.'

'No,' Karen said, 'you weren't, you were trusting. Very different.'

Bilaval gave her a hard look. 'Right, back to these two whose car had allegedly broken down. Can you give me a description?'

'Me', Karen noted, not 'us'.

'We already did. Straight after the burglary. Don't you have access to that statement?'

'Better if you start again.'

'Why?'

Karen hid a smirk, then said, 'It isn't so much the basic description as anything . . . well, unusual, about either of them.'

'You mean a swivel eye or a scarlet birthmark?'

He looked at her without moving a face muscle.

'Yes . . . that sort of thing.'

'I would know her again though I'm not sure why . . . she was the one who asked most questions, seemed appreciative of this and that, but there wasn't anything especially distinctive about either of them. Looking back, I do wonder if she wasn't wearing a wig . . . I can't be sure. And coloured contact lenses – her eyes were that unusually bright blue, you know? So maybe a bit of disguise went on. Have there been any other robberies of the same kind around here? I haven't seen anything in the papers if so – but I didn't see anything about this robbery, come to that.'

'Deliberate media blackout,' Bilaval said solemnly. 'Can't say any more.'

'Ah, I see. Then I'll shut up, obviously.' Ade made a zipped-up motion, finger to lips.

I like him, Karen thought. He's fun and he's got the measure of Billy, who would be a decent member of CID if he didn't take himself so seriously.

'Do you know if there is any information at all?'

'Can't disclose—'

Karen jumped in. 'Not so far, but we're obviously making extensive inquiries and following all sorts of leads.'

'What sorts? Forgive me – I really don't know how police investigations work.'

'No need for you to know, sir, leave that to us,' Bilaval said. 'Is there anything else unusual you remember about that night? Anything, however small. It must have been an awful shock.'

'The night they came first or the night we discovered the robbery? That was the shock. Well, obviously.'

'You'll be hearing from Victim Support, if you haven't done so already.'

'No, we haven't, and honestly, we don't need them. We just need those two weevils rounding up and having the book thrown at them. We're fine. Furious – but fine.'

Karen set down her cup. 'That was great coffee. Thanks.'

She got up. Bilaval did not.

'Bil?'

'Was it only this room they took stuff from?'

'No, as I said. The hall, the dining room, in here, the staircase, the upstairs landing. They went pretty much all over the house but they only took valuables, they didn't bother with the telly and the Roberts Radio.'

'Oh they wouldn't. These were specialists.'

'Clearly. I take it you get on to Christie's, Sotheby's, all those people in the course of inquiries?'

Bilaval looked blank.

'Auction houses,' Karen said. 'Of course we do.' She walked towards the door and waited for him to cotton on. Behind his back, Ade smiled at her.

God, yes, he was good-looking. She could have a nice harmless daydream about him, and given their respective statuses, no harm done.

Tim got home shortly after they had left.

'I hope it's not too early for a gin, because I need one.'

'I'll drink to that. I had two cops here – the cream of CID.'

'With news?'

'Nope. With a repeat of all the questions we have already given answers to but which they seem not to know about.'

'They were idiots?'

'One was. If we don't hear that they've made progress within this coming week, I'm going to make a nuisance of myself. Ask to see the boss.'

'I happen to know the boss – correction, know his sister, she's a GP and sings at St Mike's with me.'

'Come on, let's go outside while there's a touch of warmth still.'

It was only a touch and Ade went back for a fleece. 'I hate being inside – it feels all wrong. Bare. Any news from the insurance by the way?'

Tim shook his head. 'I rang the broker – they're working on it. Allegedly. It'll be all right – just takes time. Cheers.'

Ade raised his bowl-shaped glass of gin and tonic. The ice chinked. 'Who is he, this doc's brother?'

'The Detective Chief Superintendent. She is also married to the Chief Constable.'

'Then get on to them. Why put up with idiots?'

'Everybody else has to.'

Ade rolled his eyes. 'Yes, well, forget your egalitarian principles and use your inside knowledge. That's what it's for – you think everybody else wouldn't?'

Nine

Serrailler opened the door of the CID room and stood still. Nobody looked up. Those who were at their desks were focused on screens. One DI, two – no, three DCs. Someone coughed behind him and he stepped aside to let them through. Four DCs. 'Excuse me, guv.'

Two DIs. He began to get one or two furtive looks before eyes were averted and back to screens. It was calm. It was a room of silent, focused work. Apparently.

He stepped inside. 'Right. Small conference room. Everybody.'

He walked out again before he could see the exchanged glances, which meant 'Guv in a mood – probably his arm giving him gyp. Best make allowances.' He hated it even though they were right, his prosthesis was a brilliant piece of engineering and electronics and most of the time now he could pretty much forget it, what it had replaced. But the socket and his shoulder still hurt occasionally, sometimes because he had been using it too much or was simply tired. Today was that day. He took a deep breath. Don't give them too much of a bollocking, you want them onside – even if they are not the most proactive CID team or the ones with the best ideas. It happened. They would shape up, so long as there wasn't a sudden exodus and change of personnel, and he would have to start again.

Instead of going to the whiteboard and standing in front of it, he sat at the table, poured water for himself and his next-door neighbours, and waited until they were settled.

'Could someone open a window please or we'll die of oxygen deficiency?'

Someone did.

'Thanks, Andy. Right, this is a catch-up for any of you who have been on leave or working on other stuff and aren't fully up to speed. Because unless you can convince me that there is something more pressing, I want everyone focused on this, at least for now. Yes, I know, another burglary, blah blah. Except that it isn't. It'll be easier for me to give you the whole picture from the wall.'

He got up and pushed the flop of white-blond hair back from his forehead, his habitual, unconscious gesture. God, he is handsome, Fern Monroe thought. She studied him now as he flicked on the light over the whiteboard. He used his prosthesis as naturally as anyone used their flesh-and-bone arm, seemingly quite familiar and comfortable with it. How tall was he? Must be six two at least, with blue eyes which could give you the coldest of stares, of which she had been on the receiving end once or twice since he'd returned from his work in Barbados.

She refocused on what he was saying. He had indicated Ade Holland and Tim Letts's house and area, and got as far as the breakdown which had brought the couple to their door.

'It was a clever scam and a well-thought-out plan, though it isn't new. The man and woman are clearly not at all suspicious in appearance or manner. Our victims are two intelligent men who meet all manner of people in the course of their work, so they would be very likely to have spotted anything that didn't ring true.'

'Guv . . .'

'DS Parks?'

'Not sure those two things necessarily go together – you don't need higher degrees to have your suspicions about someone's behaviour.'

'True. Useful input but let me just finish. The opera tickets were kosher – good seats too, apparently – and they knew they had time to go right through the place, pick out the items of serious value, load up and leave. Nothing was damaged or broken, there was no mess and of course no prints. It was a thoroughly professional job.'

Serrailler went back to his seat.

'Now, we have nothing to go on, in that SOCOs drew a total blank. There are no CCTV cameras, though there was a burglar alarm, which the gang disabled. It's an isolated house – no neighbours to hear or see anything. They researched thoroughly, not just on their initial visit but no doubt before-hand, driving round, excluding other houses before targeting this one. They probably did an earlier recce, waiting until they knew no one was in before looking through as many windows as they could, checking out the back and the side, and so on. OK, let's think. Let's ask questions. Were they working alone?'

'Almost certainly not. They'd need a lookout plus a van driver doubling as a loader. Plus contacts with fences and high-value art rings round the country.'

'Yes. Do we think they are local?'

Several said no.

'They'll have come from – well, anywhere, but not round here.'

'But they made sure they were well disguised – subtly, though. I'm keeping an open mind about whether they're from our patch or outside.'

'Either way, guv, they won't do another like it here.'

Serrailler frowned. 'Not sure about that. Not yet certainly, but I wouldn't be surprised if they're already doing their homework, sussing out likely victims – big houses, in villages, isolated places, around Lafferton. Takes time.'

'So are patrols being stepped up, guv?'

'In a way, but honestly, it's needle in haystack time. Uniform don't have the resources to drive about the countryside, looking for – well, for what? Obviously they've had a heads-up, eyes and ears open and all that.'

'No kipping in lay-bys.'

'No reading the *Sun* parked up round the corner from the chippy.'

'All right, all right. But some of you at least come from around here, you know the sort of places, and people, they might target. Just be aware.'

'Guv, we're always telling people to be on their guard, don't let strangers in, make sure your house is well secured, night and day and specially when you're out or away. So, if they know about this sort of robbery and how it happened, they're going to be extra vigilant if they answer to the house and place description and have a lot of valuables. But if they don't know anything about this one how can they take precautions and step up their security? There's been nothing in the local media whatsoever – you need to get onto our press office pronto.'

'Thank you for clarifying the details of my job description, DC Sandhu.'

Serrailler kicked himself for scoring a cheap point by being sarcastic. He looked at the rookie DC again.

'But point well raised. I was coming to that. I have ordered a media blackout on this robbery.'

There were one or two astonished faces, a couple of head-shakes.

'I know what you're thinking but you're wrong. At this stage, let's keep them guessing. Obviously they know we've been in and they're pretty sure forensics found it all clean. But what are we doing now? We appear to think this isn't worth a press release. We've got other fish to fry, because let's face it, these guys were well insured, there was no violence. On the other hand, maybe we do know something and we're just one step behind them, waiting, watching, biding our time. They just can't work it out. So, for now, it's all under the radar.'

'Sorry, guv, but I think that's asking for trouble. They know the public isn't on the alert. We're making it easy for them to target someone else and bring it off.'

'It's balancing the risks, DC Rhodes. For now, I'm playing it my way.'

'Guv . . .'

'DC Monroe?'

'Just a thought . . . I agree with you in general but there are a few people around our patch who live in out-of-the-way houses, who are rich or at least have valuables. Wouldn't it be possible to run through a list of possibles and give them a discreet heads-up? Visit from uniform, "We've reports of one or two burglaries in the area, may we remind you to check your security?" even, "Can we send someone round to help you with it?" That sort of thing. It could go with a request not to broadcast it and . . . well, a stress on "make sure you don't let anyone you do not know into your house, however plausible" de dah de dah.'

Several people nodded.

'That's one way of going about it, good thinking, Monroe. Trouble is, man hours – how do we go about finding our well-off owners of precious items, checking them out, calling on them? Yes, of course it can be done, with a lot of time spent on the databases, but time is money and I am being told every other day to save pennies, there are more cuts in the offing.'

'What you said a minute ago, guv – this is a bit of a victimless crime, isn't it? Two gay guys, pretty well off, valuable collections of knick-knacks, cleaned out but no damage, no mess, they got a nice night out watching the fat lady sing, insurance will cough up – haven't we got a lot more serious stuff on our hands?'

There was a murmur round the table.

'I'll set aside the question of what their being gay has to do with anything, or being well off, for that matter. Plenty of people have antiques and jewellery that they've inherited and looked after for years – they're not necessarily cash-in-the-bank rich. Someone who is robbed is a victim, whether they're mugged for their wallet in broad daylight or live on the Dulcie estate and have the back door kicked in and the gas meter money nicked. Theft is theft, it's our job to investigate, make arrests and put a good enough case to CP to get them sent down. Come on, you all know this. We don't discriminate.'

'What kind of people are we looking for? Possible previous?'

'Presumably someone's checked that there haven't been any identikit jobs in neighbouring force areas, guv? Or any areas, come to that.'

Simon looked around. 'Volunteers then? None of you are up to your eyes in a triple murder.'

'The foot in the river, guv.'

'That accounts for, what, two of you? I take it no one has actually retrieved said "foot" and brought it in?'

'Liam O'Brian's out there again now, talking to the person who spotted it.'

'Or said they did.'

'Expert robberies with decoy MO. Start with the forces immediately adjacent, spread out . . . phone round, if necessary. Local media.'

'Maybe they've all got a news blackout as well.'

Simon chose not to hear.

'They know their stuff, these two. What's valuable, what's not worth bothering with . . . and they must be good actors. They kept it up for quite a while and didn't arouse a whiff of suspicion. So, not your bogus gas-meter man. I'd agree there's got to be someone behind them.'

'I think you mean Mr Big, Fern.'

'How could I have forgotten his name? Thanks, Bilaval.'

'That's one of the reasons for keeping this below the public radar,' Serrailler said. 'If there is a Mr Big – and yes, thank you, DC Sandhu – we want to flush him out.'

'Set a trap? You can be the honey, Fern.'

'I'll see you outside.'

'Promises . . .'

'These things have been done as insurance scams.'

'They have, but I don't think it's likely in this case.'

'I do and I went to interview them. Just the type.'

'Interesting point of view. Remind me, what exactly is the type of person who mocks up an elaborate heist in order to cheat their insurance company?'

'Someone who needs the money.'

'Yes. Is that how they struck you, DC Sandhu?'

'Could be, could be.'

Serrailler snorted.

'The thing is, guv, with respect, you haven't interviewed them or even met them – correct me if I'm wrong. Sandhu has.'

He looked at Fern Monroe. She had spoken carefully, and she had meant "with respect", even while calling him out. Nobody else in the conference room had come up with

38

anything worth his or their time in here. She had, and more than once.

'All right, that's it for now, but put your backs and brains into this. You know the line – "omitting no detail, however slight". I shall expect you tapping at my door non-stop during the next twenty-four hours. DC Monroe, I want a word please.'

Fern Monroe felt a shiver of anticipation, as she waited for the others to troop out. Serrailler closed the door. 'Good points you made, I'm impressed. You'll progress up the ladder fast if you go on like this. Now, on the house robbery – I didn't mention it because there was no need, but there's been a complaint, not so much that we are not doing enough – they don't know what we're doing – but that they were not interviewed by anyone at a higher level than DC. They had an initial visit from uniform on the night of the break-in, and DCs Sandhu and Rhodes went there a couple of days ago, but now they're asking for more, and I want to see the set-up and talk to them so I'm going to the house and you're coming with me. It won't be straightforward but we want to be seen making a bit of a fuss of them. They do have a right to ask.'

'Guv.'

Fern closed the door of the conference room carefully before punching the air.

Ten

'Carrie.' He stood half in, half out of the doorway, ready to say whatever it was at speed and bolt back into his office. It was how it was.

She had been dozing, the book on her lap about to slip off onto the floor.

'Are you all right?'

'Yes. I get sleepy.'

'You should see a doctor. You haven't been to any check-ups or clinics, and that's OK, your decision, but at least see the GP.'

'You can never get an appointment.'

'Rubbish.'

'When did you last try?'

'That's beside the point. You may not be able to get one tomorrow but you can surely be given one a week or ten days ahead and that would do, it isn't urgent. You should go.'

'I'm fine.'

She retrieved her book and got up. The baby squirmed about inside her like a small underwater creature. Which of course it was.

It was almost dark. They had eaten supper, said little, Colin had gone back to catch the stock exchange figures from the other side of the world. Or somewhere.

'Here. I saw something about it – interview in the local paper, I think.'

'You don't read the local paper.'

'The digest comes through to my Twitter feed.'

He handed her a printout.

'This is the thing. No need to wait about for the NHS to get its act together.'

Concierge Medical, your private GP in Lafferton. You need a GP. You call us. We come to you, the same day. And you might be surprised to learn the affordable rates for individual/ couple/family membership.

Carrie had been flipping through the pages of *The Forsyte Saga*, a book her mother had loved and so, of course, she had resisted, until she had found the battered family copy. Why did she have it? And why had she unpacked it now? Family? Did 'family' mean anything to her? Had it ever?

'You won't have to go to a surgery or wait about, whichever one covers this village will come to you.'

'You haven't made an appointment? I don't want you to decide for me.'

'It is my child as well.'

He had never said such a thing before.

'But no, I haven't. I'll leave that to you. The phone number is on the printout I gave you or you can email them.'

He went into the kitchen. A wind had got up and it caught the door and slammed it. The baby inside her gave a startled little kick.

The next night, unusually, Colin was in his bed first. There was a holiday in the Far East and their stock markets were closed.

'How was today?'

'Great. Made about seventy points.'

'You're very clever. I know it's not as easy as it looks.'

'Not easy at all – takes experience and nerve. And a bit of luck.'

Carrie opened her novel, but she had been reading more and more slowly, not taking it in and having to go back and start paragraphs or even chapters again. She could not concentrate, her brain seemed to have become sluggish, her attention always drawn back to the baby.

Colin had settled himself with three pillows and *The Economist*. They had never shared a bed. He had a dislike of sleeping within reach of another body. Carrie had not thought it strange or that it added up to anything. Sleeping and sex were two different things.

The baby fluttered a little and then thrust out a limb. Hand or foot? She could not tell. It was so near. It was a third person in the room, and yet it might have been living on another, unreachable planet, it was so unknown, so apparently far away, curled up within itself in the water and the dark.

'Who are you? What are you?' She pictured a small monster with two heads. A spider-shaped creature. A trunk without limbs. Every day, her imagination threw up new images.

She had not mentioned this to Colin.

'Are you comfortable?'

She looked at him. He had pushed his glasses up onto his forehead.

'You never complain. You haven't complained once.'

'Haven't I?'

'I always thought women did – because they had sickness or backache or stomach ache or something else.'

'Then I suppose I'm lucky. I haven't had any of those things.'

'That's good.'

'It won't mean anything.'

But he was already reading again.

'I do love you,' she said. Because she supposed that she did. He seemed not to have heard.

She had read about women who had gone mad as soon as they had given birth, and been put into psychiatric hospital. The babies were taken away because they were at risk of being harmed. What exactly the madness was like, how anyone could tell, was difficult to understand, but perhaps it began like this, with exactly her conviction that her baby was not right. No, was wrong. Completely wrong.

But that could not be the case because Carrie felt perfectly normal, was not even worried about herself, about giving birth, about any of it. She was functioning on every other level. It was simply that she knew.

She picked up her book again and an image of a baby without a face, a featureless thing, interposed itself between her eyes and the page.

Eleven

Fern Monroe took a step back, after Serrailler had rung the doorbell, and looked appreciatively up at the house. Spacious and well maintained, the window frames recently painted, the whole place roofed with reclaimed stone tiles. 'DCS Simon Serrailler. This is Detective Constable Fern Monroe.'

'Hi. I'm Tim Letts. Come in.'

He led the way through to a long, beamed kitchen. Terracotta floor. Light oak bespoke units. Two small sofas adjacent to one another, covered in old kelims.

'Ade will be back soon. He's been wrapping up a shoot and there's traffic, as ever. What can I get you? Coffee – or tea?'

Serrailler usually refused anything, but right now it would be good to look friendly.

'I'd love a coffee please . . . black.'

'And for me please. The same. But I'm afraid I take sugar.'

Tim laughed. 'Don't worry, so do I, but everyone feels they have to be apologetic about it to a doctor. Kenyan or Colombian beans?'

'Either.'

Tim opened an earthenware jar which did not have COFFEE printed on the side, took out a new packet of beans.

'Have a seat.'

Serrailler sat on one of the sofas. Fern hesitated. Sat at the far end.

As Tim set down the cafetière and a bowl of brown sugar, they heard the front door open.

'You tell me,' Serrailler said, after having drunk some coffee and paid the required compliment on it, which was not difficult because it was excellent. 'And I know you'll say you have already told half a dozen others and ask why I haven't read all the reports and your statements. I have. It may sound as if we don't do joined-up policing but I want to get as full and clear a picture of this as I can from you, the people who were here, those it happened to, and that comes best if you just tell me the whole story.' He leaned back, coffee in hand. Fern did the same.

Tim took a deep breath, paused for a few seconds with his eyes closed. Then he started from the moment the doorbell had rung and he had opened the front door and let in the couple with their story of having broken down and being stranded, to the moment they had opened the same front door, after returning from the opera, onto a house from which so many valuable items had been taken.

His recall was good. He remembered details of clothing, features, voices, and snatches of the conversations they had had more or less word for word. He talked about the interest they took in a sculpture and other precious belongings, how convincing they were, their earnest thanks. He produced the letter offering the opera tickets. There was nothing odd about it. The handwriting was ordinary, the paper too, neither looked suspicious. The woman's false signature did not look false. The address appeared genuine though it had been discovered in the first hour of the police investigation that it did not exist.

Tim poured them all second cups of coffee.

'Couldn't be better,' Simon said. 'I wish everyone who makes a statement had such an excellent memory. Thank you.'

'Anything new?'

'Yes – quite a few details, and it's good to have the whole thing set out in the right time scale. It's given me a very clear picture. It's not only what happened – that's the easy part.'

'I imagine they've done this before.'

'Almost certainly, but not around here. It seems to be a first.'

'Where do you think our things might be? Will they have been shipped abroad? I know we're insured but that's not the point as I'm sure you're aware. You can replace widescreen tellies with the identical model but not those pieces.'

'They won't have been working alone,' Fern said. 'They will have people behind them who take the stuff and dispose of it, to a network of dodgy dealers in this country and abroad.'

Serrailler nodded. 'There's very likely to be quite a gang involved in this. Our young couple just get a decent cash reward and know nothing more. If we rounded them up tomorrow they would tell us they have no idea where your stuff is and that would be the truth.'

'It sounds pretty hopeless.'

'Oh no. I've every hope of breaking up this little ring but it will take time and we will need to go carefully.'

'Meanwhile, someone else is going to hear a ring at the doorbell late one night . . .'

'They won't do this too often. They have to work out the best targets, have a carefully thought-out plan of action. These aren't smash and grab merchants.'

'But presumably you want to stop them before they do it to someone else?'

'Of course we do.'

'So why hasn't there been anything in the media? Surely a big newspaper shout-out about it, and some of those identikit . . . no, photofit, whatever – people might recognise them. They might remember something. I can't believe the *Bevham Gazette* wasn't interested. Or even local telly.'

'I put a media blackout on it. There are a number of reasons why we do this occasionally, but of course if and when the time comes to put it out there, we will.'

Fern Monroe looked as if she would say something, glanced at Serrailler. Did not.

'I guess you know what you're doing,' Tim said.

'It isn't an exact science, but in this instance I'm keeping it under the radar for the time being. Now, I'd like you to think back – before the night of the phoney breakdown. They will have sussed you out. They weren't on-spec housebreakers, they knew what you had, or at least some of it, before they even came calling with their story of the broken-down car. Have you had any suspicious visitors? Seen anyone hanging about? People offering to sell you things, wanting to be your friendly neighbourhood window cleaner? Garden jobs?'

'No, but we're both out most of the day and there are no neighbours to report on hangers-around.'

'I know you feel we haven't taken this as seriously as we should have done. We have and we are, though appearances are important too. But you've given me an admirable account now and I doubt if it could have been fuller or clearer the first time round. Thank you and I promise I will keep you informed about our progress – because there will be progress, I promise you that too. These guys will be thinking they've got away with a great haul of valuables and nobody appears to have noticed. Clever them.'

Simon got up, shaking his head.

'This was an expertly executed burglary but that doesn't mean we won't get them. Far from it. Oddly enough, the more expert and specialist the job the better. It's the handbag snatchers and the chancers climbing in through a back window who we find it harder to get our hands on, though we still often do.'

As soon as they were back in Simon's car, Fern said, 'Maybe I've missed something here, guv, but I didn't think he told us anything we didn't already know.'

'He didn't.'

'So . . .'

'They made a complaint. They didn't think Sandhu and Rhodes were senior enough to take their statement.'

'And does everybody who complains get you?'

He laughed as he wound in and out of the country lanes. 'You acquire a nose for the ones who will start kicking off if they think they're not being given top treatment.'

'I thought he was charming.'

'They're the worst. No – they feel aggrieved, and in this instance, I can't blame them. The interview wasn't the best, from what I read of Sandhu's notes. I'm surprised they didn't go all the way up to the Chief.'

'Oh well then.'

'I'm sorry?'

Fern could have kicked herself.

'DC Monroe, if you think that because the Chief Constable happens to be my brother-in-law he would back me and my team over an official complaint from a member of the public, you think absolutely wrongly. If anything, he'd come down harder on me than anyone. Our family relationship ends at the door of the station and you can spread that around as much as you like.'

'Of course. Sorry, guv.'

'That's OK. It's an easy mistake to make, but the Chief has to be seen to be above reproach on that front – so do I. And we make sure we are.'

They sat in silence until they were heading towards the bypass. Then, without planning, without its even having crossed his mind seconds before, Simon said, 'It's two minutes past. You're off duty.'

'Yaay.' She glanced at him. 'I love the job though. I really do.'

'Oh, listen, everybody's glad to come to the end of a shift, never mind how happy they are in their work. It's normal. And you're no clock-watcher.'

'I hope not.'

'So, let's debrief over a drink?'

Twelve

There was nothing wrong. Nothing in the world. Nothing could spoil this. It was just that if she had had even half an hour's warning, she would have had time to change out of her work clothes – pale grey skirt and jacket, cream silk shirt, low heels.

At least she was CID and not uniform. But he would not have asked her out for a drink if she had been uniform.

Would he?

There was nothing wrong with her grey suit. Just that she could have done a whole lot better.

Would that have been a mistake? If she had had time to change she might have tried too hard.

She talked to herself as they walked from the car down through the Lanes. This is a debrief. He wants to be relaxed, he wants to have an hour away from the station. That's what it means. It means nothing else. Nothing.

She was conscious of his height and the fact that, until they reached the pedestrian area, he walked on the outside of her. She was conscious that someone might see them, someone she knew, worked with, lived near. Listen. This is not a date, it's part of work, it's a debrief, better get back to Ade Holland's account of the events leading up to the burglary. If she was keen on her job, which she was, if she wanted promotion, which she did, if she was bent on following a swift upward path through CID, she had to be on the ball, to remember everything, to have opinions even if she didn't voice them, to come to conclusions, even if they were eventually proved wrong. She had to show that she was the sharpest tool in the box.

It was warm enough to sit on the veranda at the front of the brasserie, as a few others were. Inside was busy.

'What would you like?'

Fern had been asking herself that question and not coming up with an answer. Which was ridiculous. She wasn't sixteen, she knew what she liked and what she did not, what was appropriate and what was not. Oh for God's sake.

'A glass of Prosecco? They have a good one here. Or whatever you would like – my sister gets furious if I assume women prefer bubbly drinks. Sorry.' He smiled at her and the smile was in his eyes as well as on his mouth.

She did not know how old he was, guessed at forty-one, -two?

'Actually, I'd like a glass of Pinot Noir, if that's all right.'

'Of course it is.'

The waitress arrived and greeted him like an old friend. So he came here a lot. He gave her the same smile, Fern noticed.

'You know your wine?'

'Not a lot but I enjoy it and I never drink spirits, hate beer, so I started taking more of an interest than just white or red.'

Half an hour later and the break-in to Tim and Ade's house had still not been mentioned. Fern had a second glass of wine, Serrailler had another whisky. She could get a cab home, he was leaving his car in the square and walking home 'round the corner'.

No one else in the brasserie, walking by, in the rest of her life, existed, let alone mattered as they talked. Films. Wine. Families. Travel. Skiing – she had been twice, he had skied with Cat and Chris before they had had the children, and neither he nor his sister had been much good or even enjoyed it, whereas Chris had been all about black runs. Cricket, which Fern did not follow, football, which Simon did in a half-hearted way, out of solidarity with his nephew Sam. Books – she read a lot. So did he. Politics. Art. He talked about his drawing.

'I've wasted so much time over this bloody arm. But there's a new project – the cathedral is going to put up scaffolding and take a close look at the carved angels and saints high up in the nave roof. Have you seen them?'

'Only from below. I'm not really a churchgoer but I love the cathedral. I sometimes just go in and sit there. Is that weird?'

'No. Why would it be? Once they've examined them for any damage, rot and so on, assessed how much repair they need, then I'm going to follow on and draw each one. It'll be a different sort of record to photographs, though they will do those too. I hope I get an exhibition out of it. I should. Maybe you'd better not mention this until they've made their press announcement – they want a bit of a splash about the work.'

'Must be costing a fortune.'

'Yes, but they've got a sponsor. Have you heard of a guy called Declan McDermid?'

'Mega-wealthy, lives in a McMansion on Beauchamp Hill. Who hasn't?'

'Yes. He's given the bobby van to us – launch tomorrow.'

'And a new paediatric unit at Bevham General. Where does his money come from?'

'Manufacturing widgets, exporting widgets, God knows. Anyway, whatever he does, he gives away plenty. Just so long as it has his name on it. Are you hungry? Because I am and they do a good steak here.'

Steak frites. Well-dressed green salad. Glasses of Côtes du Rhône. Rich dark coffee.

'Did you parents approve of your career choice?'

She hesitated. 'Yes and no. No, because my dad was a copper. He died when a car he was trying to stop with a stinger swerved deliberately to hit him.'

'Oh God, I should have known that. I'm sorry I didn't.' He put his hand on hers as it rested on the table.

'I was only twelve. I do remember him, but he wasn't the reason I joined the force. No "honouring his memory" or anything. I was angry for a long time about it being his job that had taken him away from us. But maybe it brought the whole idea to mind more easily. I thought of going into forensics first.

51

I read criminology, and CID itself was a wider world. Eventually anyway.'

'Do you have siblings?'

'One sister and one brother who has Down's syndrome. He's in a sheltered community. He's fine but . . . well, it isn't regarded as OK to say this nowadays but I think it's a case of making the best of it. My sister doesn't feel the same. She went into psychiatric nursing because of David.'

She had not told anyone in the job about it. There was no reason.

'I'd be grateful if you didn't tell people.'

'You honestly think I would?' He seemed hurt. 'You wouldn't know of course, but I had another sister – Martha. She was very seriously handicapped. She died. So I'm the last person . . .'

'I'm so sorry, Simon – I mean, sorry, guv. Oh help.'

He smiled.

'One more coffee, we need it.'

They left the brasserie. She shared a house in the Apostles with Lily, who was both a cousin and her oldest friend. Lily was a dentist. They got on fine, saw just enough of one another – it worked. But Lily had a boyfriend who was becoming pretty serious and Fern guessed she might soon be moving out.

Serrailler went up to the taxi at the front of the rank, and put her into it. He kissed her on the cheek, waved her off. Turned away. By the time they were leaving the square and Fern looked back, he had disappeared.

And that would be that, she told herself. It wasn't going anywhere. Remember this evening, expect nothing else.

Expect was not the same as wish for and she wished like mad during the short taxi ride home, and then as she checked her messages and had a shower and watched the late news and got ready for bed. Lily was still out, but Kelly would be up, because she had three days off, and in any case, never went to bed early. She hesitated, her finger on 'call'.

No. Not Kelly. Not anyone, actually, because she wanted to hug this to herself for as long as she could, and besides, what was there to tell? She had been working, done an interview reassessing a case, and on the way back, the boss had taken her for a drink, which, as neither of them had eaten, merged into supper. Talk. Of course, talk.

Nothing else. Nothing to tell.

She left her phone charging and went to bed. She dreamed neither of Simon Serrailler nor of anything else, so far as she remembered, but when she woke, as first light flushed pink across the sky and through her thin bedroom curtains, he filled her mind and after that she did not sleep again but lay thinking, remembering. Looking forward. Hoping.

Thirteen

What they would have done if it had been pouring with rain nobody thought to ask. It was a mild May evening, cloudless and delightful, and the bright blue van stood on the forecourt of Lafferton police station, draped in bright blue ribbons, with two huge bunches of helium balloons attached to the door handles.

Cat and Simon walked round it, glasses of champagne in hand, admiring. The lettering on the sides read 'LAFFERTON POLICE BOBBY VAN'. Below that, in white-outlined boxes, was 'Sponsored by Declan McDermid Ltd'.

'Cost?' Cat said.

'Not sure but he gave 100K altogether. That includes fully equipping it and the first year of running costs.'

'And staffing?'

'No, that has to come out of police budget, but I think careful use is being made of voluntary overtime. The guys are very keen on it.'

'I think it's a great idea.'

'Not new – I think it was the Wiltshire force who got the first and there are a few more around the country now, but cuts have meant they have to be sponsored or paid for by fundraising.'

They wandered back to the crowd of people who were standing around, uniform, CID, assembled guests including the Lord Lieutenant, the High Sheriff and all the other worthies about whom Simon was sometimes less than complimentary.

'I'm surprised there's no royalty.

'Oh, don't worry – Declan McDermid is far more important.'

'Ah yes, Over there.' Cat glanced. McDermid and his wife were surrounded by a large and smiling group.

'Oiling up,' Simon said.

'Hadn't you better?'

'Leaving that to your old man.'

Kieron was standing in the circle. Cat felt a spurt of both pride and affection. In the run-up to her marriage, she had had pangs of misgiving, not so much because of Kieron himself but about marrying again at all. Chris was still part of her, woven into her fibres, and always would be. She had told Kieron as much, fearfully, expecting him to be hurt.

'Of course,' he had said. 'Of course. It never crossed my mind that you wouldn't. Listen, you knew him for, what, more than twenty years, he was the father of your children. I'm not his replacement, I never could be and would never expect to be. I just hope I can make you half as good a husband, that's all.'

She had not had a further moment of doubt and now, looking at him, she realised not only that she loved him and was happy, but that things got better and better as they settled together, and even better still, her children were fine with him, though Hannah had spent the least time in his company. But nevertheless she had welcomed him, partly, Cat thought, because it meant she was free to be away herself, at her performing arts school, without worrying that she ought to be spending more time at home with her mother. Not that anything had ever been said, and Cat would have cut out her own tongue rather than do so. But if it had only been herself, Sam and Felix, things would have more difficult and she would have been lonely, in spite of them, and of her brother and her work. Now, it had all bonded together. Even Simon . . .

She looked at him. He had said that he was pleased about her marriage, he liked Kieron and certainly respected him as the Chief. But Simon was an oyster, good at hiding his real thoughts and feelings. She was never one hundred per cent sure she knew what he was thinking.

Simon had gone over to join the group standing with Declan McDermid and what was presumably his wife, a woman in her fifties. 'Glamorous' was probably the word, Cat thought, watching. She had bouffant hair which had been dyed blonde, very expertly, she was well – too well – made up, she wore a lot of jewellery.

Cat moved across to listen in to her conversation with Simon.

'I'm Cindy McDermid and I'm sure you're something important in the police, only I haven't yet had the pleasure of meeting you.' Her voice had Estuary English intonation and she was looking directly and admiringly at Simon. 'I am so ashamed! Of course you're a Chief Inspector, you've got the look that goes with it.'

Cat was about to judge Cindy McDermid, prior to dismissing her, when the woman turned.

'Hello! I'm Cindy McDermid and I'm afraid . . .'

'Dr Cat Deerbon – also Mrs Kieron Bright.'

'Aww, the lovely Chief Constable's lovely wife to go with him. And you're a doctor not a cop, that makes a change round here. Come and talk to me, tell me all about what kind of doc you are. Have you got a drink? It's really good champagne, quite fizzy.'

She took Cat's arm and led her to a group of chairs on the other side of the van. 'I need to get the weight off my feet – these shoes cost a bloody fortune and they're really not comfortable, you should get comfort as well as style in my book. Do you mind if I take them off for a mo?'

'You go ahead. Not many things worse than aching feet. Sit down.'

'I can't wait. Here, can we have two of those, sweetheart?' She reached out to a passing waiter with a tray of glasses, took two, and winked at him. He was about Sam's age, with a certain amount of acne. He blushed and fled.

'To be frank with you, Carol—'

'Cat – short for Catherine, but only my father ever calls me that.'

Cindy put her hand on Cat's arm. 'So sorry, I always get names wrong, Declan is forever telling me, he never forgets a name, never. Once met . . .' She sighed. 'Where was I?'

'You were about to be frank.'

Cindy let out a yelp of laughter.

'I was. To be frank then, Cat, I'm not very good at all this, these dos. I've learned to get through them, I like people, I like talking to them, don't get me wrong, and I always want to support Dec, but these dos when you say hello to so many and you – well, I mean I – forget their names straight away . . . it's a bit of a trial.'

'Especially when your feet hurt.'

'Especially.' Cindy looked at her with such sudden warmth, such open friendliness, that Cat saw a different woman, and was ashamed of herself for assessing her on a quick look-over as a bit common, a bit brash. She was neither of those things. She had created a front for herself to get through 'these dos' but she was unconfident, she felt out of place, and what she wanted most was just this, a conversation with one other person and to be able to relax, perhaps to confide, to feel at ease. At home.

'I like doctors,' she said now. 'I suppose it comes from watching too much telly . . . *Casualty, Holby,* I love them. Do you think that's funny?'

'Of course not. Why would I? The more people who take an interest in my profession the better. Though those dramas don't always tell it like it is.'

'Oh, I'm sure. I actually watch all the real ones as well – *24 Hours in A&E, One Born Every Minute* . . . What kind of doctor are you, Cat? Do you work at Bevham General?'

'No, I'm a GP. I've been one for a long time, though I used to be the MO for the old Imogen House hospice as well.'

'I bet you're good at your job, I can tell. You've got that some-thing about you. What surgery are you at?'

'Actually, my job has changed over the last year.'

'Tell me. I want to hear. I'll just keep an ear out for when they start the ceremony, you know, Declan cutting his bit of ribbon, I'll need to be there standing by him for that.'

She settled back in her chair, a woman waiting for a good story.

Ten minutes later, she knew almost everything there was to know about Concierge Medical and someone was coughing into a microphone to test it for sound.

'I've got to get up and put these bloody shoes on, Cat, but listen, I want to hear more, I'm really interested – can I get in touch with you? How do I do that?'

They walked towards the assembled crowd. Declan McDermid, in a double-breasted suit, was looking around for his wife. 'I'll catch you later.' Cat slipped over to Kieron. Simon was among his colleagues, standing next to a young blonde woman with a sharp-featured, intelligent face.

'Chief Constable, police officers . . . ladies and gentlemen – does that sound all right?'

Serrailler was surprised that McDermid seemed so diffident, given his confident, upfront profile, his shiny blue suit with emerald-and-red tie, his general air of importance. There had been a big feature about him, and in particular about his philanthropy, in the *Bevham Gazette* and he had come across as the expert self-publicist. He had talked expansively about the Bobby Van project and the party he was throwing tonight, he seemed obviously proud of himself, and yet on meeting him, Simon noticed how little his personality matched the image, how quietly spoken and even shy he was.

His voice was clear enough but he was still hesitant, and he looked down or at the microphone, or the bobby van, rather than at the assembly. His accent, unlike his names, was neither Irish nor Scottish but south London. Several times, he looked at his wife who was standing next to him, as if not only for support but for reassurance. Flash he might seem, but flash in his true persona he was not.

'This bobby van . . . I'm proud to have had the chance to provide it. I've been on at the police here for longer than you might expect asking what they could make best use of with a bit of extra money. They were quite bashful. Now the hospital aren't – you maybe know that I donated a scanner to them a few months ago, but when I asked them, they were straight back with a shopping list. And why not? Well, but then someone told someone else and it got through to me eventually . . . about these bobby vans. There are a lot of old people in this city of Lafferton which has such a smart look to it what with all the new shops and blocks of apartments, but you'll find poverty here and loneliness here just like anywhere else, and when old people are lonely and a bit isolated then they're vulnerable – or they feel it anyway. They're frightened someone might bang on the door pretending to be the meter man and they don't know who to trust, they keep their pension money in cash in a drawer and their bits of valuables in another drawer upstairs, and they ought to have proper security locks and chains and window bolts, but even if they can afford them, they don't know how to get them fitted . . . they're not stupid, they're just out of touch. Then there's people being attacked in their own homes . . . small domestics can turn nasty but maybe if someone comes to check early enough it'll get sorted out. You are all busy, and I know maybe you don't think you can do much in these instances, but now you can. The bobby van is equipped, ready to go, the bobby van officer can go round and help them before anything kicks off. There's it in a nutshell . . . well, more in a mixing bowl.'

Applause. Some laughter. Some muttered asides. The trays of champagne circulated again.

'Mr Big,' Fern whispered to Serrailler. But he shook his head.

'I thought that. I've sort of changed my mind.'

'OK . . . generous anyway.'

'Yup. Got to go and congratulate. Oh – something I meant to ask you but it's all a bit public here.'

'No one's eavesdropping.'

But he was already halfway across to the McDermids, noticing as he went that Cindy was deep in conversation with Cat again.

Fern looked over towards him several times, but eventually let herself be commandeered by a small group of CID who were proposing to leave in five minutes for the Maharajah, Lafferton's newest and reportedly best Indian restaurant. But Serrailler had said he wanted to ask her about something and she hugged the thought – it had not sounded like anything to do with work.

'Is the . . .'

'Is the what?'

'Nothing. Come on, let's go.'

Of course he wasn't going with the rest of them for supper, of course not, and they would none of them had suggested, or

59

wanted it. She looked at him again, as he stood with his sister, the Chief, the McDermids, and then she slipped away with her colleagues.

'If you want to ask me anything, give me a ring. I'm not doing a hard sell – if Concierge isn't right for you, fine.'

Cindy McDermid put her hand on Cat's arm. 'Oh, don't you worry, love, it's right for us, I can tell you that. We've had a lot of trouble with Declan having to have his heart checked and whatnot, and it's always a wait, though we go private for hospital stuff, but now I've found you I'll be filling in your form tomorrow. And maybe you can pop round and collect it, have a cup of coffee or a drink and I'll show you the house. We've only been there a year – Declan had it built just the way we wanted and that took time, but it's perfect now, it's everything we'd planned. Do come. I've so loved meeting you, Cat, and talking to you. I know when you're our doctor it has to be a bit formal, but we can be friends otherwise, can't we?'

Cat looked into her slightly anxious eyes, full of warmth, full of a touching friendliness. She had barely spoken to Declan, got little sense of the man – except that he was less self-confident than he had seemed. A man who liked to do good things with his money and liked people to know it, but she did not blame him for wanting to throw a party. It had been enjoyable, he was generous, and maybe the resulting publicity would encourage others.

Yes. Good people. Genuine people. She was looking forward to visiting.

Fourteen

'I expected them to have a chauffeur,' Kieron said, as they stood outside the station waving the McDermids away.

'Flash car all the same.'

'I'm off,' Simon said. He would walk home. 'Night, you two. I'm not in tomorrow – going up scaffolding to spend a day with the carved angels.'

'You be careful.'

'Don't worry, I've had health and safety crawling all over me.'

Cat's phone buzzed.

SO lovely to meet you. Will have the medical forms signed tomorrow. Call in. Kettle always on. x Cindy

Cat smiled and read the message to Kieron. 'I wonder if she's one of those women who are devoted to their husbands who in turn are also devoted to them but always working.'

'Like me?'

'No. I've got an absorbing job. Haven't time to miss you. I just suspect that she's rather a lonely woman, in spite of it all.'

'She took a shine to you. But who wouldn't?' Kieron waved to a couple of the last guests. The bobby van was being driven slowly round to the back of the station.

'Is McDermid the one backing the cathedral project to restore Simon's carved angels?'

'I thought it was Heritage Lottery.'

'It is but they ask for matching funding.'

'Then it probably is him.'

'Are you going round to the gin palace tomorrow?'

'I don't see why not. I always have visits which take me down that side of the bypass.'

'Christ, what a bloody idiot!' Kieron leaned on the car horn as a car far flashier than the McDermids' undertook them and a lorry, with inches to spare, and screamed off into the darkness.

'Where are the police patrols when you need them?'

He muttered something rude.

Cat tapped into her phone. *Cindy, thank you. Would love coffee. Might have to be an early one – 10? Let me know. Cat*

Fifteen

She had to visit a ninety-year-old who had just come out of hospital but he was comfortable, cheerful and being well looked after, and Cat was on the road again by nine thirty, heading to see Cindy McDermid, going over what their meeting had made her suddenly aware of in relation to herself. She had always had several good women friends to have lunch or coffee with on days off, sometimes fellow members of the St Michael's Singers, and she valued them greatly. But in the last few years she seemed to have had less time for that sort of social break, after Chris's illness and death, her role as a single parent, the various problems and crises in her work life, Simon's attack and recovery, conflicts with her father. Then had come marriage to Kieron. So, did she have friends still? Not acquaintances, not family, real friends? She understood why Cindy McDermid had seemed so eager to know her, invite her home. She was lonely, which Cat, who treasured her own company when she could get it, never was. Had she a family? She would doubtless find that out and more within the next ten minutes.

The house was a rather raw new build, brick and stucco, with electronic gates and an imposing entrance, steps and pillars and lines of small lollipop trees.

The gates were open when Cat reached the house. She drove in and parked up. A ginger cat sat on the top step, miaowing, but ran off when Cat leaned down to stroke it.

There was a big lion knocker on the front door, and an old-fashioned brass bell, which, when Cat pressed it, rang chimes. On either side were stone urns full of scarlet geraniums, together with two bristle boot scrapers and two pristine snow shovels. Perhaps someone, probably not Cindy, polished these every day, like the step in front of the door, which was white like icing on a cake.

There was no reply to the bell, so she lifted the lion knocker and banged it a couple of times. It was very heavy and sounded loudly inside. No one came. There were no footsteps or voices. No sound at all. Maybe Cindy had forgotten and gone out.

Cat wandered round the outside of the house. The garden at the back was extraordinary, very formal, very Italian, very designed, with more urns, flights of steps, lily ponds, statues, fountains, lollipop trees and shaven lawns. More scarlet geraniums. It had an oddly lifeless air. Did anyone ever sit on the curved stone benches or take a drink out to the gazebo with its domed roof and pillared sides?

She went back. The cat had disappeared.

Her phone rang, and she went to the car to answer it, save the details of two more calls she had to make, and send Cindy a text saying she was at the house and could stay until ten fifteen.

She updated patient notes on her laptop and sent them across to Sandy, who kept the practice records.

The cat had reappeared on the top step. Cat went up and rang and knocked hard again. The sounds died away, and then the echo of the sounds. The entrance hall was probably high-ceilinged and spacious, without furniture or soft flooring. There was no answering sound. The cat brushed against her leg.

And then she heard something. Or perhaps not. Or perhaps.

It had come from the house, a voice but not a voice. A sound that might have been a cry, something that was possibly not human. Another cat. The cat that was outside the door now had its paws up against it and was asking to be let in. Then the cry again. Cat turned the brass handle and the door opened easily.

The cat shot between her legs and raced up the stairs leading from what was, exactly as she had imagined, a wide, handsome hall with a cupola above that let in the light, and black-and-white tiles in lozenge shapes on the floor. It was the perfect imitation of a grand English country house except everything was new, shiny, clean.

But she had only a moment to take it in because she heard the sound again, a muffled, strangulated noise, coming from above. She took out her phone and kept it firmly in her hand as she ran up the stairs. On the landing the ginger cat was now wailing, but behind that noise and the faint muffled murmur, there was a strange and disturbing silence, which had a depth to it that signalled more than the emptiness of a house whose occupiers had gone out.

Two doors were standing open. One led into a small room fitted out as a library with a curious mixture of matching leather-bound books, spines exactly aligned and which looked as if they had never been taken from the shelves, let alone read, and a hotchpotch of paperbacks. But no one was in the room and it seemed undisturbed until Cat noticed two small alcoves with shelves for ornaments. The shelves were empty.

The cat was trying to trip her up now, weaving in and out of her legs, then leading her through an open door opposite.

It was a handsome, brilliantly light sitting room with another cupola and a row of tall, sashed windows. Cat took in the sight of a woman lying on the floor, a lot of blood, and a man tied to a straight-backed chair, with more blood, on his head and face, and a gag tight round his mouth. His eyes were half open, and he moaned before his head slumped suddenly to one side.

The cat was back at her feet now, distraught, eyes huge, still wailing.

'Emergency. What service do you require?'

When she had summoned ambulance and police, Cat untied the gag from Declan McDermid's mouth and checked his breathing and pulse. Both registered, though the pulse was weak and thready. The wounds on his head and the side of his face were extensive and deep, but the bleeding had stopped, probably some time ago.

She knelt beside Cindy. She was still wearing the clothes from the previous evening's party. The blood on and around her had come from severe blows, made by something heavy, to her head. Her cheekbone was smashed, and her nose, one eye had been beaten in. She had no pulse and she was not breathing. Her body was cold. Cat touched her cheek gently.

She rang Kieron but got both his and his secretary's voicemails, then dialled Simon with the same result, before remembering that he would by now be on a scaffold in the roof of the cathedral, drawing pens and paper block in hand, sketching a medieval carved angel. He would not reply for the rest of his working session.

From the bypass, the wail of the ambulance and police sirens came up to her, as she stood beside Declan, holding his hand and talking to him quietly. The paramedics would take over. Then, as the vehicles turned off the main road below the house, the room was completely silent again. There was no movement of air. Even the cat, sitting at Cindy McDermid's feet, was like a cat-statue, stiff with shock.

Sixteen

It was not a job for anyone with a poor head for heights. Serrailler was sitting on the plank flooring of the scaffold high up above the nave. If he looked down through the metal rods he could see the pews, the black-and-white tiles of the floor, and small figures moving slowly about, heads back to study the stained-glass windows, the fan vaulting of the roof, which was above him, and the organ pipes.

He was close beside one of the carved heads of angels, each one of which was set, in its turn, above a carved rosette, and each rearing out from its roof strut, as if it were about to launch into flight heavenwards. He was cramped, just able to balance his sketchbook on his knees and lean against the pillar. He was also warm. Looking across to the opposite side he could see a man and a woman painstakingly cleaning two of the other angels with fine-pointed tools, cloths and brushes, to prise out the grime of centuries. Once, they had waved to Simon. Once, the girl had disappeared down the four long ladders which led from the top of the scaffolding to the nave floor, and returned, climbing carefully back up, half an hour later. Once or twice, he noticed some of the people who were looking up catch sight of them, or of him, and point them out, or stare. Or wave.

Simon did not usually undertake commissions. He preferred to work at what he found, bumped up against or, even more likely, had become fascinated by, often almost at random – bones, birds, buildings, weirdly shaped trees, people. He had drawn his nephew Felix more times than he could remember, because he had such a beautiful but slightly irregular face with an expression that was usually serious and thoughtful, but occasionally blazed with sudden joy or broke up with laughter. He had drawn his mother after death, and his sister Martha, the cat Mephisto, but never the Yorkshire terrier Wookie though he had no idea why the little dog, of whom he was quite fond, did not appeal to him visually. But the medieval heads of these angels were remarkable, not because of where they were, but because of who they were – depicted as angels but in fact the faces of the medieval people who had worked on the building of this cathedral for decades, who had been in the few streets and many fields around Lafferton in the twelfth century and perhaps earlier. They had been copied and transformed in status from the carpenters and stonemasons, housewives and barrow boys, monks and priests and nuns they were in everyday life, to these holy beings, ethereal and timeless, who were angels and yet still and eternally human. If you had walked past the one he was drawing now in the twelfth century street or marketplace, you would have recognised a neighbour, a cousin, a stallholder, nodded to him in greeting.

Now, Simon took his finest pen nib – he was drawing in ink – to work on the strands of the man's eyebrows and lashes. He was absorbed and totally happy, in his own elevated bubble, even unaware of the cramp in his legs.

Then, footsteps were coming along the planks. He held his pen still. Maybe someone was bringing him coffee. The girl opposite had done so first thing that day, from the enterprising new coffee bar in a van, set up outside the main gate – real coffee from freshly ground beans. 'I've brought you Kenyan,' she had said, a plain girl, with a beaming smile which made her pretty. 'They do Guatemalan, Nicaraguan – just let me know.'

'Kenyan is fine. It smells amazing. Thanks – how much?'

'On us this time. You can buy the next lot but I don't mind going for them. I like running up and down the ladders.'

'Go carefully.'

'Trick is, just go, don't think about where you're putting your feet, definitely don't look, just go and your body's instinct will guide you.'

'Hmm. Sorry, I don't know your name. I'm Simon.'

'Sally.'

But this time, it was not Sally.

'Morning, guv. Sorry about this but your phone's switched off.'

He knew that a uniform would not have been sent, given his location and that he was off duty, for something trivial.

'What's up?'

The PC was even taller than Serrailler, bent almost double and staying well away from the wall of scaffolding. He was also keeping his eyes focused straight ahead.

'You're needed, sorry, and it's urgent. Break-in and murder.'

'Where?'

'The McDermids'. I'm taking you straight there.'

'Right, let's move.'

The constable hesitated, panic in his eyes. 'It's . . . guv, would you mind going first?'

'Sure. Don't worry, this isn't for everyone, I know, but take it slowly and backwards.'

It wasn't the easiest descent, even for someone with a good head for heights, and he appreciated what it had cost Combes to climb up there and down again. Back on the ground, he told him so. And then they moved.

The entrance gates to Declan McDermid's house were wide open, but there was a uniform on the gate and crime scene barriers across the entrance.

'Stop here, I'll walk up to the house. You get back to the nick. Thanks, Combes.'

'Guv.'

It was overcast but dry and the drive had well-clipped low shrubs lining it on either side, in between which were lights, some of the many which lit up the property after dark. There was a CCTV camera on the pillar at the entrance and Serrailler noticed another over the front porch as he reached it. The front door was also taped, with another PC on duty.

'Guv.' He reached to unhook the tape.

'Morning. Who's here already?'

'DS Parks and DC Monroe. The Chief had gone off early, over to the far side of the county, but he's returning as soon as he can.'

Simon stepped back and looked at the door, the pillars, the lion's head knocker, the gleaming brass knob. Nothing seemed to have been interfered with, there were no obvious signs of any break-in or even damage, though the SOCOs would be over every last millimetre and if there was anything to find they would find it.

'Morning, guv. Sorry, I know it's your day off.'

'Not your fault, Graham. Fill me in.'

'They were both found in their sitting room upstairs. Mr McDermid was in a chair, bound and gagged and in a poor way – bleeding from the head, nasty injuries, but he was still semi-conscious. He was rushed off on a blue light and I haven't heard anything. Mrs McDermid was on the floor and she'd been dead a while.'

'Who found them?'

'Well, actually, guv, it was Dr Deerbon. She's still upstairs.'

'No, she's coming down,' Cat said.

She looked as calm and efficient as ever, but Simon saw the aftermath of shock in her face. She had seen plenty of badly injured, dead and dying people in her time but he doubted if she had been the first on the scene of anything like this.

She touched her brother's arm. 'You want to go and have a look? There are two CID already up there.'

'Leave them to it. Are you OK for a few minutes? We'll go outside.'

'Sure, I've put my calls onto Luke. He'll take over until I let him know. Yes, outside would be good.'

They walked round the corner of the house to the garden and one of the benches overlooking the fountain.

'Stately home. It's all a bit raw – Cindy said they'd only finished it a year ago.'

'All right, tell me.'

Cat began with the arrangement, made by text message the previous evening, to have coffee with Cindy McDermid, fill in the Concierge forms, then she moved straight on to her arrival.

'It was the cat that really got the wind up me in the end – a nice ginger cat, but it was so nervy, it knew there was something very wrong.'

'Had the place been knocked about?'

'Not so far as I could see. There's no mess in general. Just the blood, on the carpet, on the chair he was sitting on. The rug at his feet. She was in a pool of it.'

'Was she dead when you found her?'

'Oh yes. I'm not a pathologist but she'd been dead a few hours – maybe four or five?'

'What sort of state is he in?'

'Bad. He isn't a young man and this sort of thing can have knock-on effects, apart from the immediate danger from his injuries.

'Shock.'

'Shock. Blood loss. Heart attack, stroke – obviously he'll be closely monitored. I don't think he'll die from his injuries unless he has a fractured skull or brain damage, and from my superficial observation that looked unlikely. They'll do an MRI and then you'll know more.'

'Are you all right?'

'Yes. But it was nasty. You can imagine. We were only with them a few hours ago. Was this a planned thing, do you suppose?'

'I haven't taken it in yet, but there appears to be so little damage and no signs of forced entry, unless they broke in somewhere round the back out of sight. The gates weren't bashed in. It looks pretty well planned.'

'The gates were wide open when I arrived but they're electronic. I thought those always closed automatically after someone went through, in either direction.'

'They do – unless they've been disabled.' Simon stood up. 'Someone will come over to get a formal statement from you. You're the key witness – the only witness. This evening?'

71

'I'll be finished around five but I have to collect Felix from choir. I don't know when Kieron will be back. Will tomorrow morning do?'

'Not really. Can you call into the station then? I'll get everything I can from here before I go over to Bevham General. I need to talk to Declan McDermid as soon as he's allowed to see me.'

'Might be a while, Si.'

'Jesus, what is this all about?' He was suddenly furious. 'Bastards. What had poor Cindy McDermid done to deserve that? No, don't bother to answer.' He gave her a quick hug and saw her into her car.

'Do you think he knew them? That he maybe let them in?'

'It's a possibility. The other is that the scumbags were already in the house when the McDermids got back and surprised them, that Declan tried to stop them taking things and so it got violent. They panicked. But I'm only speculating, don't say anything. There's a lot of work to be done on it, but if he is in a fit state to talk to me, that will get us a long way.'

He watched Cat drive off and returned to the house, taking the imposing staircase slowly, looking around, but nothing seemed out of the ordinary. The sound of voices speaking quietly led him into the sitting room, where two SOCOs in spacesuits were on their hands and knees.

'Morning. Has Mrs McDermid's body gone?'

'Soon as the pathologist confirmed death, guv. She said to say she'll do the PM straight away and phone in.'

'Who was it?'

'Dr Donato,' Fern Monroe said, coming into the room. 'Hi.'

Simon frowned. 'Good morning, DC Monroe.' He turned straight back to the SOCO.

'What have you got so far?'

'No prints. We haven't been round all the windows at the back of the house, and there are quite a lot, but the first uniform on the scene said he could see no sign of a break-in. They wore gloves, they wore rubber shoes. They were experts.'

'Mrs McDermid?'

'Beaten about the head, they both were. Blood on the carpet, on the wall here, close to where she fell, on this chair edge, and all over the chair he was tied up in, on the belt used to tie him and the scarf they gagged him with. This is going to take a while, guv. I'll shout if we find traces of anything at all that could identify them but don't hold your breath.' She leaned forward again, and continued to brush millimetre by millimetre along the crevices between the polished oak floorboards.

Fern Monroe had gone to the window and was looking out, and Serrailler was about to speak to her again when the DS appeared.

'They disabled the CCTV and the alarms and those are pretty state of the art. They also froze the electronic gates. They got in with keys and the alarm code. Must have sussed that out before somehow.'

'Tyre marks?'

'Maybe.'

'Don't tell me – the McDermids' own car, my sister's car from this morning, and then the world and his wife.'

'Gravel's churned up right and left, yes, you're right, guv, but even if their tracks had been untouched we don't often get much – this sort of large-stoned gravel doesn't hold the impress of tyre marks. Even if it did, you'd only be able to narrow it down to a 4x4, or, most likely, our old friend a white van.'

'Anything disturbed in the rest of the house? Take me round.'

On the landing Andy pointed to spaces in the alcoves where ornaments must have stood, empty shelves, faint marks where pictures had hung.

'Monroe?' Serrailler called.

Fern came hurriedly out, expression blank.

'What do you reckon?'

'Guv?'

'Conclusions?'

She hesitated and then said, 'Professional.'

'Yup. And?'

'More than one.'

'Because?'

'Professionals accessing large houses with plenty of valuables and who kill one person and badly injure a second don't work alone. Guv . . . one thing. The two guys we went to interview out at Ash Farm – Tim Letts and Ade Holland?'

Serrailler nodded.

'Do you think this could be the same gang?'

'Do you?'

'Probably, yes. Nice big house, the owner's well known locally and known to be rich, so there must be plenty of valuables. The house isolated, though not in the same way as the farmhouse. They came when they knew the owners were out.'

'At the reception.'

'Only . . .'

'Only?'

She looked troubled and then shrugged. 'No. Nothing, guv.'

'Right. Good thinking anyway. When you get back to the station, go through the file about the Ash Farm robbery and the scam they set up, see if anything, anything at all, seems to marry with this.'

Fern hovered at a window, standing well back, until she saw the patrol car taking Serrailler to Bevham General turn out into the road. She had wanted to suggest that she drive him there herself but thought better of it. Perhaps he was regretting their drink and supper together, or perhaps it had meant absolutely nothing beyond just that, a drink, supper, and she was making a fool of herself. But at least no one else had an inkling about that and, whatever happened, she intended to keep it so. He was a very different man on duty this morning, as was only right of course, but she felt a chill emanating from him and not just because she had been a bit too informal.

Was she imagining all this? Cindy McDermid kept appearing in her head, a friendly, warm, not altogether relaxed woman, in uncomfortably high heels, wobbling slightly, clutching a glass of champagne, glancing at her husband, being supportive, being proud.

'For Christ's sake,' she muttered, shocked when she thought that the images were the last of Cindy alive and cheerful. Violent death. You never got used to it. It always got to you, often weeks later. But although the road accidents and the drownings and the house fires were shocking, two sorts of violent death were unquestionably the worst – those of children, and suicides. A violent death after an unprovoked assault, like this one, came next on the list.

The quiet work of collecting went on for the rest of the day – samples, prints, dust, fluff and a thousand other things no one ever thought of as being part of their daily lives in their own houses. The sun slanted in at first at the front of the house, then at the side, finally through the windows at the back. Uniform officers changed guard, some CID came, others left. The house in which the McDermids had been living and happy twenty-four hours earlier, where they had dressed for the bobby van presentation evening, seemed to be held in suspension. One of the officers had found the ginger cat lurking under the stairs and tried to coax it out but it had stared at him from huge eyes and made an odd noise in its throat, a hissing growl. All the same, Ben liked cats, as he liked all animals, and he sensed that it would not come to him but it might to a food bowl. But whether it did or didn't, it surely could not stay in this empty house on its own. No one had called in or telephoned. If there were staff, they seemed not to come on Thursdays.

He went into the kitchen and opened the two big fridges and found a tin of Tuna Delight for Cats. He put what was left into the bowl on the floor and tapped it with the fork. At first, nothing happened. He stepped out of the way and waited. Still nothing.

'Ben? Where are you?'

He left the food and crossed the hall towards the stairs. As he did so, the ginger cat shot through the kitchen door and DC Sandhu came in from outside.

'Any news?'

'Not here. SOCO are still hard at it. I've just tried feeding the cat. Poor thing, it can't stay here on its own.'

'Can't it?' Bilaval said vaguely.

'No. We ought to find out if there's a daily or a housekeeper or someone. There's got to be a list of numbers.'

'No. People have those on their phones.'

'Not old people.'

'True. But they weren't – aren't that old though and he's a business guy.'

They went up to the sitting room where forensics were finishing off and preparing to move to the stairs and hall.

'Nothing more for us at the moment,' the DS said. 'I'll take you back, Ben. Bil, there's been a breaking and entering in St Luke's Road. Sounds like small stuff, back window broken, people away, doubt if it's anything to do with this, but there's a neighbour you should go and talk to – break-in was at 24, neighbour at 26.'

'Who shall I take?'

'No one's free. You're on your own. Now let's get out of here.'

'Any news from the Super?'

'No. He might be talking to McDermid. Or more likely sitting by his bed waiting for him to come round. Bugger of a job. He'll have to break the news about the wife to him as well. Wonder if they've traced any family?'

They stood on the top step for a moment, looking down the drive. Apart from the low hum of traffic on the bypass, there was no sound, no disturbance. Nothing. Only the strange, familiar atmosphere that always crept in and settled like a fog in the aftermath of a murder, as if violence and rage and blood and fear had somehow been impressed upon the very air.

Seventeen

Later, Cal would tell him that she was not surprised, it had to happen and she was half glad it had. But he had never spoken about it other than on a practical level – would he continue to have pain from his arm, would he ever reach the point where the prosthesis became second nature? She had answered as well as she could, while reminding him that she was not an expert and he should ask his physio those questions, or even the surgeon who had removed his arm after the sepsis. He had not done so, he had got on with it, and was lucky to have had had few problems and the minimum of pain.

But this was not pain. This was different.

He showed his warrant card at reception, and was pointed to the lift. It took him to the fourth floor, after which he crossed a covered way into the new block. ITU had been moved across into it the previous year, expanded and given a special budget to make it the best in the county.

People came and went in scrubs, overalls, civvies, badges dangling round necks, carrying things, not carrying things. A wheelchair. An empty trolley being pushed past. He wondered if he would bump into Sam. Probably not – it was a huge hospital. It was quieter up here than in the main lobby, where there were shops and crowds, noticeboards, tannoys and the sound of the lift bells ringing every few seconds. He walked on, following the procession of signs, dark blue lettering on white. Nothing was unusual. He felt as he had felt all morning.

ITU.

He went through the doors. A short corridor. A light reception area with a long desk. And a different feeling. A tension in the air. No rush but something else, some sense of importance and seriousness. Here, people were at various stages between life and death. Here, they spoke quietly. Here machinery beeped and bipped. Here, people moved in a different way.

It was none of those things and all of those things, but first, as he walked towards the desk, it was the smell, the smell of every clinical area in every hospital. Antiseptic. Medication. Other things.

The smell overwhelmed him. He felt his throat constrict. His heart pounded from normal to insistent, hammering. He was hot, and then cold and his fingers, the fingers of his own real right hand, tingled. He could not breathe. He had to gulp air down. His legs turned to some strange soft, rubbery substance and might not hold him up. He put out a hand to steady himself but there was nothing to hold on to.

'Are you all right?'

He could feel himself sliding down the wall and then being supported, walked to a chair, sat down. His pulse being taken. Voices seemed to recede and come near, echo and shout. He was in a half-nightmare, but most of all, he felt a sense of impending doom so great that he wanted to scream out for whoever was holding his arm to save him.

Things blurred and voices came and went and then he was lying down.

'God . . . what . . .'

'It's all right. I'm putting an ECG tracer on you. Do you have any chest pain or pain anywhere else? Does it hurt to breathe?'

He could not breathe.

'I don't know . . . not chest pain.'

'All right, take a couple of slow deep breaths from your diaphragm . . . not high up in your chest, breathe from deep down. Slowly. That's good, that's good . . . and hold it for three seconds . . . now breathe out slowly. Slowly. That's better. Now just breathe normally for me.'

She was young, too young, no nurse should be as young. And a young man, though not quite as young. A stethoscope, and then pulse again. Something in his ear and quickly out again.

'Can you tell me your name and why you're here?'

Everything cleared. The blind was whipped up and the light came in.

'Detective Chief Superintendent Simon Serrailler. My warrant card is in my jacket, inner pocket. I'm here to see Declan McDermid. He's in ITU.'

'Ah. Just lie still while I look at the trace. More deep breaths if you feel light-headed again – you shouldn't now.'

'I need to talk to him.'

'Not sure you can, but let's just get you sorted out before we look into that. When you sit up, I want you to drink a glass of water.'

'I need to talk to Declan McDermid.'

'You can talk all you like, he won't answer, he's under sedation.'

Serrailler sat up.

'Don't rush it.'

'I'm fine. How long will he be like that?'

'No idea. Right, you're OK to go. ECG is good, everything else is good. I recommend you get a drink and something to eat.'

Outside the cubicle he was back in the orbit of bleeping, blipping machines.

'You OK now?'

'Thanks, fine, but I'm really here to see—'

'Mr McDermid, yes.'

'Two minutes only and I'm counting. Room 9. And you see your GP.'

Going down the corridor, past drawn curtains, past closed and then open doors, machines not only bleeping but pulsating green or white, on off, on off. The smells. He stopped. Deep breath. It made no difference. He wanted to run. He turned round and touched his hand to the wall.

'You,' the doctor said behind him, 'are having panic attacks. You can get those sorted out, you know. As I said – your GP. He can refer you.'

79

Serrailler moved away from the wall and went on, angry but forgiving because he was a junior doctor, he knew nothing about him. He had no mental health problems and he had definitely never had whatever a panic attack was in his life.

Room 9. The door was open. A nurse was adjusting the drip.

He stepped back quickly, as the walls of the small room seemed to balloon out and then in again. His vision blurred.

'What can I do for you? It's relatives only in here.'

He forced himself to step forward again. 'It's OK, police' – he fumbled for his warrant card.

'All right, but if you're thinking of talking to him . . .'

'Still not awake?' He looked at her intently, to avoid having to look at the machines, the drip, the bed, even the figure on the bed, attached to various tubes and wires.

'No. Maybe in a few hours.'

'I'll come back . . . tomorrow probably.'

'That'll be your best bet.'

'Thank you, thanks a lot . . . Nurse . . .' He tried to see her badge.

'Hughes, Sister Becky Hughes.'

She came down the corridor with him. He felt normal again. He could see the sky out of the windows ahead.

'Will you be on duty tomorrow?'

'Depends what time you come.'

'You tell me.'

'Ah now.' She smiled as she turned towards the computer to log her results. 'That's for me to know and you to find out.'

He went out of ITU feeling better but needing coffee. The League of Friends cafe was busy but he got a corner table, an Americano and a ham salad roll, and tried to work out what had happened to him. Panic attack? Why? The attempt on his life? But he remembered precious little about it. The period in his own ITU bed had been painful, boring, alarming, by turns, but he had never thought that he was unable to cope, because he always coped. In his own way, his own time. Coped.

He dismissed the junior medic's diagnosis because as soon as he was halfway down the coffee he felt better, flooded with energy, his mind working efficiently, as he thought back over the time he had spent at the McDermids' crime scene. Low blood sugar, he remembered his mother saying when he had come home, with his brother and sister, at the end of the school day, pale-faced and cross. She had poured tea, toast and honey and home-made cake into them and, as she had said, watched them revive like wilting flowers given fresh water.

But he knew there had to be more. He checked his phone. Forensics had drawn a complete blank in terms of anything save Declan's and Cindy's blood – no prints, no marks, no one else's blood or other fluid containing DNA. It was as if the place had been sterilised.

Cindy had died from the blows to her head, which had fractured her skull, and from blood loss. The pathologist had not quite finished but estimated her death as being between six and seven hours before Cat had found the body.

There were also various notes about the absence of tyre marks in the drive, the dismantled alarm system and so on, none of which were any help at all to the team.

He had finished his roll and the surprisingly good coffee but he did not leave. He had the crime scene in his head, and from there he was tracking back through the hours to the moment they had watched the McDermids drive away from the reception at the station. They had been cheerful, had enjoyed themselves, they were proud of the evening. They liked doing good things with their money for the local community, and they liked people to know it, and Simon did not blame them for that, and nor did anyone else. Yet somehow, they seemed to have had made enemies. Or had they? The robbery had clearly not been random, it was meticulously planned and carried out with professional skill, but it was surely not any sort of personal vendetta. So why the violence? Why beat Cindy McDermid to death and tie up and badly injure her husband?

'Do you mind if I sit here?'

He looked into the face of the nurse who had been checking on Declan. She held a tray with a salad and an apple, a mug of coffee and a doughnut, and she was smiling at him, a slight, ironic but not unfriendly smile.

'Of course not. I was just going to get another coffee – could you keep my place?'

She sat down. 'With pleasure.'

Serrailler went over to the counter, smiling to himself.

Eighteen

'Guv?'

He was still in the hospital car park when his phone rang.

'On my way back. No joy with McDermid, he's still sedated. Any news your end?'

'They didn't find anything at the house except Mrs McDermid's phone – it had been dropped and skidded across the polished floor and under a chest. Anyway, it was retrieved. Damaged, out of battery . . . not too many contacts surprisingly, but we found the housekeeper – Mrs Pauline Mead, lives in Bevham, on the Lafferton edge. Want us to go?'

'Address?'

'45 Larch Close, Deepdale—'

'I know it. I'm three or four minutes away from there so I'll see her. Wonder why she didn't come to the house this morning.'

'Day off?'

'Very likely. Thanks, Andy. Anything else?'

'Looking for relatives – no one with their surname on the phone so it's going through and checking each contact.'

'Who's on that?'

'DC Monroe.'

'Right.'

He drove off wondering about both Sister Becky Hughes and Fern Monroe, knowing he had no serious interest in either but would be happy for a date or two. It had been a long time.

*

Deepdale was a pleasant area of Bevham, once separated from it only by woodland and fields. It still had a touch of rurality about it, mainly because although the houses were typical 1930s suburban semis, with the odd large detached among them, the gardens were disproportionately large and there were old hedge-rows lining the canal, which ran through Deepdale on its way to Lafferton.

45 Larch Close. The house was neat and the front had been repainted, the double glazing on the windows looked new. Simon parked and looked at it for a moment before going up the path. It was quiet apart from some muffled traffic noise from the main roads. A squirrel shot up the trunk of a chestnut tree and bounced along one of the branches. A dog barked from a back garden.

He hoped that Mrs Mead was not on her own and, even more, that she had already heard the news. He remembered knocking on all too many doors, as a uniform and then with CID, his stomach clenched tight, glancing at his colleague for reassurance as they heard footsteps coming downstairs into a hall, or along a passage, sometimes the rattle of a door chain. A face. Enquiring. Distracted. Worried. And then the look. Dread. Denial. Bewilderment. Shock.

The door opened.

'Mrs Pauline Mead? Detective Chief Superintendent Simon Serrailler, Lafferton CID. I wonder if I could have a word with you please.'

He realised that he should not be doing this alone, he should have got Andy, or Fern Monroe, anyone, to stand there with him, for her as much as for him. It was the form. The way things should be done.

She simply waited for him to speak. She looked neither worried nor surprised.

'May I come in?'

'I hope this isn't about Gary, because if it is, I don't want to know, nor will Michael – that's my husband. We gave up on our son many years ago, and you'd be wasting your time going to anyone else in the family either. Gary's a waste of space.'

'It isn't about your son.'

'Oh. Well, come in then – I'm afraid everything's in a mess because we only got back from holiday this morning, I'm in the middle of unpacking still. We flew into Heathrow at six.'

She led him into a tidy, pleasant sitting room, with doors onto the long narrow garden which was clearly the garden of someone who loved it, worked hard at it and must be proud of it. There was no mess, just an open wheelie suitcase and a couple of airline carrier bags on the sofa.

'Been on a cruise,' Pauline Mead said. She had been waiting to tell him – to tell anyone. 'Caribbean cruise. It was out of this world. Just a bit of a comedown, back here . . . bit of a shock to the system, if you follow.'

'I do.'

She would be in her early fifties, small, nervy, with short, greying hair, shrewd eyes. A nice woman. The sort of woman you would trust to look after your house.

'May I sit down, Mrs Mead?'

There was something in his tone of voice. He saw that she had picked it up. Her expression changed.

'Something's happened, hasn't it?'

'I'm afraid so.'

When he told her she became absolutely still. And ashen. She sat looking at her own hands, and he had a rush of recall of other times like this, and it was so often the same – silence, stillness, pallor, before tears, before cries and questions and desperate denials as the facts began to penetrate below the first layer of consciousness, to be gradually understood. But never accepted. Never ever truly accepted.

'What should I do?' She looked at him with the eyes of an anxious child.

'It would be really helpful if you could come to the house with me, Mrs Mead. You are the best person to tell us what things are missing and if there have been any other disturbances. Could you face doing that?'

'Today? Now?'

'It would help us enormously.'

85

'The trouble is, my husband's taken the car to get some shopping, there's nothing in—'

'I'll drive you there and get a car to bring you back, of course.'

'Oh. I see. Then I should, shouldn't I? I should do this for them. They're the best employers, you know . . . they paid for us to go on this cruise. I've worked for them exactly ten years now – first in the old house, then in this – and they wanted to mark that, make it an anniversary. Can you imagine anyone else doing that?' Her eyes filled with tears abruptly. 'Who could do this? What sort of people could do this? They're animals – no, worse. Animals wouldn't do it. Oh!' She put her hand to her mouth. 'Tigger. What's happened to Tigger?'

'Is that a ginger cat? He's fine – I think one of our PCs found some food for him in the kitchen.'

'I wonder if . . . should I go to the hospital first?'

'No, because Mr McDermid is sedated – they'll let us know when he can see anyone. Do they have family, Mrs Mead, because we need to be in touch with them, obviously.'

'No. Cindy – Mrs McDermid – she had a sister and an elderly mother but they both died a couple of years ago. There's nobody. Which has always seemed sad because they have – had – they have so much to give and I don't just mean money – they give away plenty of that. But affection, attention . . . they'd have made wonderful grandparents. Still, if Gary is anything to go by, they're better off without. Anyone would be. Do you have children, Mr . . . sorry, I forgot the name.'

'Simon Serrailler. No children of my own but plenty of family otherwise, yes, a sister and a brother, nephews, a niece. I should have asked you if I could make you some tea or just a glass of water. I'm so sorry. Would you like it before we go?'

How long was it since he had done that? Making tea was what family liaison officers did most of the time, making tea, sitting and drinking it, washing up, making more. He had not been an FLO but he had made plenty of tea in unfamiliar kitchens.

'I think I would. I feel a bit . . .'

'Sit down again. We'll have some tea and you can try and get your head round it all. It's not easy.'

'There'll be milk in the fridge, my neighbour got it in and . . .'

'I'll find everything.'

He did and took the tray into the sitting room. Pauline Mead was standing at the window.

'Are you the gardener?'

'We both are . . . we're out there more than we're inside. Thank you for this. I shouldn't expect to be waited on.'

Serrailler was all too aware that climbing up the ranks could so easily mean losing touch with people, which was why something so simple as making tea now was important, as much for him as for her. It was why he still liked to do some interviews himself, why he did not always send his juniors on a routine call. One of the chief reasons he had become a policeman at all.

'Have you any idea about who could have done this?' Pauline Mead asked, as people always did.

'Not yet but it's early days. They were professionals – left everything clean, no fingerprints, not the slightest thing that could have identified them. Most burglars make tiny mistakes, leave some trace, but these were very careful, which makes our job difficult but not impossible. It's never impossible. When we get to the house, I'd like you to go into every room and look around it. You know it better than anyone except the owners themselves, you'll spot what's unusual, what's missing . . . and can you also think of anything – anything at all – that happened recently and that might seem odd? Someone calling at the house? Someone phoning? People or vehicles hanging about?'

'It isn't a place you can hang about near, is it? You'd be seen. And the gates only open to let in a car when the intercom button inside the house is pressed, unless you've the code, like I have.'

'The gates were wide open first thing this morning. Someone had left them like that.'

'They can't have, the gates close themselves.'

'Maybe the system was disabled. The alarms were.'

She set down her empty cup. 'They worked it all out, didn't they? For God knows how long, they were planning it. To rob, to murder—'

'No, I doubt if they meant to do that – or even to be violent at all. I think they were surprised – the McDermids came back before they were expected. And when people are caught in the act – caught off guard – they can quickly turn nasty.'

Pauline Mead looked stricken, with distress, with grief – and with anger. Her face had changed, she had aged in front of him. It happened. He remembered that it happened.

'Mr McDermid's in a bad way but they don't think it's hopeless. I'll know more later.'

'I'd say that's good, Mr Serrailler, of course I would, except that Cindy was everything to him, there's no one else and I wonder how he'll even begin to cope without her. He won't want to live. That's a terrible thing to say, I know, but I'm sure of it. Oh . . . can you . . .'

'Do you feel OK?'

'Yes. But I have to ask . . . have they . . . has she . . . Cindy, I mean . . .'

He slowed. 'Her body was taken from the house this morning. There's nothing distressing to see.'

'Oh. Thank you. It's just . . . I've never seen anyone dead.'

How many times had he? From his first week as a rookie PC until this morning? How many and in how many different states? Death by accident, from suicide. Death by drowning, strangulation, stabbing, gunshot, carbon monoxide poisoning, burning. Or simply from natural causes. His sister Martha. His mother. Others he had seen in the course of work, because even for a cop, the most common death was still a natural one.

They came through the gates and Serrailler stopped and switched off the engine. The forensics' van had left but there was a patrol car, parked next to Andy's Golf.

He put his hand on Mrs Mead's. 'Take as much time as you want, walk around outside for a bit . . . whatever you find easiest. When you're ready to go into the house I'll come with you.'

She looked at him. 'You've been very kind to me, very thoughtful. Thank you. You've made it – well, it isn't easy, of course it isn't, but as much as it could be. Has anyone ever told you what a kind man you are? I hope they have.'

She was surprisingly composed, going slowly from room to room. Serrailler followed her and gave her all the time she wanted, did not ask questions or interrupt, but as she spotted this or that space where a picture or an ornament was missing, he noted it, once or twice asking her for more details. It was clear that everything had been checked out beforehand. Nothing trivial was taken. The biggest space was in the sitting room. The wall opposite the door was empty and there were several drill holes visible.

'Oh. She's gone. I know she was very valuable,' Pauline Mead said. 'To be honest, Mr Serrailler, she wasn't to my taste. I mean, I know she was very famous and a wonderful film star and all that, and how she died, but that wasn't what I'd choose to have all over my wall.'

'Whose picture was it?'

'Marilyn of course – not one but about six of her, arranged like postage stamps on a sheet, if you can imagine it.'

'Painted or photographed?'

'Well, it looked like a painting but it must have been based on a photo somehow – I've no idea how they do these things.'

Andy Warhol? The famous series, arranged, as she said, like a row of stamps, the portrait of her head and shoulders, the pouting mouth and the blonde smooth hair, waved at the bottom . . . that Marilyn.

Just an original Warhol print would make the entire burglary worthwhile.

'Was there a lot of that sort of art?'

'Yes – very modern taste Declan has, though honestly, I know Cindy didn't much like them. She once said the Marilyn pictures had grown on her but they never grew on me. Her taste was very different, she liked the lovely watercolours . . . there were four in her bedroom – English country scenes, and another of the sea . . . I suppose they've taken them.'

'They knew what they were coming for. Where did Mrs McDermid keep her jewellery?'

'She didn't have much of that actually . . . her wedding and engagement rings, and another diamond eternity ring she always wore. She wasn't one for precious stones. She loved her big necklaces but they're not worth much. Costume jewellery really. The rings would have been on her fingers.' She turned to Simon. 'What – where would they be now?'

'I'm not sure . . . If they took them from her, I know how upsetting the thought of that is. But otherwise any jewellery is carefully removed and kept safe at the mortuary. Nothing goes missing, Mrs Mead. And in case you were wondering – because a lot of people do, when the post-mortem is done . . . you understand that a post-mortem has to be, don't you?'

She nodded, but did not meet his eye this time.

'Everyone is respectful . . . aware that this is a person, an individual, someone missed and loved and whose death may have been sudden and shocking. I really can reassure you.'

'Thank you. Will . . . would . . . I wonder if I could see her. I told you I never have but if . . . I would like it to be Cindy if I do. She was a wonderful employer and friend to me. Not just someone I worked for.'

'I'll find out. Mr McDermid would normally be asked to identify his wife's body but he isn't going to be in any fit state to do that for a while.'

'Then could I do it? Is that a strange thing to want?'

'No. Absolutely not. Of course. I'll get in touch with them in a minute. But we haven't finished going round the house, have we?'

'No, but being new, it doesn't have any cellars or attics so it's just the spare rooms now, and Declan's study, and the library – not that they read much but Declan thought it was what a gentleman should have. He came from an ordinary background, you know, and this house meant a lot to him. He designed it himself. Cindy went along with everything he wanted but she's never been bothered really. He likes the signs that he's moved up in the world and why not?'

'He's certainly been a great public benefactor.'

'He gives so much money away, you can't believe. He's an example a lot of other people could do to follow. That couple – the lottery winners.'

'In Up Starly?'

'Them. Nobody ever hears of them giving away a penny. Spend it all on flash cars and designer stuff. And they still have

90

blazing rows in the street, in the garden, in the middle of the drive among those cars the size of ocean liners. Of course they get asked for money all the time, every local charity goes to them, and you don't expect people to give to every scrounger, but they wouldn't put ten pence in a collecting box for orphans. It takes a Declan McDermid to hand out twenty-pound notes to beggars in the street.'

They were back in the entrance hall, from which two decorative figures had been taken.

'I'm presuming Mr McDermid is well insured.'

'That I couldn't tell you. But I'm sure you're right. Maddy would know – she's his PA. Oh my God, she won't have heard, will she? Will it be on the news?'

He had not yet given the press office permission to release the information, and if Cindy McDermid had not been killed, he would have considered a news blackout on this robbery as well, at least in the short term. But a murder had to be reported, even if details were initially kept back.

'I'll ask one of the team to go over there. But if he didn't turn up at his office this morning, presumably someone would have rung?'

'Maddy would have rung his mobile and left a message, I suppose. I'm not sure, I never had to deal with anything like that. I wonder if I could go home now, Mr Serrailler, I feel all over the place.'

'Of course. DS Parks can take you and then go on to the company offices. And thank you very much indeed. You've not only been helpful and made a big difference to a lot of things – you've been extremely courageous. I know it hasn't been easy and I wouldn't have blamed you if you hadn't been able to face it today. So thank you again. I mean it. Not just empty words.'

Pauline Mead's eyes filled with tears, and after a second's hesitation, he put his arm around her shoulder.

Simon stood alone, hearing Andy's car drive off, reminded of what was important. It was not just the crime or who had perpetrated the crime, not only the first victims, but the effect that crime had upon an ever-widening circle as it touched them, family, friends, neighbours, those like himself who dealt with it, and so on to the surrounding community. Everyone, as they found out, was somehow affected. Lafferton would have to take in the shock of this violent robbery now, and the death of Mrs McDermid, people would look over their shoulders, make sure their front doors were locked and bolted at night, and wonder why – why good people like the McDermids? And who next?

The buzz of a message coming in interrupted his thoughts.

Declan McDermid conscious and stable. Visit for 10 minutes max. Sister B

Nineteen

Cat wondered how she had coped with home visits in the days when she was on call regularly and often out at night, and without the benefit of satnav. Her patch now, working for Concierge Medical, covered the area surrounding Lafferton which included several villages whose names resembled each other – Starly, Starly Tor, Up Starly, Starly Dean. But satnav had failed her today and she was now facing a reverse up an unmade lane, at the end of which she had found not the expected Starly Lodge but a deep and impassable ford. Concierge Medical had a number of patients in the Starlys and two of them had requested visits today. After what she had found at the McDermids' house, her partner Luke had suggested she take the day off. But she had told him she was fine to continue and she had meant it. She had been shaken, but she had also been twenty years a doctor, and was battle-hardened. Cindy McDermid's murder had upset her because she had only just met and taken to the woman. The sight of bodies, whatever the cause of death, did not disturb her.

Starly Lodge seemed not to exist and she would probably have to ring in and ask for more directions. She got out of the car and walked down to a small wooden footbridge over the ford. Sunshine touched the surface of the water, and Cat caught a glimpse of magical bright blue as a kingfisher flashed downstream.

I am at work, she thought, but there is this. She had taken to her new life from the beginning. It was more than work, it was a privilege. Every day she checked the initial list of visits that had come in while she was getting up and making breakfast, talking to Kieron, seeing him and Felix off. She would be on the road and out into the country by eight. Her area was wide and much of it rural, though some of the villages were large – Starly had almost turned into a small town, with several hundred houses recently built on what had been fields until a couple of years ago. But as she enjoyed driving and knew that she was a better doctor for being able to spend more time with her patients, she felt infinitely happier than she had during her last, unsatisfying years in an overstretched GP practice in Lafferton, under pressure to get through every surgery as fast as she could, miserable in her cubbyhole of a consulting room and often at odds with her fellow doctors. They had lost enthusiasm, were submerged in paperwork and boxes to tick, longing for retirement. Two of the women were still enthusiastic and dedicated, but they both had young families and were part-time. That did not make them bad doctors but it was difficult for them to make any ongoing relationship with their patients, and besides, one of them had told Cat that ongoing relationships were in the past and no longer relevant. Concierge had no surgery building, each of them worked from home and consulted one another via phone and email apart from their monthly meetings.

The kingfisher was now sitting on an overhanging branch, looking out for food. A little higher up, the stream ran shallow over the stony bed. If she waited she might have a chance of seeing a dipper, competing with the kingfisher for prey, but she had to get to Starly Lodge. There was no phone signal here at all, so she reversed slowly up the lane, hoping she did not pay with a stiff neck the next day.

She found the house with help from a dog walker. It had clearly once been the lodge of the grand house which was the hub of Starly Park estate. It backed onto the old deer park, with its great oak, ash and beech trees. This was a beautiful place, but the small bungalow in which her last patient lived was proof that Luke had been right – Concierge members would by no means all be rich and living in big houses. Many preferred to save on something else in order to pay for good GP services when they needed them, though Cat still regretted that the state of general practice was so bad that this alternative was necessary at all. She dared not imagine how fiercely Chris would have argued against it.

Her message about the call had read, *Pregnancy problems, no details.*

The man who opened the front door scrutinised her.

'I'm Dr Deerbon, to see Carrie Pegwell?'

'Do you have any ID?'

She had never been asked that before. 'I have the details on my phone. And my medical bag. No other ID, I'm afraid.'

'Perhaps you should think about acquiring some. Anyway, come in.'

He led her down the hall and into a sitting room which overlooked a rather unremarkable garden and, beyond it, the park.

'Mrs Pegwell? Hello, I'm Dr Cat Deerbon.'

The woman was pale. Pale hair, pale skin, even pale eyes of washed-out grey. She could have been twenty years old, or forty, or anything between. She was lying on a sofa beside the window and did not get up. Her pregnancy was very visible.

'You won't want me to stay?' The man, presumably her husband, stood in the doorway. He had addressed her, not Cat.

She shrugged.

'I'll be in my office.' He went out without glancing at either of them again.

The woman did not speak, only stared out of the window but apparently without interest. There was no expression on her pale face or in her pale eyes. 'Depression' – the word came to Cat readily enough.

'I gather from the message I got that this is to do with your pregnancy?'

'Yes.'

'Do you already have children?'

'No.'

'So how have you been? How many weeks are you?'

'I'm not sure. I can't believe I can get any larger – look at me, I'm an elephant. I hate what it's doing to my body.'

'You look fine – about eight months?'

'I look horrendous.'

'You don't actually, you look blooming. But tell me – what do you think you look like when you're not pregnant?'

The shrug again. 'Nothing special. I've got a decent figure. I've never been fat. I am too fat now though, aren't I?'

'No. You look good to me.'

Which was not the whole truth. The woman emanated a listlessness and apathy which were not usual.

'Apart from thinking you are huge, how do you feel?'

'All right. I suppose I'm lucky. I haven't felt sick. Or anything else.'

What was this about? Something other than the pregnancy?

'May I take off my jacket?'

'Please do. I'm always hot now. Is that normal?'

'Perfectly.' She looked more closely at Carrie Pegwell. She was very still. Her expression gave nothing away.

What is this?

The door opened and the husband came in carrying a tray on which were tea things and two glasses of iced water. He set it down without speaking and went out again.

Usually Cat refused the offers of drinks which were made at every house and which would have kept her bladder permanently full, but as the tray had been brought and she knew that she would have to give the woman time, she thanked him warmly as he went out, and poured cups for them both.

'Have you lived here long?'

'Not long. A few months. I'm not sure I like it but it's nice having the park.'

The very soft voice went with her overall paleness.

Cat drank her tea.

'Why did you want to see a doctor?'

Sometimes directness was the only way.

'Colin said I should. See someone anyway. He found your details. He made the appointment.'

'But you weren't so sure?'

'I have a bad feeling about it.'

'About what exactly?'

'This baby.' She went on looking out of the window and not at Cat.

'In what way "bad"?'

'That there's something horribly wrong.'

'With it or with you or with both of you?'

'Oh, I'm all right. It.'

'Do you know the sex?'

'No. How would I?'

'Didn't they ask if you wanted to be told, at the twenty-week scan?' Cat knew that they would have done.

'No. I didn't – I mean, my husband doesn't want to know.'

'And how do you feel about that? Would you like to find out?'

The shrug. 'It doesn't make any difference. I just have the . . . it's not a feeling, I know. I know there's something wrong.'

'Did the radiographer mention this?'

There was a slight pause before she shook her head.

'They're very skilled, you know. Of course, there are some things that scans don't reveal but not many now, the technology is so far advanced in detecting all sorts of things, serious and not. So they didn't express any worries, even faint possibilities?'

A movement of her head which Cat took to be a shake.

'Have you had any odd symptoms that make you think there's a problem with the baby? Sickness, bleeding, pain?'

'No.'

'Is it being active – moving about and kicking?'

'Yes.'

'Have you fallen or had any kind of accident? Have you been ill with a high temperature?'

'No, I told you, I'm perfectly all right, it isn't me.'

'Have you any history of neonatal problems in your family? Do you or your husband have a sibling or a cousin with any sort of birth defect or unusual condition? Some things are genetic, as I'm sure you know.'

'I'm not sure. I don't think so.'

She was depressed – depressed, troubled, listless, apparently uninvolved in her pregnancy, even indifferent to it. Tread carefully then.

'Your feeling of anxiety isn't unusual. All women worry a bit, but when the scans are clear that ought to be totally reassuring. You don't feel that reassurance, do you?'

She shook her head.

'This may sound a harsh question but I need to ask it if I'm going to be able to help you, Carrie – may I call you that?'

She nodded.

'Do you want this baby?'

She turned her head and looked directly at Cat for the first time. 'Not if there's something wrong with it.'

'But the overwhelming likelihood is that there is nothing whatsoever wrong. So if you have a perfectly fine healthy baby, as I have no doubt you will – do you still want it?'

'It's a pointless question. I know it isn't fine. I just know. So what am I going to do? I need you to tell me. I can't even think of having a . . . a damaged child, so what am I going to do?'

There was no emotion in her voice, and her face still had no expression on it. Her eyes held no tears.

'I think the first thing we do is get you another full scan. I'm not concerned that the previous one missed anything but I am concerned about you and why you're so troubled about this. Another scan, at which you can ask every question you can think of and more besides. After that, your mind will be at rest when you give birth to a completely healthy baby. And perhaps we can talk a bit about how you gradually learn to control your anxiety. We can do that once you've had the scan. Would you like me to arrange it for you? I can refer you privately, but if you want to go to the NHS again, then your midwife will have to decide if she feels that another is justified.'

'Please, you fix it. I want it done as soon as possible. A private one.'

'Right. I'll contact them.' She stood up but Carrie did not, only looked listlessly at Cat, still apparently detached from it all. 'I know it's easy for me to say don't worry, but I think your anxiety is out of all proportion. I really am sure everything is fine. Go outside for some of the day – don't sit in here brooding. Does your husband know how you feel?'

'He isn't really very interested.'

'In you, do you mean? Or in the baby?'

'I'm not sure. I don't know what he feels. Thank you for coming. I know you do your best but, you see, there is something wrong. I'm quite sure. Do you think I'm going mad?'

'Absolutely not.'

But Cat knew that her reassurance had slipped over the woman's head like the stream over pebbles.

Twenty

'Is Sister Becky on duty?'

'She finished half an hour ago but she left a note in the book that you can see Mr McDermid. Ten minutes.'

'I know the room, it's fine.'

'I still have to take you.'

'Keep an eye on me.'

She laughed. 'I wouldn't dare, you being the Chief whatever. In here.'

She was friendly and cheerful, and, he saw, both married and pregnant. He made a note to check when Sister Becky was next on duty. And then he saw Declan McDermid and everything else dropped away.

He would look even worse in the next day or two when the bruising on his face and arms came out, but already his face was swollen, his right eye almost closed up. His left arm was in a sling, and his hair had been partly shaved away so that his head wounds could be cleaned and stitched. There were a lot of them, plus contusions and more swelling where stitches had not been necessary. The nurse bent over to help him take a drink of water while Simon sat beside the bed. She nodded to him before turning away to check the monitors.

'Declan,' Simon said. There was no response, other than a movement of his eyelids. 'Declan, can you hear me? It's Simon Serrailler – Lafferton Police.'

He thought there would still be nothing, but then McDermid opened his eyes, in so far as he could.

'It's all right. Just relax. I'm not staying long but I want to ask you a couple of very important questions now and the rest can wait. I'll come back tomorrow.'

'Simon . . .'

'Serrailler. Yes.' And he touched the back of the man's hand.

'What . . .' But saliva dribbled out of the corner of his mouth and he tried to lift his hand to wipe it away. Simon did it for him.

'Declan, I am investigating this awful thing that happened to you and if you can possibly tell me anything it will help. Did you get a look at the men who did this to you? And did you recognise them? Even vaguely. Had you seen them before?' He spoke very quietly, bending closer to the man and leaving his own hand on his.

'Not . . . no. Nobody I ever saw before.' His voice was clear even though it was obviously an effort for him to speak. 'Didn't know them.'

'How many were there?'

'Two. I think. Or three? It's . . . shadowy.'

'I understand. But definitely two men.'

'Yes. Not sure if . . . yes, two. Where's Cindy?'

There was a silence and then the nurse caught Simon's eye as she went to the bed and started to make a business of checking the drip stand.

It seemed wrong and both cowardly and unkind not to answer the question at all.

'Time's up, I'm sorry. You can come back with your questions tomorrow.'

Her tone of voice dismissed him without argument, but as he went out of the room, a doctor in scrubs was about to go in.

'Can I have a quick word?' Simon beckoned him further away, before saying who he was and why he was there. 'Are you looking after Declan McDermid?'

'Well, I'm the registrar not the consultant, but more or less. Have you just been in to see him?'

101

'Only for a few moments. There are some questions I want him to try and answer but he isn't in a fit state today. I can come back but it isn't that. He asked me where his wife was.'

'Ah. No one has told him yet – I think it ought to be one of his family so we were waiting.'

'He has no family – they didn't have children, and so far as we've been able to find out, there are no close relatives, no siblings. They have a lot of friends and acquaintances in the community and presumably he has plenty connected with his work. It's possible some cousin may appear of course.'

'Or not. Now that he's conscious he will have to be told.'

'Will you do it?'

'If you prefer.'

'Listen, I'm perfectly willing but it doesn't seem entirely appropriate.'

'OK, I'll see if I think he's ready.'

Twenty-one

Cat had an hour before she needed to pick up Felix from cathedral choir practice, and go home. It had been a difficult day, beginning at the McDermid house and then trying, not very successfully, to puzzle out what the true situation was with the Pegwells, then referring a ten-year-old boy to hospital with suspected meningitis. Her last two calls had been to the worried well. She had also been into the police station to make a statement about the McDermids.

She was two minutes away from her father's place and she had just the right amount of time free to call in and have a cup of tea with him. He had been in the new apartment for a few months, and after helping him move, Cat had barely seen him. Work. Family. Si coming back from Barbados and living at the farmhouse. She had managed to get down to London to see Hannah, who was in the final stages of rehearsals for a new musical based on a David Walliams story about a boarding school for rebellious girls and hopeless teachers, in which she was playing the second lead. Hannah described it as 'St Trinian's only worse and without the hockey sticks'.

But Cat had not managed to see Richard. 'And I wonder why that is?' she said aloud to herself as she headed up the drive leading to what had once been a maternity hospital, and which had been so well converted into luxury apartments, with communal grounds, and lounges – even a small – very small – cinema. Her father had bought a ground-floor flat at the side of the house, overlooking the river as it flowed out of Lafferton on its way south. He had French windows, a small garden with a view, sitting room, two bedrooms, kitchen if he preferred not to use the restaurant, Wi-Fi, satellite television and an alarm system. She pulled into the visitors' car park, wondering if all this might have helped to make him less curmudgeonly.

'Ah, Catherine. I wondered who could be pushing the door-bell so vociferously. Come in, we're on the terrace.'

We.

Richard was looking – Cat floundered for the word. Smug. Yes. And 'dapper', which had always been a negative description in her mother's book. 'I never altogether trust a *dapper* man.' He wore a blue linen jacket, darker blue trousers, a blue-and-white-striped shirt. A cotton handkerchief tucked into his breast pocket.

'I don't think you've met Philippa?' He knew perfectly well that she had not.

'No,' Cat said, 'I don't think I have.'

She was half a head taller than Richard when she stood up, a woman with a nice smile, a firm handshake. But there was a reserve too, as if she would be pleasant but hold back any deci-sion about friendliness. She wore a cotton frock, a shirt-waister – the sort of frock Meriel had always worn in summer, for home, for shopping, for gardening, for everything except work. She had had a selection of them. They came out in early May, often accompanied by a cardigan, and were put away again at the end of September. Was this anything at all to do with this Philippa – no surname as yet – having become her father's latest friend, if that was what she was?

'No tea on the go, Catherine, but if you need a cup do make yourself one.'

'No.' Philippa stood quickly. 'Of course not – I'll make it, Catherine, you stay and talk to your father.' And she went into the kitchen and closed the door.

'Are you on call from your new practice, visiting a patient here?'

He spoke in the way he often did when not wishing to discuss something else, in a conversational tone, as if she were someone he had met in the street. She knew it so well, that breezy manner, had known it since childhood and recognised it for what it was, a smokescreen for his real situation, or motive.

'No. I came to see you.'

'Ah. And how is everyone? I haven't seen Felix for too long – bring him over, Catherine. I want to talk to him.'

'The trouble is, school and choir and music lessons take up so much of every day.'

'All the same, I should like to see him. And how is the hospital porter?'

'Loving being a hospital porter. Don't worry, Dad, no one knows he's your grandson, it won't reflect on you. In any case, I don't think many people at the hospital remember your name. Everything changes.'

'Of course people remember me. How is the new job?'

'Not so new now, but it's fine. Concierge works for me – and more importantly, for the patients.'

The kitchen door opened. 'I found some biscuits, Richard, I hope that's all right?' Philippa said, carrying in the tray of tea.

'Find whatever you like, my dear, the kitchen holds no secrets. Nor do I, for that matter.'

Cat gave him a swift look. No one held back more about himself than her father.

Philippa was what Meriel Serrailler would have called 'well preserved' – she must be seventy, looked ten years younger, with a beautifully clear skin, hair subtly highlighted, slim figure. She was putting her best foot forward, perhaps slightly on her guard. Like Richard, giving nothing away.

'I would like to know more about how Concierge work.'

'I've got one of our brochures in the car, I'll get it for you when I go. If it doesn't tell you all you need to know please get in touch with me and just ask.'

'Doctor turned saleswoman,' her father said with the sly look on his face she loathed.

'No, just a doctor hoping to explain the benefits and then letting the enquirer make up her own mind. We're busy and getting busier – taking on two new doctors in fact. We don't need to push for patients.'

Richard held up his hands in an 'I surrender' gesture. Cat wanted to lead Philippa out of the door, sit her down somewhere and fill her in about the man he was. How sad, she thought, how appalling that that is how I feel about my own father.

They chatted politely for another ten minutes, she finished her tea and got up. So did Philippa.

'I'll come out to your car with you and get this brochure,' she said.

Twenty-two

He had called the team together and got all the updates, such as they were, on the McDermid case. There were no useful results from forensics.

'Clean as a whistle,' Andy said. 'It's as if they sent in a team to scour it like an operating theatre after they'd finished.'

There were no vehicle tracks or sightings, no reports from members of the public about any unusual activity before or after the break-in.

'So we spread our net wider,' Serrailler said. 'Anything from neighbouring forces, and let's get on to customs at the ports in case they've driven straight down and been stopped boarding a ferry.'

'Why would they be? Customs wouldn't have anything on them.'

'Probably not but it's a van and they do spot checks for illegals. You never know.'

But somehow, they all did know. Customs would not have stopped and searched and found, even assuming the van had driven to a port in the first place.

'OK, empty garages, warehouses, derelict industrials – you know the routine. Let's get out there. This is the only sort of policing that bears fruit in the long run. And I want two people on the phones to the antique dealers, art dealers, especially those interested in the sort of stuff McDermid collected – I've emailed over details of some particular items to DC Monroe. Anyone in this country – will be mainly London – and then abroad who is a specialist in these please contact them. Otherwise, I'm going back to talk a bit more to Declan tomorrow, try and get at least something from him, though I don't expect he'll remember much and he's now been told that his wife died so he'll be in shock over that. It's a slow business but we'll get there . . . just remember about not leaving stones unturned. Thanks.'

He went straight out and down the street to the Cypriot cafe, got a double espresso and, realising how long it was since he had eaten, one of their special honey pistachio cakes. It was sunny, so he could have sat at a table outside, but he didn't want half the station stopping to chat and went to one in the corner.

After drinking his coffee quickly and ordering another, he started to go over the McDermid case step by small step, from the moment he had arrived at the house. But he found that he could not focus properly, his eye kept wandering round the cafe, to the posters on the walls, out of the window to the sunlit street. He felt light-headed, which was probably because he had gulped down strong caffeine on an empty stomach, but when he took a bite of his cake he was suddenly unable to swallow. His throat seemed to close up, though he could breathe perfectly well and he had no soreness nor the dry scratchy sensation which preluded a cold. He just could not swallow the cake.

He had pins and needles in his hand. He was breathing fast. He felt hot, he was uncomfortable inside his collar, as if his neck had started to swell.

He had to get out.

Out. Round the next corner. Not back to the station. Round another corner. Here. Safe. He went in through the high wrought-iron gates. Stopped. There might not be any signal here. Stupid. Why wouldn't there be?

He walked along the middle path to a bench. No one else here. Not really.

As he pushed his flopping hair back from his forehead he found that it was damp.

'Si? Hello?'

'Are you . . .' His voice sounded odd. He cleared his throat. Again. He had been clearing his throat all the way from the cafe.

'Si?'

'Are you driving?'

'No, I'm waiting for Felix. What's up?'

He cleared his throat again.

'Is something wrong?'

'Yes . . . . I don't know . . . I feel . . .'

'What?'

'Am I having a heart attack?'

'Tell me what's happening.'

He tried to list everything and there seemed to be so much, he could hardly think of any part of his body which was not behaving strangely. Differently.

'Slow down. Listen. Take three deep breaths from your diaphragm . . . slowly . . . then let them out even more slowly. You haven't mentioned any of the things which would give me a red light for a coronary. Just keep breathing like that. Three deep breaths.'

He managed them.

'Chest pain?'

'Yes.'

'Are you sweating?'

'Yes. But it's warm and I just had two espressos.'

'Where are you?'

'Sitting on a bench. In the cemetery.'

'Stay there. Felix is just coming down the path. I'll be with you in about six minutes. Stay sitting. If the chest pains get worse, lie down on the bench. Undo your tie and loosen your collar. And keep taking deep breaths. I'm coming, Si . . . and you're fine. I'm not worried – if I were I'd be calling an ambulance.'

Twenty-three

Simon was still sitting on the bench. He had talked to his sister on the phone and she had told him she was on her way. He was expecting to see her hurrying into the cemetery. But instead she rang back to say that Felix was being sick.

'Are you feeling better?'

'I . . . yes. My heart's still racing.'

'That's panic. But I really can't come now, Felix is vomiting by the side of the road.'

'It's all right. I'll walk back to the station.'

'Your legs will feel like jelly but that will pass. OK, Felix? Simon—'

He was the one who cut off, before he stood up and waited to see what would happen. Nothing did. His head felt as if it was full of cotton wool but as he started to walk that cleared, though his heart still raced. He remembered the deep breaths and stopped again. Took two. Three. Waited.

Better.

It wasn't until he reached the gate that he began to feel annoyed, an annoyance which grew until it became resentment and rage, that his sister had abandoned him because her son was sick, that he might have been dying, that . . .

He passed the Cypriot cafe. The window seats were occupied by CID but no one glanced his way. He kept his head down, got out his phone and pretended to check it, went on as quickly as he dared. It could happen again and he would not know how to

110

handle himself among other people. It seemed to overcome him at random and without warning. Cat had not actually seen him when it was happening, so how could she be sure that he was not about to have a heart attack? No, he knew that himself, he had dealt with people in cardiac arrest. But there were other things, strokes, early signs of a brain tumour, probably things that affected the central nervous system about which he knew only a little.

His phone rang for real, as he was going through the station door.

'I'm home and Felix seems fine now. You OK? Are you still in—'

'No. I'm just going into the office.'

'What's happening?'

'Work, I imagine.'

'Simon, listen to me—'

'I'm fine. Got to go.'

He went in and upstairs straight to the gents. No one in there. He looked in the mirror and his eyes stared hugely back at him. His hair was plastered to his forehead with sweat. His tie was pulled open and his collar unbuttoned.

'Guv.'

He turned on the cold tap and bent over the basin as the sergeant went into a cubicle. Water all over his face and neck, and then his hair.

His shoulder ached.

'Oh,' Alison, his secretary said, as he opened the outer door. 'Is it raining?'

'No.' He saw her clock that his tone of voice meant the subject of his wet hair was not open for discussion. 'The hospital rang. Declan McDermid would like to see you – apparently he's much better.'

'Anything happening?'

'No. Full pathologist's report on Mrs McDermid is waiting for you. Nothing new from forensics.'

'I'll get over to BG now.'

'Are you back in after that?'

'Depends.' He did not go into his own office but as he went out, he said, 'Thanks, Alison. Keep them sweet, will you?'

She nodded. The boss had looked odd, as if something had put him off his stride. That was unusual, and she thought he had not looked well, though she couldn't have said in exactly what way. And why the wet hair? She liked Serrailler, he left a lot more to her initiative than her previous police bosses, but he was not particularly easy to read.

Twenty-four

Cat did not stir when her phone rang. Kieron had to reach over her to answer. He tried to wake her gently but it was wired into her to surface and be fully alert in seconds.

'Dr Deerbon? It's Colin Pegwell. My wife is in pain – has been for an hour or more. I think you ought to come and look at her.'

No please, no apology. 'When you say "pain" can you give me an idea of what kind?'

'Well, abdominal – I suppose this is childbirth? I'm not experienced.'

'You mean she's in labour now?'

'She seems to think so.'

'This is a bit early. Could I have a word with her?'

'Isn't that just wasting time? You could be halfway here by now.'

'It would help me assess what's going on.'

He made an impatient sound and she heard him take the phone into another room, then mumble with his hand over the receiver.

'Hello?'

'Mrs Pegwell, it's Dr Deerbon.'

'Oh, please come, please, I'm sure I'm having the baby any minute.'

'I'm on my way but don't be frightened, it's early and it may not be labour.'

'It's so painful and there's all the mess . . . the water—'

113

'Your waters have broken? Your husband should have told me that straight away – you don't need me, you need an ambulance. I'll phone now and also the labour suite and give them your details.'

'But you'll come as well, please, I need you.'

'No, you don't, you need the ambulance to get you to hospital as quickly as possible. Now, try and stay calm, remember your breathing . . . It'll all be fine. They do amazing things with premature babies in the NICU now – we just want you there.'

She disconnected before the woman could panic or plead with her any more, and phoned the ambulance and then the hospital labour suite. Kieron came in with tea as she finished the calls.

Chris had always believed in the magical properties of tea, including its power to induce sleep and in spite of his usual insistence upon scientific evidence. She propped herself up on the pillows again and picked up *The Small House at Allington*, the Barsetshire Chronicles being her favourites for soothing rereading. Kieron drove her mad by reading either a dozen new thrillers in a week, the sort, she said, which didn't touch the sides, or nothing at all other than newspapers and police reports. She was older and wiser than to try and change him, on this as on most other fronts, as she had once tried to change Chris, who had read nothing.

Tonight Kieron did not pick up a book, but turned on his side and was asleep within a couple of minutes. Cat envied him. Once she was awake she found it very hard to go back to sleep. She sipped her tea and dived again into nineteenth-century country village affairs. The phone rang.

'Colin Pegwell. Where is the bloody ambulance? And where are you, Doctor? Is this what we pay you for?'

'Please try to stay calm, you won't help your wife if you're so agitated. Just remind her about her breathing, stay with her and talk her through. The ambulance team knows it's urgent – they will get to you as quickly as they can.'

'So should you.'

Cat did not trust herself to say any more, just pulled on the jeans and sweatshirt she always kept ready for night calls, and left. She was sure that by the time she got to Starly Lodge the

114

ambulance would have been and gone, but there was no point in antagonising Colin Pegwell and having him infect his wife with his own panic. The roads were deserted and the journey took her a bare ten minutes. Lights were on, car outside. No ambulance.

'Well, at least you're here.' He held open the door. But she had been wrong about anxiety and panic. He looked as detached as if he had been letting in the cleaner. Detached and irritable.

'I just asked for an update on the ambulance – they're very busy but they'll get here as soon as they possibly can.'

'Bloody public services.'

'Well, I'm here now, I can check what's happening.'

'A lot of pain is what's happening. I hope you can give her something for that.'

They were heading up the stairs and she did not reply, but she could hear Carrie Pegwell making soft little moaning sounds.

Her husband stayed in the doorway. 'You won't need me.'

'It's your wife.'

'No, I'd be no help. I'll go and wait for the ambulance.'

He ran quickly down. It was a long time since Cat had encountered a man like him.

Carrie was lying on the bed with a sheet over her and what Cat saw first was how frightened she was. She was holding her body tensely and every time she felt pain she tensed it more, and arched her back slightly, clenching her fists.

Cat sat down on the bed beside her and took her hand. It was clammy.

'What happened, Carrie – can you describe it from the beginning?'

'I had backache all evening . . . down low. It came and went.'

'Only in your back?'

'Yes. I got a hot-water bottle and that helped.'

'Did you take anything?'

'No. Colin said I shouldn't.'

'When did the pain move round to your tummy?'

'It didn't, it's still in my back, it's really bad.'

'Right. I'd like to check you, if that's all right. Can you lie on your side first of all?'

115

She felt the young woman's back gently, then her stomach, and as she did so there was a contraction. Carrie winced and tried to draw up her knees.

'Now can you turn onto on your back?'

The baby was still, but its heartbeat was strong through the stethoscope. The contractions were not regular or fast.

'Is it going to be born?'

'Not yet, but you are in labour. Can you do your breathing exercises? They'll help a lot.'

'I don't really know any. What should I do?'

'The ones you practise in antenatal classes.'

'Oh. I haven't been to any of those.'

'None at all?'

'I didn't want to. I wouldn't want to sit with a lot of other pregnant women who would look at me and I'd have to look at them. It's a private thing.'

'But no one there judges you – they're all in the same boat. The classes help with everything – the pregnancy itself, anticipating labour, learning about it and how you can cope . . . breathing. And they involve your partner. He needs it, it's a different experience for him, but they're still very involved.'

'Oh, Colin doesn't want to be there, he said so from the start and I'm glad, I don't think he'd get on well in this sort of situation.'

Cat said nothing. The state of the Pegwell marriage was not really her business but she was concerned that a young pregnant woman was clearly without support from the one person who ought to want to provide it. Chris would not have dreamed of missing the births of their children. Even her father had helped deliver all of his.

'I need to go to the loo – can you help me get down?'

But as she moved, she cried out and rolled back onto the bed. Cat took her hand and held it. The sound of voices came from a television. And then the ambulance arrived.

The two paramedics came upstairs. Their calming, steady, ever-cheerful presence still reassured Cat, after all her years of dealing with emergencies, and since the beginning of her career they had become more and more skilled and informed, and better equipped.

'Hello, I'm Poppy, this is Duncan. What's been happening?'

Cat was briefing them as Carrie gripped her hand through another contraction. 'You need to get her in quickly.'

'I want to stay here, I can't move, I can't go into hospital.'

'You'll be in the best hands there, Carrie, and these two are going to have you in quickly and safely.'

'As soon as we get you into the ambulance you can have some pain relief.'

'Please, no, I want to stay here.'

'Carrie.' Colin Pegwell had come in and now he stood looking down at his wife, though without touching her. 'Listen to me. You are going to the hospital.'

She was silent.

'Are you going with her, Doctor?'

'No,' Cat said. 'You are.'

He hesitated. 'Won't I be in the way?'

The paramedics exchanged a glance.

'Can I have a word while they're getting your wife ready to go?'

On the landing, she turned to him, working to restrain herself from showing the anger she felt. 'Your wife is in labour. She is fine and she will go on being fine, but she needs to get to hospital, as you obviously understand. This is her first baby, and everything is strange – she hasn't been to any antenatal classes so she's had no preparation. That makes it even more frightening for her. She needs you with her. You can't just sit here at home and wait for the phone to ring with good news, Mr Pegwell – that is what our grandfathers did but it isn't what's done now. She needs you. This is your child too, you know.' She waited for an explosion but the man looked suddenly deflated.

'Yes. It's just that it has been very – very difficult. She isn't – she doesn't want what she believes this child is going to be.'

Cat put her hand on his arm. 'Listen, pregnancy is a strange business sometimes. I took her worries about the baby's health seriously but I'm sure that's all they were, worries.'

'Premonitions.'

'No. The mind plays tricks, and once she became convinced about this and because she was so anxious, she let it take hold.

The only thing that is going to put it right is the arrival of a healthy baby – and you need to be there to share that relief and joy with her. I'm not unsympathetic to your feelings, you know, but I promise you it will be fine – you will be fine. All three of you.'

Poppy came out. 'Ready to go but she doesn't seem to have an overnight bag. Can you help?'

He hesitated again. Looked at Cat.

'Yes. I'll try.'

She waited until the house was locked up and the ambulance was pulling away, before saying a prayer of thanks as she headed home.

Twenty-five

'*How* much?'

Shenda turned the magazine round to show Agneta, who leaned forward. Her eyes were getting worse but she hadn't time or money to sort out glasses, not until she'd been in the job six months and was permanent.

'One thousand pounds! My God, Shenda, that is terrible, that is just wicked. Bad. Wrong.'

'Oh, I don't know. It's silly money, I wouldn't pay it for a handbag, but I don't see how it's wicked.'

'When people are hungry.'

'Yeah, but if you go down that road . . .'

'A lot of people go down it.'

Shenda offered her bag of crisps to stop the argument. She liked Ag. She was a lot better than some of them who'd come to work here and lasted five minutes. Agneta got on with it, she was good-humoured, the customers liked her and her English had got a whole lot better. Maybe it was her religion, Roman Catholic and regular at it, that made her always on the side of the underdog. Deep down, Shenda knew she was right, always standing up for those worse off than herself, always worried about the ones who hadn't got a decent job and somewhere to live.

'Shenda, promise me, you won't really use this money buying a bag, tell me please.'

'I might.'

She saw Agneta's shocked face and laughed. 'You kidding? Of course I won't but it's all right to look.'

'OK. Anyway, this – gamble.'

'Lottery.'

'Yes. This. You win five thousand pounds, Shenda? You have to save this money.'

'I will. Most of it. I'm going to enjoy some as well.'

'Good, but now you to tell me how I do this. The lottery.'

Shenda dug about in the bag of crisps to save herself answering. She wanted to kick herself for having mentioned the money at all, but five thousand pounds in one go was a lot to get excited about. The ones over in Essex had been practice, small beer, Jake had called them rehearsals. They had worked fine but she had only got five hundred pounds which had paid for their holiday, her share. Jake never told her how much went to him but of course it would be a lot more. He kept her out of the details, better that way he said. She just acted out her part. She'd enjoyed the acting. She thought she did it pretty well and maybe one day she could do it as a job. How hard could it be doing the same thing on one of the TV soaps, just a small part? Better than loading up plates of all-day breakfast and carrying trays of tea and coffee and cleaning bloody tables.

The five grand had been a very big surprise. Whoever was behind it all – and she had no idea who – wasn't mean, though God knows how much he made out of selling everything – hundreds of thousands probably. Next time, she'd ask for ten.

Because there would be a next time, she was sure, and why not, when it was just stuff and the insurance would pay up? The doctor and the photographer wouldn't have empty shelves and spaces on the walls for long. Thinking about them, she had a slight twinge of guilt, simply because they'd been so nice and friendly. 'Idiots,' Jake had said as they'd walked back to the car in the rain that night. 'I mean, would you just let people in like that?'

She hadn't answered.

It had been a bad moment that morning when Ag had asked if she could borrow her make-up mirror and she'd just said, flying out of the kitchen, 'In my bag, help yourself.' She hadn't thought twice and Agneta was as honest as the day.

She had come upon the fat roll of notes and grabbed Shenda by the arm as she'd come back with a tray of dirty dishes.

'Shenda, you are mad, you shouldn't carry all that money in your bag just like this, anyone can see, anyone can take.'

Agneta was shocked and went on and on about not leaving it in her bag, not carrying it around, and how someone could hit her over the head on the way home and take it.

'Who's to know I've got it? Unless you put the word around.'

'Shenda, I would not do this, ever!'

'I know that. It's fine. Two new tables taken, Agneta, you need to get out there.'

In a lull after lunch they'd looked at the bag in the magazine and then the cafe had filled up again and from then on it was non-stop, there wasn't time or space in her head to worry. Soup and a roll, dish of the day, roast of the day, fish and chips, ham salad, the never-ending permutations on eggs, bacon, sausages, tomatoes, mushrooms, baked beans, but there was generally a breather between three and four, and then it was rush till closing at six, after which it was clearing up, cleaning, washing down, chairs on the tables, and so much racket she could pretend not to hear whatever Ag was trying to say to her.

With any luck she could rush off as soon as she'd finished, saying she was meeting Jake, they were going out. But Agneta stopped her by the cupboard

'You will tell me, help me do it as well, I am happy to work, I like it, but money like you win would be so much help, Shenda. Please.'

Shenda took a breath. 'Tell you what, it's a bit complicated, why don't you give me one pound every week and I'll do it for you?'

'Only one pound?'

'Yes. I mean, you can do more but I wouldn't, you might spend more than you should.'

'You just do one pound?'

'Yes, only not till Friday, don't give it me now, Ag.'

'OK, thank you, I give you one pound, you win for me.'

121

'Listen, it's luck, it's not—'

'Of course, sure, but look what happened to you.'

Abruptly, Agneta gave her a hug.

When Shenda got in from the cafe, she went straight to shower, to get rid of the smell of cooking. She also put her clothes in the wash and pulled on leggings and a fleece. Jake was out. She never asked. If he had anything to tell her, he would. There wouldn't be another job for a bit, they were very careful, so it was the cafe for now, but the money was there for a bit of a spend, and they might have a good night out as well.

Shenda got a can of lager, and settled on the bean bag, remote control to hand.

'Bevham Police say that while they do not know what the motive for the attack on Mr and Mrs McDermid might be, they are working on the suspicion that the criminals were carrying out a planned robbery and were disturbed by the couple returning home unexpectedly. They were subject to an extreme level of violence, as a result of which Mrs McDermid died at the scene and Mr McDermid is in intensive care, though his condition is said to have improved overnight.'

Shenda zapped the sound and sat for a few minutes, staring at the silent television set. She felt cold, cold and frightened. But no, surely not. It was horrible but it couldn't have anything to do with Jake or anyone he knew. Could it?

It had never crossed her mind that anything they'd been involved with or ever would be could lead to harm, to people being hurt. To someone being *killed*. Jesus.

They were cogs in a wheel whose size she didn't actually know, just two cogs who took orders. They play-acted. They had broken down and they needed to call the AA, they'd walked till they'd found this house, lights on, car in the drive, people at home who might just let them use their phone. Batteries in their mobiles had died, or no signal round here, or dropped the phone in a ditch in the dark, scrabbled around but couldn't find it. It helped if it was raining. And actually it had been fine, the photographer bloke had been easy, laid-back, come in, coffee and biscuits . . . nice. All she had to do was go to the toilet and look around on the way. She had to be good at remembering things, because there wasn't going to be a chance to write anything down. They'd practised, in shops and galleries, noticing, remembering what and where. The hardest bit would be knowing what was valuable and what was not, but actually that had been easier than she'd expected, because you just could sort of tell, by the look of something or the way they'd got it displayed. She had been told they wouldn't take big furniture or heavy oil paintings, and that china ornaments and small pictures, silver objects and clocks were what she should be looking out for. She'd even got some books out of the library about antiques and how much they could be worth. Those had been an eye-opener.

She jumped up suddenly, shaking herself. Stuff, that was all, it was just stuff, but now a woman was dead and she had to find out, and if it was something else altogether, she wouldn't feel like she was feeling now, sick inside and in a lather.

The phone kicked straight over to voicemail. 'Jake, call me back. It's really important.'

She made a cup of tea, got out two Jaffa Cakes then put them back in the packet.

'Jake, will you pick up? I need to talk to you, it's urgent.'

She flicked around the channels to see if there was any more news, then looked online. The *Bevham Gazette* had a newsfeed and it was there, at the top, but there wasn't any more than she'd seen already, no details. The police weren't saying anything new.

'Jake, where the bloody hell are you?'

She couldn't just sit down and wait, there had to be somewhere she could find out more. Then she remembered that sometime during the wait outside the doctor's house, Jake had had to use her phone because his battery had gone and that's how he got through to Chaz. She scrolled up and down. He had said from the beginning that she didn't need to have any numbers, he was dealing with all that side of it, so if she hadn't been so nervous and on edge she'd have taken the piss out of him when his phone had died.

There. A number she didn't recognise, right time and date. Her heart banged.

She thought a text was better than a call. *It's Shenda. Jake isn't home, not picking up. He with you?* She was about to press 'Send', but added, *Sorry 2 bother you.*

She did herself beans and a fried egg, and they were eaten and the dishes washed before there was a response.

'What you doing trying to talk to Chaz?'

'Where are you?'

'Out. He's not best pleased. What you making a fuss over, Shend?'

'I saw about that woman, on the news.'

Silence.

'Jake? That one who was murdered in a robbery and her husband's in hospital in a bad way. That woman.'

'And?'

'It's not got anything to do with you, has it? It wasn't you or Chaz or anything, was it? The woman was beaten to death, Jake—'

'Oh for Christ's sake, Shenda. What do you think I am?'

'I'm beginning to wonder.'

'Nice. Hang on . . .' Hand over the phone. Muffled voices. Hand off. 'Got to go, babe. See you later.'

'When? Tonight, next week, what? Because this woman being killed has really got to me, and I want you to tell me it has nothing to do with you or Chaz or anyone else, that's all. Jake?'

'Drop it.'

'I won't drop it. Is Chaz there? I want to talk to him, I want to ask him if you won't say. I'm not staying involved in any of this and he can have his money back as well.'

'Don't be stupid.'

'You or him, one of you, tell me now or I'm going to the police.'

'You what? Now you're being really stupid. Hello, officer, I've got five grand here, I got it for being mixed up in a robbery.'

'It's not funny.'

'Grow up, Shenda.'

'I mean it.'

There was a slight scuffling noise and then Chaz came on. 'Shenda, you listen up. Shut it, all right? Shut it, and keep it shut.'

124

Twenty-six

'You'll notice a change,' Sister Becky said. She was at the computer behind the desk. She smiled at him, which ought to have gladdened his heart. Why didn't it?

He hesitated. A part of him wanted to stay and talk to her, find out if she was spoken for – she wore no rings. A bigger part knew he should get on with his job and was indifferent to her private life.

He turned away and down the corridor, and as he went into the room, the sun shone straight into his face so that, for a second, he was blinded and had to pause, before he could see that the bed was empty and Declan McDermid was sitting in a chair beside the window, looking out.

'This is a good sight,' Simon said. 'You're obviously feeling bottor.'

'Yes. I seem to be.'

In one sense he was much improved. He was pale, with bruising and stitches and his hair had been partly shaved off, but he was not the man who had been hooked up to machines and barely able to speak to him. He was in pyjamas and dressing gown and his tone of voice was firm and clear. There was a closed-down expression on his face, though, and his eyes were without light.

'May I sit down?'

'Of course.' Simon moved the upright bedside chair and set it opposite.

'I'm so sorry about your wife. It was an appalling event, and needless to say, we're putting everything into finding who did this. But your loss is dreadful, never mind who or how.'

McDermid had not looked him in the eye, but as he did so now, Simon saw not only pain but bewilderment, a questioning, as if he were being asked why he could not change everything, work some miracle to undo what had been done. It was like looking into the eyes of a hurt and confused child and it struck him with a rare force, given that he had been over twenty years a policeman and the tally of the things he had witnessed was long.

'They tell me I can leave here in a couple of days. I'm doing all right.'

'That's good news. Hospital is not the place to be now. You want to get home.'

'I can't go there. I don't think I will ever go there again.'

There was no reply he could give but Serrailler had heard variations of this often and understood. He also knew that the feeling did not last.

'We have a flat in Bournemouth. Faces the sea. Cindy loves it there, she'd move there . . .' He choked on his words. It was better to let him recover himself in his own time.

'I can think everything through if I go to Bournemouth.' He sighed. 'Is there something I will have to attend – some – an inquest?'

'There will be an inquest, yes. The coroner decides who should attend and it is likely you will be asked because you are the next of kin, but principally because you were there when it happened. Which brings me to why I'm here, Mr McDermid.'

'Questions.'

'I'm sorry.'

'You've to do your job.'

'Do you feel up to answering? I can come back but it's very important to move this investigation forward quickly – time really does matter, questioning a witness soon after the event can make a big difference.'

'You carry on.'

'Can I get you anything? Some tea? I can go and fetch it.'

'Just – maybe a glass of water.'

He got up and went to pour it and McDermid sat very still and silent as he did so, continuing to look out of the window but not, Simon was sure, seeing what was there. Seeing God knew what.

'We have to start at the beginning and the moment you drove away from the reception at the police station. But rather than my firing lots of separate questions, it would be best if you can just tell me everything in your own words.'

'Yes.'

'And take your time. If you want to have a break, just say.'

'Are you going to write it down?'

'I'll be recording it.'

He had hit record but expected to wait until McDermid had organised his thoughts, and whatever recollections he had. Instead, he began speaking at once, without turning his gaze from the window.

'We enjoyed the evening, I know that. It was very – satisfying. I felt very glad to have done it, and everybody was appreciative. I do remember that. I'm not the best person in crowds, not the best. But I enjoyed it and Cindy did but then she's . . . she was . . . an enjoyer, she likes dressing up and going out, I should . . . I should take her out more.'

Abruptly, he began to cry, bending his head and sobbing without any restraint. Serrailler pulled some paper towels from the dispenser and had to press them into his hand. He waited then, and after a while, the sobbing turned into a paroxysm of coughing.

'All right, that's enough for today,' Sister Becky said, banging in through the door. 'He's taken a step forward but it'll be ten steps back if you press him with questions.'

But McDermid was shaking his head. He took some water. 'It's fine, please, I want to get this over with, I need to. I'm all right.'

She frowned at Serrailler. 'I'm not far away and if I hear anything I don't like . . .'

'I understand. I'll keep it as short as I possibly can. Carry on when you feel up to it, Declan. Let's move on to coming home.'

When he spoke again, his voice was stronger, as if he had drawn on some reserves.

'The gates were open and they're on an automatic control, so when we left they would have closed. I thought there could have been a power cut – some of the lights were out, I remember that. I said to Cindy that it would be the power.'

'Was there a vehicle in the drive?'

'No . . . I don't know. I'm confused about that.'

'It's likely they had a van round the back. Better than having it in full sight. You parked and then . . . ?'

'I put the car in the garage, and there's a door that leads from it straight into the house. Useful . . . at night, if it's raining.'

He took a huge breath and more water. Simon waited, trying not to take in the usual hospital noises from the corridor, which awoke a flutter of panic. He leaned back in the chair, trying to calm himself.

'We . . . I remember going in through the garage door. I remember that. Cindy was behind me. I can . . . I'm sure of that. I can . . . sense her there, I can smell her. I can – I could smell her perfume. Her hair.' Declan had his eyes closed and he was shaking his head. 'It's blank. It's just a blank after that. I've tried. Once I came round, I started to work on remembering but it's all just a blank.'

'No sounds? No voices?'

'Nothing. There's nothing. It's frightening, isn't it? I can't understand how I don't know what happened to my wife and I don't know why I couldn't save her. I'm sorry.'

'You have absolutely nothing to apologise for, and not remembering a traumatic event like this is quite normal. Bits and pieces may come back to you eventually, gradually, or they may not. You had an awful blow to the head and more, add shock to the concussion and it's no wonder you don't remember. I'm not going to press you. All you need to do is call me if you do remember anything, the tiniest thing, and don't be afraid it might be too trivial. It can't be.'

'I want to go home. Can you take me home?'

'Your leaving hospital is up to the medics, Declan. I haven't any say in that.'

'I keep wondering if I can face it. Should I go home? Tell me.'

'I can't do that. I can only suggest that you stay in here until you feel able to make a decision, whatever it is. If you want to go back to your house, I'll gladly come with you but if you want to go straight down to your flat in Bournemouth, at least for a while, you should.'

'How do you know we have a flat in Bournemouth?'

McDermid looked completely bewildered. This was not going to be easy, Serrailler thought as he got up.

Twenty-seven

'Wint, I need to talk to you.'

'You're not giving in your notice, please tell me you're not, this place can't run on fresh air and you're good. Or is it a pay rise?'

'No, it's not and I am not leaving, Wint, but it is important, can you turn that off?'

Winston rolled his eyes but the potato chipper ground to a halt.

The kitchen was gearing up for lunch as well as getting out breakfast. There should have been more noise with Agneta and Shenda and Lois banging in and out, crockery, cutlery, pans, machines, but it had been a slow morning and Lois had had a call from school to say her son was unwell, would she collect him?

'When I was at school, you was ill you got on with it or you went into the office and sat there till you felt better and if you were sick they gave you a bucket. Now, come and collect, every little sneeze, teachers don't want to know.'

'Wint, if Lois isn't coming back in today and Shenda hasn't turned up yet, how am I going to do this all alone? OK, so it is quiet now but it will go mad soon.'

'Lois is taking Callum to her mother, Shenda'd better get here any minute.'

'Has she called you?'

'No and I've got to chip these potatoes.'

Agneta went into the cafe, took two orders for coffee and toast, and money from a full breakfast. Shenda hadn't come in this morning or phoned, which wasn't like her, but Agneta hadn't worried about it. Anything could have happened, but she was worried now. She was about to get her phone out when three tables came in and then it was the early lunch rush. Lois came back. They were flat out. It was nearly three o'clock before there was a minute's break in which Agneta could eat something and phone Shenda. It went at once to voicemail and she left a message, but the voicemail was still on after her third try just before the cafe closed.

'Hope she's here tomorrow or I'll have to find someone else,' Winston said, swabbing down the kitchen surfaces. 'If she's ill, that's OK, but I have to know, I can't just grow another pair of hands now, can I?'

'It isn't like Shenda, Wint, come on. She's reliable.'

He shrugged. 'Well, we'll see tomorrow.'

She had never been to Shenda's flat and it wasn't easy to find. She biked up and down several streets and retraced her route twice before finding it, on a corner between two parking areas which had construction hoardings up, though there was no sign of any construction. 7C was up a flight of steps on the outside of the building. It was a quiet street but the block itself was noisy, with children wailing, televisions and sound systems blaring, loud voices. She could not see any of the windows, they must be on the other side, and the front door had no glass, so it was difficult to tell if anyone was in.

Agneta knocked, then saw a bell. Nothing. She banged again, pressed again. Shenda was obviously not there. She was about to turn round, not wanting to stand about here on her own, when without warning the door opened wide, making her jump. He was quite ordinary, that was the first thing she noticed about him – medium height, medium brown hair, unmemorable face, blue shirt, jeans. Bare feet. He looked at her and said nothing.

'Is this . . . 7C?'

'Why?'

'I am trying to find Shenda.'

131

He shrugged. 'Not here.'

'But she lives here?'

'Did.'

'Sorry?'

'Moved out, and no, I don't know where.' He stepped back. 'OK?'

'But I work with her and she wasn't in today.'

'Can't help you.'

'Are you . . . the new person in the flat? Only it's all very quick and I am worried. Do you – did you know Shenda?'

'Can't help you.'

There was nothing threatening about him, but then he took one step forward and stared at her and Agneta turned and ran down the stairs very quickly. When she reached the pavement she looked back but the door could not be seen from there. There was no sound. He had not followed her.

Twenty-eight

The woman had tapped on the door and opened it in one move. Her face was unfamiliar.

'Carrie Pegwell?'

Carrie turned her head. She had been looking out of the window to the tiny figures busily moving about far below.

'I'm Serena. Can I have a chat with you?'

'You've come with some results, haven't you?'

'Results of what?'

'Whatever tests have been done.'

'Have you had some tests?'

'No, she has.'

'Your baby? Sorry, I don't seem to have her name down.'

'She hasn't got a name yet.'

'Ah, right.' She sat on the end of Carrie's bed. She had her hair in dozens of tight little plaits and braids, with beads threaded through. Did she wash the beads as well, did the beads stay there for good, did they have to be redone when the hair grew?

She was not wearing a uniform, just a blue lanyard with a badge, her photograph, some print Carrie couldn't make out.

'I always think a baby's name either comes with them at birth or you spend ages trying different ones on. You'll get there. Well, you'll have to when she's registered.'

She laughed. Carrie looked out of the window again.

'Can I have a peep at her?'

One of those people. Knock but just come in, ask to look but then just go over to the cot and peer at her.

'She's a little beauty. So sweet. How much did she weigh?'

'I don't . . . it's on the card.'

A sharp look. Carrie was used to those.

'What was her Apgar score?' But that was on the card as well.

'So . . .' She hitched herself back on the bed. 'You'll be taking her home any time now? Today, tomorrow?'

An ambulance raced up the main drive, blue light whirling round, but silently. It was too high up to hear any noises and the windows were double-glazed.

'Carrie? May I call you Carrie?' Everyone just did. Why ask?

'Who are you exactly? I know your name – I mean, where are you from?'

'I'm really here to make sure you're happy before you go home, and to answer any questions – not medical questions, Carrie, but how you feel about what it will be like at home on your own with a new baby because the reality is always so different. In here you're sheltered a bit, you've got a bell to ring if there's the slightest thing. So, do you think you're prepared?'

'Why wouldn't I be?'

'You're not breastfeeding.'

'No.' How did this woman know?

'So – you've been here nearly a week and you yourself are quite fit, the obstetricians have you one hundred per cent. And the baby is fine.'

'Is it?'

'Why do you ask that? Are you worried about something? Because I can assure you there is absolutely nothing wrong with her, Carrie.'

It was as if the woman could see inside her head.

'You can't stay here any longer, you know.'

'We're paying.'

'That really isn't the point, is it? Your place is at home now. With your daughter. And your husband. What does he think? Colin, isn't it?'

'What about?'

'He must want you home, surely. Proud father?'

134

'I don't know.'

'Carrie . . . what's the matter? Everyone is concerned about you. That's why I'm here. Are you feeling overwhelmed by this new little person and all the responsibility? Or just apathetic and low? Maybe you should have another blood test in case you're anaemic or have an infection lurking.'

'I don't.'

'Postnatal depression is very real and devastating and it can take the edge off all your joy in that lovely little girl.'

'I'm not depressed.'

'You can talk to me. I understand completely.'

'No. No, you don't. No one does.'

There was a long silence. She is waiting, Carrie thought, so that her silence will wear me down and I'll crack and pour it all out.

She wouldn't.

Another ambulance came in. A little flock of birds flew across the concourse.

'I wish you'd talk to me.'

'What about?'

'How you feel.'

'I'm fine. You're right, I should go home. I'm fit and well, aren't I?'

'You both are.'

'No.'

'Sorry?'

'You don't understand, do you? She isn't all right. There's something very wrong with her. I can see it. They don't seem to be able to and now you can't. I thought you were the experts.'

Serena slid off the bed, went to the crib. 'May I pick her up?' Carrie shrugged.

She bent over and touched her finger to the baby's face, before scooping her up into her arms. She looked at her intently, with a sort of awe.

'Carrie, she is absolutely perfect and quite beautiful. Look at her. Look! Open your eyes. Now take her.'

'No. Not now. She needs to sleep.'

'She needs you to hold her. Cuddle her. She needs to be close to you, to hear you and smell you and know you're there. Take her, Carrie.'

Silence for a long time, until Carrie said, 'Please will you tell the sister I am going home tomorrow?'

She wondered when the Serena woman would leave. She wanted her to put the baby down. And suddenly, she wanted to be with Colin, in their house, with a passion.

'That will be for the best, Carrie, but I think you should talk to someone before you go.'

'What about?'

'That you're not very confident with the baby, perhaps? It does come but it's daunting, I know. Is she feeding well?'

They had handed the baby to her and then a bottle and she had put the teat into the baby's mouth and she had sucked it empty. They had shown her how to get up wind. They had weighed the baby and told her the weight.

'I think so.'

'You know that they always lose a few ounces from their birth weight before they start to put it on again? That's normal. She's doing really well.'

At last she did put the baby back in the crib, swaddled it in the blanket. Stroked its cheek. Went.

Carrie looked down at the ambulances and the wheelchairs and trolleys and the people sitting on benches far far below. Once, she glanced quickly at the crib. The baby lay on its back, a few strands of fair hair showing beneath the white hat.

Twenty-nine

'Then you go like this when the caller shouts, "Turn around and a dosey-doe."'

Rod was doing the steps.

Sam pulled back, Rod tripped, someone came in the door and they ended up in a heap.

'Bloody hell, Sam, I could of broken my leg then.'

'Shut up, that's my pager. And the phone.'

'Porter to SCBU please.'

'I'm on the stores rota, and they're all screaming at me.' Rod was banging out through the door.

'Hey, where's this? SCBU?'

'Special care baby unit – fourth floor west.' His voice went away down the corridor.

Sam had never been up to SCBU, even with a linen trolley, which was the first job you got when you started as a porter. They gave you linen and miscellaneous supplies before they gave you people.

'Very wise,' Cat had said.

Corridors. Lifts. Lifts. Corridors. Swing doors. A covered way. Lift. Corridor. SPECIAL CARE BABY UNIT. SIDE A

'At last.' 'Nurse Lydia Spence', her badge read.

'I've never been up here. Took me a bit long, sorry.'

'Right.' She glanced at his own badge. 'Sam. Hold on here a sec.'

Sam stood in the corridor, looking through a long window that gave onto a room full of cots with perspex sides, like plant propagators, he thought. Tiny, very pink creatures lay in them, most attached to monitors and tubes and lines, all wearing little knitted hats, some naked save for nappies. He could not take in how small the one nearest to him looked – he guessed it measured the same as a school ruler, from the tip of its head to its very pink feet.

'So small . . .' he said.

'Oh yes. But little fighters, every one of them. Right, in here.'

A waiting room. Blinds down at the window. Three upright chairs. No one. Just one of the perspex cots.

Sam went closer.

It was wrapped in a shawl. A pink knitted hat. A white sheet. There was a red label attached. He bent over and read it.

'"Carly Primrose Dennison".' A date of birth. And today's date.

'Will you take her down? Paperwork's all done but here's the form. The parents were with her, but they had to leave, they have two other kids and they don't live close.'

'Am I taking her on this?'

'How else? It's the same as a trolley, just smaller. What are you thinking?'

Sam hesitated. He didn't know what he was thinking. There was just something that didn't feel right.

'You know your way from here to the mortuary?' The nurse was not cross, just brisk and rushed off her feet, like all of them.

'I wonder if . . . couldn't I carry her?'

She looked at him, her expression changing. 'I don't see why not.'

'It seems . . . just seems right, somehow. More . . . I don't know. She's so tiny and it's so . . .' He couldn't go on. For the first time in the job, he had to swallow back tears.

She touched his arm. 'Of course it's all right, Sam . . . just put the form in your pocket.'

She picked up the tiny body, rearranged the shawl and the hat, and then handed her to Sam.

'She weighs nothing,' he said. 'It's like holding a bird.'

The sister opened the door for him and watched him as he went out, slowly, carefully, and away down the corridor.

Thirty

'McDermid is coming out of hospital tomorrow. He said he'll be in touch with me if he remembers anything. Returning to the house may stimulate some recall, or it may not. Nothing else for now. Press conference tomorrow at eleven, but it'll be a stalling op, there's nothing to tell them unless it comes up tonight. Anything more?'

There were mutters and headshakes and they broke up, tired of there being nothing, on the brink of losing heart.

'Guv . . .' Fern was hanging back. 'The auction houses and fine art places . . . there's been nothing at all on the robbery stuff from the doctor's house but I had a message to call back on those Warhol prints they took from the McDermids.'

She was well aware that she hadn't anything to tell him, no excuse for keeping him in the room which had now emptied, no news. The request to call someone back was likely to be nothing, just a courtesy from an art dealer wanting information from the police as much as the other way round. Maybe he needed a nudge. Maybe he needed a little reminder that she was here. Not waiting exactly, but . . . yes, come clean. Waiting.

'And?'

He looked at her with impatience and a certain coldness.

'Thought it might be something.'

'Well, you won't find out if it is or not by standing here chatting to me, will you? Go and get on the bloody phone back to them.'

She fled, her face on fire, angry with him, angrier with herself.

'Bastard,' she muttered under her breath, banging through the swing doors into the CID room.

It was almost half past six and Simon found nothing urgent on his desk or in his messages. He could go home. He felt exhausted, as if he had been up for several nights, as in the old days with the Met when things kicked off at midnight, shift after shift. But this was not the sort of tiredness easily remedied by one long night's sleep, it was more like having been drained of energy – energy and enthusiasm and interest in the job, something he had never known. Perhaps he should book an appointment with the MO, get a health check and overhaul. Perhaps there was something. A virus, an infection. Something wrong with his blood. His heart. His mind.

As he went out, he saw a familiar car parked. He stopped. She did not wave or call out, just waited, the window wound down.

'Hey,' Cat said.

'You OK?'

'Of course. Kieron is in London overnight and Felix is away for a week at a wildlife centre. I have a couple of ribeye steaks. Follow me.'

'No, I can't, I have to—'

'No,' his sister said, starting the engine. 'You don't. See you back there.'

He waited until she had turned into the road and gone out of sight, before following her but then taking the left turn, in the direction of the cathedral and home. The last thing he wanted was to spend an evening with his sister being either inquisitive or bossy. The first thing he wanted was to be in his own perfect space with the door locked against the world.

The town square had been pedestrianised, with only access for taxis and buses, so that he had to make a detour past the Hill. It was busy and he was held up at temporary traffic lights, and as they finally turned green, where he should have gone left he drove straight on, to the roundabout and the bypass. He felt in some odd way that he was under orders and that his own decisions had been overruled.

There were more lights, where the bypass was being resurfaced, and the traffic went to single lane, which had been causing congestion in Lafferton for several weeks and would go on doing so for several more. Simon reached the farmhouse minutes behind his sister.

'Are you on or off duty?' Cat asked.

'Technically I'm off now, but you know it doesn't work like that, we're in the middle of a major investigation.'

'A beer or a glass of red?'

'I'd actually like a Scotch.'

'Then mine's a large gin. I'm definitely off tonight.'

'How's the job going?'

'It's good. Yes.'

For several minutes, they avoided talking by being busy, Simon getting the drinks, Cat flattening the steaks, salting and peppering them, picking out some new potatoes.

'Right, fifteen minutes. Bring our drinks into the den.'

Behind her, carrying the glasses, he knew exactly how to play this, as he pretty much always knew how to handle Cat.

'So . . . what exactly happened in the cemetery?'

Simon swirled his whisky round the bottom of the heavy glass, held it up to the light. 'Look at that – tawny. Like honey.'

'Si.'

'What? Oh, that . . . heat, low blood sugar – you've always preached about that but, you know, I've realised that you're right, though it pains me to admit it . . . not having eaten, too many espressos, running up the station stairs a few times, it really does—'

'Simon.'

'—make you feel weird. Dizzy and . . . well, you know. Like Felix gets when he does his breathing wrong playing his oboe . . . he told me his ears went buzzy—'

'Simon.'

She did not raise her voice, she held her glass and looked at him steadily. And waited.

'What? As I said. I wouldn't mind your take on Declan McDermid. Went in to talk to him and physically he's on the mend, they're letting him home tomorrow probably – well, when I say "home"—'

'Simon.'

'For Christ's SAKE!'

After the crash of glass hitting the wall there was a long silence. Simon stared at the mess, his heart racing, his hand shaking. Cat looked at him for a while, her expression one of love, understanding and patience, before she got up to fetch a dustpan and brush and clear up the glass. She returned everything to the kitchen where she poured a replacement whisky. The cat Mephisto had fled in here from the sudden noise, and was now smelling steak. She covered it with a dish.

Simon was sitting as she had left him.

'You probably needed to do that, but, you have to talk to me, and if you can't talk to me, to someone else. I mean it.'

'I'm not going to a bloody therapist. I don't need one.'

'Then talk to me. At least just tell me what's happening. You don't ring me like that for nothing, and you know it. If you tell me what your symptoms were I can help you.'

'Symptoms.'

'Yes.'

He looked at her. 'You sound like a doctor.'

'Tell you what – bring your drink into the kitchen while I cook the steaks. Talk to me there.'

She hoped he might find it easier if she was doing something, not sitting with her attention focused only on him.

He was silent for a few moments, and then he got up. But sitting at the kitchen table, fresh glass in front of him, he just said, 'It's no big deal. Honestly. I told you – I hadn't eaten, I'd been rushing about, I had too many espressos.'

'Bullshit.'

'Well, it's what I've heard you preach about a thousand times.'

'Hypo because of low blood sugar, yes, and that won't have helped, but it is also the least of it, as well you know. You said you had chest pains.'

'I did not.'

'Didn't have them or didn't say you had?'

He didn't answer.

'You had pins and needles in your hands and arms.'

'Singular. Hand. Arm. And no, I didn't.'

Cat pulled the cord on the extractor fan, to take away the smell of frying and make conversation impossible while her brother calmed down again, as well as to give herself a moment to think. She knew him, and always had, as a man who was understanding of any stress-related issues his fellow cops or anyone else might have, sensitive and patient. Yet he could not give himself the same treatment, would dodge the issue, bury it, evade it.

Ten minutes later, they were sitting with medium-rare steaks and glasses of wine, in silence. Wookie scratched at the door and Cat let him in, to join Mephisto, already bedded deep in the cushions, on the old kitchen sofa. Simon ate. Drank. Looked at his plate.

Throwing her own glass at the wall seemed an appealing option. But Cat knew better.

'Si, please . . . just listen. I just want you back to your usual self. You know that since the attack you have been pretty much a hundred per cent physically. But you are still mentally and emotionally below par and it's not getting better, it has got worse. You've seen it happen to other cops, for God's sake, you know it's pretty much standard. You've tried to treat it yourself and to a certain extent, like when you went up to Scotland, you've done that, but it's got a grip. It's got itself deep into you. Call it PTSD, call it delayed shock, call it whatever you like, names don't help and they don't much matter in this case. Call it nothing. But you can't go on like this because it will affect everything – work, home, relationships, and most of all you, your own self. You're the one who will come off worst if you don't do something. And I don't understand. You're not stupid, you get all this. Are you afraid of what will happen?'

'I'm not afraid of anything.'

'Yes, you are. You're afraid of IT. Please. You are the son of doctors, brother of doctors, you're in the police force, which isn't burying its collective head in the sand about this sort of thing any more, they're slowly getting to grips with it. So are the military. But you have to cooperate. The attack and the whole thing with your arm was awful, a bloody nightmare, but this is becoming a lot worse. You make me bloody furious but I'm the closest person you've got, so let me in. TALK to me.'

For a few seconds, it could have gone her way. He sat quietly, perhaps even taking in what she had said, taking it to heart. The tension between them was taut as a wire, she felt as if she could reach out and feel it. Please. Please, Si. She looked at him and saw how tightly he was holding himself in, how the skin was stretched across his cheekbones, straining across the back of his hand where he was clenching it. She wanted to hug him yet knew it would not be well received. But at least, when he had worked his way through the hedge of his own prickliness and pride, she was sure he would start talking.

Instead, he got up and walked out. The front door opened and closed, she heard his car start and the tyres hit the gravel. A couple of seconds later, there was loud noise as brakes were stamped on. Two sets of brakes. Two cars.

Cat wondered if she had to panic or be furious, but before she had settled for either, the front door opened again. Voices. Laughter, even. Wookie jumped off the sofa, tail going round like a propeller.

'Hi, Ma, nearly had a major RTA on your hands, I just told Uncle Si, he should arrest himself for careless driving. Sheesh.'

'Sorry, sorry.' Simon, back in the kitchen as if nothing had happened, and behind him, Rosie Chen, petite, exquisite, fourth-year medical student, and Sam's girlfriend.

'Any supper left?'

'No, Sam, I told you, we will do it. Your mother doesn't have to cook for us. Hello.' Rosie hugged Cat, so did Sam. Simon had his back to her, bending to get beers out of the fridge and when he turned round, he gave her a winning smile, the smile she had known since they were small children and he had wanted her to do something, or needed forgiveness without having to ask, his charm, like the smile, on full-beam.

It had always worked but this time, she decided, only for now because the kids are here and the whole mood of the evening has changed. She was putting the conversation they were going to have on hold. That was all.

Food. Drinks. Talk. Rosie's sweet smile. Sam's happy face. Kieron rang her and heard the laughter. Felix sent his daily text, as required by the accompanying teachers, to say he'd had a great day and seen an otter. She glanced at her brother as he was explaining something to Rosie, who listened intently, with a small frown of concentration. And she wished passionately that Simon could find his way through the thorn hedge, which was not entirely of his own making but to which he had certainly added plenty of layers, and to which he was still stubbornly refusing to take the pruning shears.

Thirty-one

'Winston, listen to me.'

'I am listening to you.'

Agneta went nearer to him. 'What are you going to DO?'

Winston stepped back from the machine. For a moment, he looked as if he was in pain.

'Ag . . . I don't know. I'm sorry, girl, I'm not heartless, all right? I'm not taking this as if it's just . . .' He clicked his fingers. 'I'm worried, like you. I don't know what to do though, you see? You and me both. What to do?'

He sighed and returned to the blender, which whirred on, the batter hitting the perspex sides and pouring down.

'I don't know either, Wint. Where is Shenda? This is not normal and there is something wrong, we both know.'

Wint nodded, wiped his brow with the back of his hand, adjusted his white hat, and sighed again. Then he switched off the blender and reached for a baking tray.

'Perhaps she's just gone off. It happens.'

'No. Shenda is not like that and you know it. I am not like that, Lois is not like that. We work hard and we like it here and we wouldn't let you down, we wouldn't just not come in and not tell you. Believe it.'

He leaned on the table. 'OK, I believe it. Now, one more time, what do you want me to do?'

'Go to the police.'

'They won't want to know.'

146

'Why? In my country—'

'Yeah, well, maybe yours is different but the police here won't be interested, trust me.'

Agneta left the cafe just after six o'clock and was padlocking her bike in the racks outside the police station at twenty past. There were two people in front of her at the desk, and a woman with a black eye and cuts on her face, sitting on a chair. Agneta did not want to stare at her, but she saw the blank look in her eyes, the way her shoulders were down, the scruffy parka, and she wanted to hug her.

The man at the counter left. The woman who was next started to talk to the desk sergeant and did not draw breath for what felt like half an hour. Agneta glanced round again at the one with the injuries. Caught her eye. Smiled and got nothing back except a stare.

It made her shiver, made the odd feeling she had about Shenda worse. She had had it for two days and when she got these feelings they were right. She trusted them. She smiled at the woman again.

'Evening, miss, how can I help?'

'Oh. Hello. I have to tell you that my friend is missing. She's not been to work for two days now, and she hasn't phoned or messaged, not to anyone.'

'Right. I'm very sorry to hear it. Let's have some details.'

He sounded sorry too. Winston was just wrong. Agneta was changing her opinion of Winston as a good man and a boss who cared about them.

She told the sergeant everything in detail. At first she was going to keep quiet about her visit to Shenda's flat but when he looked at her with such a kind smile, such encouragement, she remembered what she had always been taught, that a lie was a lie not only when you said something untrue but when you concealed the truth.

He was careful. He listened. He wrote. She felt a surge of confidence.

'I won't want you to wait now, but we'll need to be in touch with you so make sure you keep your phone switched on. This is the number, right?'

He read it back to her.

'Yes.'

'Last thing – do you have a photo of her?'

'She hates having her picture taken. I wanted one of us all outside the cafe in the sun when it was my birthday but she would not and this I don't understand.'

'Don't worry, people are funny about a lot of things. And people go missing and they're found, or they just turn up safe and well, happens every day, but that doesn't mean we won't be taking this very seriously. I'll pass it on straight away to CID and we'll go from there. You'll hear from us but if your friend does come back meanwhile you will let us know immediately, won't you? Important that you do.'

In the station, Sergeant Boyd hoped for a moment free of people in front of him, in which he could finish the short report on the missing girl and send it out, as an alert. He did not have that moment. The doors swung open and a man wielding some sort of weapon – he barely had a chance to see what – flung himself onto the woman with the facial injuries, who had been sitting for half an hour waiting for her CID support officer. Boyd pressed the alarm and clambered over the counter as a machete flashed against the light, and then everything happened in a confusion of screams, shouts, yelled abuse, fists, blade, blood, the man and the woman on the floor, doors opening and officers pouring out, and through it all the wail of the emergency siren.

He was strong, he was agile, he was in a foaming rage and he had a lethal weapon. He was off the floor, kicking out, flailing with the machete, slashing an arm, a face, a head, sent crashing, pulling himself up on hands and knees, still fighting, still raging, the blade swinging right and left. More officers came two at a time down the stairs, four of them throwing their bodies onto his, pinning his arms and legs, trying to dodge the weapon. At last, a taser hit him and he was squirming, jerking convulsively. Then still.

Thirty-two

Her clothes were wet. That was the first thing. And she saw that it was almost dark. Her left leg was painful, and her right shoulder. She put up a hand to her face, and then the back of her head. Her hair felt sticky. She had a headache. Her eyesight seemed misty.

After a few moments, she sat up slowly, felt giddy and was suddenly and violently sick.

She was outside. She felt around her and touched rough grass. Wetness. Soil. Somewhere in the far distance a dog barked, somewhere she could hear traffic but all around her it was not only quiet but hushed in some odd way. She sat up again, more carefully. She felt less dizzy but cold and shivery.

Where. Why. What.

Frightened. She was very frightened, consumed with it, yet did not know of what, only that she was made of fear and that she had to go. Had to get somewhere else. Her skin felt as if it had been scalded.

Who. When.

Who.

She had to find out who. She could not stand but she could roll over and then get onto her hands and knees, though it took a long time. Not minutes not hours.

Days.

She began to crawl, inching herself over the long, thick, coarse, wet grass. Mud. The rain was cool on her head, washing her clean.

149

As she crawled slowly, slowly, it grew completely dark so that she couldn't see the ground she was crawling on, only managed to feel her way forward. There were tussocks of grass under her hands, for a long time, until she came up against a wall. She collapsed back, her head aching badly now, but at the same time her mind was becoming clearer, in flashes which came and went and each time seemed to push the fog further away. The first flash was of a car. It smelled of oil and stale cigarettes. Another flash and there was a hand over her mouth. Another and she was stumbling forward. Being pushed. She reached out now and touched the wall, though it couldn't be a wall, and felt something round and cold, heavy, smooth, and her hand went through it. A tube. A hole. No. A pipe. The opening to a pipe. She traced her fingers round it. Inside it was wet, water dripped onto the back of her hand.

Her clothes were soaked. Her jeans. T-shirt. No shoes. No socks. Nothing else.

She wanted to go to sleep. Her arms were stiff and yet she was shaking.

Eyes closed. Lids. Head dropped.

Noise. Cars. Too loud. Lorries grinding and straining. She leaned over and felt with her left arm. Tussocks of grass again. She moved her fingers down and it was not far, not deep, she could climb up. Scramble. Was she in a deep ditch then? That was what it felt like.

It took a long time and it was painful and twice she had to stop and once she slithered back and once she closed her eyes and the blackness had swirling stars and she was sick. It took hours. All time. Nothing of her or in her was without pain and the pain was increasing, weights pressed down on her and stakes pushed up and little electric currents sizzled through her brain like lightning shocks.

She moved again and rolled over and stopped. There. She was there. The ground was cold but the grass was shorter and hard peas of gravel scraped and pressed into her palms.

The noise of the lorries was louder. Lights washed over her then and away. She knelt and looked ahead and across and behind her, until more lights swept up and blinded her and they were like the sea and she closed her eyes and fell forwards as first a car, then a van stopped, doors opened and slammed, feet on the tarmac, voices, more voices, more cars, and later blue lights.

Shenda closed her eyes.

Thirty-three

'Will you hold her?'

'Why, what are you doing?'

'Going to heat the bottle.'

Colin was halfway to his office but he came back and took the baby from Carrie. He held her awkwardly. They both did. Carrie went into the kitchen but he followed her, and she did not want that, she wanted to be alone.

'She's awake. Her eyes are open.'

Carrie did not answer.

'She doesn't cry a lot, does she? I understood babies cried most of the time.'

'That's because . . .'

'What?'

She banged the microwave door shut, turned the knob, pressed 'Start' and did not look at him at all and did not reply.

'I thought they cried half the night but she never cries.'

'She cries.'

'Not loudly enough to wake me up.'

There were blackbirds on the grass, a young one and a parent, peck, peck, peck for worms.

'Can I put her back in her cot? I need to get on.'

Carrie shrugged and went on watching the blackbirds.

She did everything on autopilot. She had no feelings of any kind, she neither loved nor hated the baby, but simply did not relate to her at all. Colin would not talk about it but she knew

152

that he was irritated. He could not see that there was anything wrong, kept on reminding Carrie that they had both been given a clean bill of health by the hospital before they left, and otherwise he shut himself in his office surrounded by his screens.

She took out the bottle, tested the milk's heat on her inner arm, got a clean muslin from the drawer, one movement, two, three, four, tick them off.

In the cot in the sitting room the baby lay, eyes open, trying to focus on the world. Her fair hair seemed to have been brushed lightly across her head with a fine paintbrush.

Carrie did not know what was wrong with her. There was nothing to see, smell, feel, hear. Everything worked. She drank, slept, filled her nappies, cried a little, made soft murmuring sounds. She lay still, in whichever position she had been put.

Carrie lifted her, held her, put the teat to her mouth, then looked out of the window. The blackbirds had gone. A pigeon was on the grass. A blue tit was in the pink shrub on the left. Sunlight, then chasing, shifting shadows. Sunlight again.

The baby snuffled as she drank, as if her nose was blocked. Sneezed once. Went on feeding.

Carrie did not talk to her.

She wondered how long it would be before something happened, something showed, and then people would believe her. People. There were none.

The baby's eyebrows were barely sketched in. Her eyelids were violet, closed in concentration.

Did her skin seem clammy and pale or was that a trick of the light? Her tiny body when naked had no flaws, no marks. She did not think she would have known it in a row of other babies.

A small splutter and milk ran down onto her lips. Carrie wiped it. Another, but then the pink mouth fastened onto the teat again, puckered round it like a sea anemone, and sucked furiously.

She had read that when babies were not right, they could not suckle properly, that was a clear sign.

The fingers curled into a fist and uncurled, curled again in the ecstasy of feeding.

Had she gained weight? Had she lost it? She looked no different.

If she became fat, flabby, loose-skinned, if she grew but in size only, that would be a sign. If she did not focus. If she lay inert.

She did not cry except when she was hungry, did not always sleep, lay squinting at her own fingers. At the side of her crib. At her mother?

Mother.

It meant nothing.

Let it show soon and be over.

Whatever it was.

In the office, Colin looked from screen to screen, followed the moving letters, numbers, red, green, scrolling, scrolling. Money there money gone money given money taken pounds dollars euros yen, and suddenly, a shoal of money landed, thousands wriggling in the net and held fast with a click.

The image of the baby came between him and the screens, though he did not understand why. As he decided to lock in his considerable gains and close down, Carrie called him.

'Someone's at the door. I can't go . . .'

Perhaps if he had not been in such a good mood, buoyed by the day's trading, he would not have asked Dr Deerbon in, and certainly not without asking Carrie.

'Did my wife call you? She hasn't told me.'

'No, but I was literally passing the end of the lane after another visit and I remembered that she must be at home with the baby by now, so I thought I'd check all was well, but if it isn't convenient, of course that's fine, I'll get on home.'

Colin held the door open. 'I have no idea if she will want to see you.' It was true. Carrie seemed to him no different, in her attitude to the baby, than she had been before its birth – if anything, she was rather more detached and distant, mechanical in all her dealings with it, saying little to him. He did not know what was normal, even for his wife. 'But come through.'

She was standing staring out of the window at the garden and did not turn when Cat came in. The baby was in a crib set against the end of the sofa, not close to her.

'Hello. I hope it's all right – I'm on my way home.'

'Yes.' There was a pause, it was several seconds before Carrie glanced round. She looked neat, hair carefully tied back, T-shirt and skirt clean. Her face was not made-up but Cat did not think she had worn any the last time she had visited. Perhaps she never did. Certainly she showed none of the obvious signs of being depressed – or even in the usual messy turmoil of looking after a new baby.

'May I look?'

'Of course.'

'What's her name?'

'She hasn't got one.'

'You haven't registered her yet then.'

An anxious look crossed Carrie's face so fleetingly that perhaps it had not been there. 'No.'

'How are you feeling?'

'I'm all right.'

'Are you getting enough sleep?'

'She's very good.'

Cat stood beside the cot, thinking, waiting for Carrie to open up to her. But she did not. Would not. She was robotic, hardly there in the room.

'May I pick her up?'

A nod.

The baby was soundly asleep and barely stirred when she was touched, and lifted. Held.

'She's beautiful, Carrie.'

She was. She was also pale, perhaps too pale? She was deeply asleep, made not the slightest sound when Cat touched her cheek though she was breathing.

'How much does she weigh now?'

'I'm not sure.'

Cat carried the baby to the sofa. 'Come and sit down a minute.'

Carrie hesitated. 'It's all right,' she said. 'We're fine.'

The baby lay still. She felt heavy. Limp? No. But there was something. Something.

'How often are you feeding her?'

'Every four hours. And she finishes her milk, nearly always. The hospital said every four hours but she doesn't wake as often as that.'

'How long? What's the longest time between feeds?'

A silence. Then Carrie came over and took the baby. 'I would like you to go please. I didn't ask for a visit. We're fine. We're all fine. Now will you go please?'

It was clear to Cat that even when help was in front of Carrie, when she could have talked freely and in complete confidence, she was unable to accept it.

Cat drove down the lane to the river. It was a grey day, not cold, but with a fine mizzle over the undergrowth, on the wooden bridge. In the air. She got out and stood for a moment but her hair and coat were quickly damp.

She was their GP, Colin had signed them up, and when Cat had advised them to sign with an NHS practice, for the neonatal services they would need as much as for emergencies which A&E covered, he had listened but been non-committal.

There was something about the baby but nothing obvious, nothing Cat could pin down. She would have liked to call out a neonatal paediatrician but doubted if she would be able to persuade Carrie to agree to it and it was Carrie she was more concerned about, because of her mental and emotional state, which had not been good in pregnancy but had now deteriorated. She seemed not so much postnatally depressed as detached and uninterested. Her husband had not reappeared during Cat's visit, as if he were nothing to do with it all.

She started the car. A second and specialist opinion was what was needed, urgently.

Thirty-four

POLICE IN MACHETE MAYHEM

Seven officers were injured, two of them seriously, when a man charged into the front reception area of Lafferton police station yesterday evening, wielding a machete, and attacked a woman who was apparently waiting to see a member of the force. Sergeant Alastair Boyd (34) pressed the emergency alarm before leaping over the desk in an attempt to over-power him, as other officers answered the call and poured into the area. The man was seen to swing the weapon about him at random, catching several police officers, four of whom continued their attempts at restraint. The man was eventually tasered and pinned down.

Thirty-five

The machine hummed faintly and she lay still inside, and because she was not aware of how narrow the scanner was and how tightly she fitted into it, she could not suffer from her usual claustrophobia, which would have had her screaming in terror, sweating, desperate to be pulled out.

Inert. Eyes closed. The ventilator sucking regularly, in, out, in, out, mimicking her normal living breath. And she was living, of course she was. She just did not know it. She knew nothing and it was better that way, for now.

Three of them on the other side of the glass window.

'The swelling has gone down, but fractionally. No other signs of significant brain trauma. Jaw is fractured, there, and below the right ear. Several teeth gone but none of this is very important. It's the tissue swelling I'm worried about.'

An arm went out, a finger pointed. 'There's some bleeding . . . quite small but it is there.'

'Yes. Not extensive – but you're right. OK, we continue to monitor her, continue the sedation for the next twenty-four hours, then have another MRI. I'd like to see the swelling reduced more and that area of bleeding gone – or at least not any bigger. My hunch is it'll just disappear. Five ribs broken, which means she'll need pain relief when she does come round.'

'Could she still have a pneumothorax?'

'Never say never but unlikely. Right, she can go back to ITU.'

Chairs scraped back, and they were away, black-and-white images, shapes and dark patches, faint lines running down the cloudy grey, still in their minds until the end of the corridor, and another cubicle, another broken figure to be put back together.

Half an hour later, the nursing shift was handing over. 'Still no idea who she is?'

'Nothing.'

'Well, she's got to belong to somebody, she's got to have been missed from somewhere, surely to God.'

'The trouble is, because Lafferton Police aren't fully functioning and Bevham are trying to cover all bases, missing persons reports tend to drop down the batting order, unless it's a child. What's the news anyway?'

He adjusted the drip. Checked a monitor. Looked back at the young woman on the bed. In here, it was quiet. Under control.

'Nobody's dead though one's in a right mess. I think he was the cop who reached him first and tried to disarm him, but you know, you don't argue with a machete. Haven't got a grip on the others because of the RTA.'

'What is it with the last couple of days? Did you hear about the snake attack on the guy who kept two pythons in his spare bedroom?'

'And a crocodile in the bath?'

'No, just four tarantulas in the kitchen.'

'He's dead?'

'Not quite.'

'It's an ill wind.' He looked down at the girl again. 'She'll live, is my hunch.'

The ventilator breathed and the monitors beeped and the girl on the bed slept, aware of nothing.

Thirty-six

'Mr McDermid?'

The police officer had pressed the new intercom button at the gate three times before it was answered, rather uncertainly.

'Sorry . . . who is it please?'

There was something endearing about the apologetic voice. She had not expected a highly successful businessman to sound so hesitant, but perhaps it wasn't surprising given the violence of the attack. 'My name is DC Jenna Rhys. I'm from Lafferton Police. Could I come in please?'

'Oh. Yes. Do you have news?'

'It would be easier to talk if you could let me in.'

'Ah. Apologies. Yes. Hold on, I have to work this out. It was shown to me several times but I don't think I got the hang of which button, which light, you know?'

'Maybe press the button below the green flashing light? Is there one?'

'Yes. I see. Thanks. Here we go. I think.'

The buzzer on the gate sounded and the lock clicked. Jenna went through, as McDermid opened the front door. His hair had not yet grown back fully where it had been shaved at the hospital and he looked shaky, as if he was not certain where to put his feet as he descended.

'Please come in. I know your face, don't I?'

'We met at the reception – the bobby van.'

'Yes. Right . . .'

160

'I've come to see how you are and if I can do anything for you, anything at all. I'm officially your FLO – family liaison officer.'

He led the way across the hall and into a warm, beautifully appointed kitchen. The sun was coming in through tall windows, touching the primrose-yellow walls and deep ochre cupboards.

'I'm sorry, I have to sit down. I'm recovering well but I seem to get dizzy now and then.'

'I do understand – you had some nasty injuries and shock. Maybe you shouldn't have come out of hospital so soon.'

'Maybe . . . I've been down to Bournemouth, to the flat we have, I didn't think I wanted to be here without my wife, but when I arrived, I didn't want to be there either. The place seemed to belong to someone else. It was . . . we had so many happy times there but I couldn't sit staring at the sea. I couldn't spend so much as a night in it. I had to come home. This is home.'

Without warning, he started to sob, letting the tears fall and not attempting to wipe them away. But he said, 'I am sorry. I am sorry.'

Jenna put a hand on his shoulder. 'No need to be sorry. It's good, you need to cry. Everyone does after this sort of terrible shock – everyone. Now, can I make you tea or a coffee or something else? I'm here for as long as you need me and if you want to talk, fine, if not, that's fine too. Is anyone looking after you?'

'We have . . . yes, but I think – I don't know. Our housekeeper, Pauline, she came while I was in hospital. She's very good. I don't know what to do. I don't know what to do next . . .'

'Are any of your family available to come and stay?'

'We didn't have any children, you see, and Cindy lost her sister two years ago, and I didn't have any siblings. So it was just us, really. We didn't marry until we were in our forties, didn't meet – I – Cindy had been married and divorced long before, I'd never . . . I was only interested in building up the businesses, the company, and what was that all for?'

'I can answer that, Mr McDermid – you have been incredibly generous, a real local benefactor, as well as providing work for a great many people.'

161

'Thank you. Cindy always said that . . . providing the jobs, keeping people in steady work, and the rest – I've been very fortunate. Cindy is dead. I can't understand it.'

'Who could? Who can understand what happened to her? It was a dreadful thing.'

'They should have killed me as well. No, no, I don't mean – I mean instead of her. She'd have known how to carry on, she'd have made a proper job of it. I don't have the first idea what to do next. It would have been better.'

'Can I make you that coffee?'

'No, I should . . .' He started to get up. Jenna stopped him, and started to look for things.

'Your Chief Superintendent was going to let me know the moment there was any lead to who might have done this but he hasn't been in touch. He said it might take some time. It doesn't matter about the things they took, you know, what are things, what's stuff? But they won't be able to sell some of that artwork easily.'

Jenna brought mugs of coffee to the table.

'They weren't chancers, Mr McDermid, they knew what they were taking, they'll have the dealers in sight, just like they would have done with that other one – that was pretty unusual stuff as well, some older things, silver and so on. Apparently there was a clock, three hundred-odd years old. Very rare.'

Declan had been stirring his coffee but now he stopped, spoon frozen.

'I don't think I know what you're talking about. What "other one"?'

'There was another robbery before yours, same pattern, same MO.'

'I must have missed hearing about that, my memory is still a bit patchy. I don't think I read anything about valuable clocks.'

'You wouldn't have, there was a news blackout on it. Nobody was injured so we could do that. Once there's been anyone hurt or . . . or sadly passed away, then obviously it's in the public interest.'

'You mean murdered, you mean killed, Miss Rhys. My wife was murdered. I'm sorry. I apologise, I didn't mean to shout at you, that was very rude. I am so sorry.'

'It doesn't matter at all. You can say anything to me and if shouting at me helps to relieve your feelings, then you go ahead. Truly.'

She stayed another hour, made more coffee, until the house-keeper arrived and Jenna felt she was no longer needed. If she had been needed in the first place. It was a funny business being an FLO. You never really knew. Sometimes she felt they couldn't have coped without her, they were all over the place. This time was different. It had been a terrible thing, Declan McDermid was still in some shock and he hadn't fully recovered from his injuries. But she had felt out of place. She might report just that, in her debriefing.

Thirty-seven

'Winston . . . oh my good God . . .' Agneta burst through the door into the kitchen, waving her phone, switching to shouting in Polish in her panic. 'Oh my God, look at it, look at it.'

'All right, all right, calm down, Ag, here, sit here.'

'I can't sit, I don't want to sit, I have to go to her, I have to go.'

'*Sit down*. For crying out loud.'

'Look, will you? Look.'

'Bloody hell!'

'You see?'

The picture was not the best but it was still quite clear that the girl photographed lying in the hospital bed, eyes closed, tubes and wires coming from her arm, chest, mouth, was Shenda.

Thirty-eight

The smoked salmon was the best he had ever eaten and now the Wiener schnitzel almost melted in the mouth. Spinach and fries on the side. A gin and tonic before, a glass of white with. The Wolseley was as buzzing with life, talk and deals as usual at a midweek lunchtime.

Serrailler sat opposite Marcus, owner of the gallery that showed his work, and ought to have been entirely relaxed, happy and content. They had walked the few hundred yards here down a bustling Piccadilly, it was a perfect London day, sunshine and warmth but with a breeze to lift the diesel-heavy air up and away. It was the part of London for which he always kept a large corner of his heart, and usually he looked forward to a day off here with great pleasure.

He had not been able to get to sleep until one, and at four, he had woken and sat up in a single beat, his heart racing and thumping, his head, hair, chest damp with sweat, strange, lurid shapes dancing through bizarrely coloured flames in front of his eyes. After that, sleep had been fitful and he had got up early and gone for a run before driving to the station. London was a nightmare, everything shot past him, everything blared and shouted and screeched, so that he had almost turned round and caught the next train home. Instead he had gone for a coffee to try and calm himself. He was in a lather crossing the road, the opposite pavement was wavering, the bus going by rose and lifted from the tarmac. He had started

165

to wonder if he had something wrong with his eyes. Or his brain.

Marcus had been waiting in his office with more coffee, shown him round the present exhibition, of small abstract bronzes, resembling those of Elisabeth Frink but more delicate. They were mysterious, beautiful, with here and there a greenish patina or a topaz sheen. Two-thirds were sold.

Simon could not focus on them clearly, he paced up and down the gallery, glanced out of the windows into the street, looked back, flinched at the way the spotlights seemed to become more intense and then fade, over and over again.

'You OK?'

'Fine. I had flu . . . doesn't seem to have cleared completely. But I'm fine.'

'You need a good lunch. Nasty thing, flu.'

Walking down to the Wolseley had been difficult because he had been on the outside of Marcus, close to the edge of the pavement and the taxis and cars and vans and buses and bikes hurtling past his shoulder. He had an urge to step off the kerb in front of a vehicle, and then a terror that a motorbike was going to mount the pavement and plough into him. He wanted to move, to put a safe distance between him and the traffic, to walk on the other side of his companion, which would make him look peculiar, would raise concern and questions. He wanted to shout out.

It was an overwhelming relief when the restaurant doors opened and he could get inside, and then the inside was like the third ring of hell, booming with voices that rose and rose, crazy with the toing and froing of waiters and greeters and customers, crash, clatter, china, cutlery, boom of the doors swinging behind him.

He drank his gin quickly and the great high-ceilinged room settled and steadied and he ate his salmon easily, when he had been afraid that he would choke on it, that he could not swallow.

Marcus gave him a quick, anxious glance, but when he spoke, it was not about health, it was about art. Art and business.

'When am I getting enough for your next exhibition, Simon? The sketches are wonderful. Are you adding anything to the angel heads – pillars, stone carving? Anything else medieval would work so well. We could open here but perhaps send the exhibition up to Lafferton, if there's anywhere to show?'

'The cathedral has a new visitors' centre. Might work. Or the crypt, maybe. Not sure. The light in the centre is ideal. I haven't thought beyond the angels at the moment. There are twenty of them, but yes, plenty of other things could work. I've drawn the pillars and the Romanesque carving on the font and the rood screen quite often. You've seen the sketch-books.'

'Could you work them up from the sketches?'

'I'd start again. But it would take a lot more time, Marcus.'

'How much more?'

'I do have a job, you know.'

'Still . . .'

'A year?'

Marcus shook his head. 'Take all your holiday at once. Six months max?'

'Tall order. And I doubt if I could do that anyway.'

'Sabbatical then.'

'I had a lot of time off after the attack.'

'That was different, surely.'

'Let me see. I have to tread a bit carefully. I can't ask for special favours now.'

Marcus leaned back. For the moment, drinks and good food had a steadying effect.

'I'd like to draw this place. It's one of my favourite rooms in London. Used to be a car showroom.'

'I know. I remember it.'

'I'd like to catch the movement – him . . . see how deftly they handle the trays . . . look, they pass one another like a ballet. Everyone focused. Everyone knows his job and does it, they're a perfect team. But a painter would do it better.'

'No, you're wrong. Charcoal. And pencil.'

'Charcoal and pen.'

'After the angels.'

'Maybe.'

Marcus looked at him closely over his glass of wine.

'What?'

'There's something you're not telling me.'

'What sort of thing would that be?'

'Not sure. The job. Family. Women.'

'Nope.'

'Health.'

'I'm fine.'

'OK. How's the arm?'

Simon reached out and extended it, picked up a napkin, then a salt cellar.

'The brain sends out the signals to this just as it does to my real arm – only a trifle slower. When I was in Scotland, my young friend Robbie asked if I could pick up a pin with it. I couldn't then but I can now.'

The waiter took away their plates.

'Double espresso, and, what, a Laphroaig? I know you're not a port man.'

'Just the coffee.'

Marcus gave the order then leaned forward slightly. 'Good job it wasn't your drawing hand, all the same.'

'On the whole.'

'Sure you're all right, though?'

Simon made a dismissive gesture with what Robbie had called his 'bionic hand'.

He did not want Marcus to pursue the subject. The effects of the alcohol were wearing off and he felt the heavy thump of his heart again, the rising mercury of panic. He had to drink his coffee fast, and get out.

He knew that Marcus stood watching as he dashed off down St James's Street, for no good reason except to get away, to move. He stopped beside one of the Palace guards, a stitch in his side. The man presented arms. Turned. Marched. Turned again. Marched back. Robot, Serrailler thought, which was hardly fair. He had done his own share of marching.

The sun was out. Tourists were taking their selfies in front of the motionless man in his bearskin. Men in suits. Men with leather cross-body bags. Why was he standing here?

He went off down Pall Mall, to walk the long way round to his hotel in Covent Garden, aimlessly, and without enjoyment. Suddenly, London terrified him again.

He slept the rest of afternoon. Woke, showered, read, watched the news, ate in the Brasserie Max among the early drinkers at the bar, the usual scattering of Americans. This was also one of his favourite places, he had brought so many dates here, it had the best of love-associations, with Diana in the old days, then with Rachel, but those memories had turned dry and stale. Now he seemed to have no feeling for anything or anyone. He thought about his sister and his mind swerved. They had fallen out, she was annoyed that he would not do as she thought he should, and had said so, he knew he could not go down the path of therapy and endless talk. It would never work for him. He was not that kind of man. He had to get out of this himself. It irritated him, that he felt weak and vulnerable, was suffering a hangover from his attack and its physical and mental consequences. The guardsman in his scarlet tunic, marching up, marching down, had perhaps been in a war zone not long ago, where his friends had been killed, had lost legs and their young minds. What was a scrap with some villains and the loss of his less-necessary arm, the good fortune of a state-of-the-art prosthesis? Put in perspective, it was little enough. *So, what was wrong with him?*

He sat at a table in Monmouth Street drinking coffee and a Laphroaig, watching the people on the street. When he had been a rookie copper in the Met he had patrolled round here, in the era before hipsters with beards, riding fixed-gear bikes.

His phone buzzed. Cat. He ignored it.

Television. Another drink. His book. But he had not been able to concentrate on any book for weeks, and that was not normal, that was not him. He had tried easy thrillers, straightforward travel accounts, old favourites, novels he knew so well he could quote paragraphs from them, yet in which he always found something new, some unexpected insight.

He had read for ten or fifteen minutes before giving up on every one.

169

Trying to remember which book he had last read right to the end, he dozed off but was wide awake again at midnight, went out and began to walk fast, but without any particular destination, he was simply covering the ground. Restless. Running away, he thought.

Plenty of others were walking but they had a purpose, they were restaurant workers, kitchen staff and waiters, fast-food servers, baristas and barmen, heading for late buses and home, cleaners, coming in to work in floodlit, empty offices. But as he walked away from the West End, and so east, beyond the Strand to Fleet Street, and further, into the City, the streets emptied. The clocks of ancient churches, there in the time of Dickens and Dryden and Defoe and Pepys, rang the hour. A police car shot past. An ambulance wailed. A bar released its last drinkers onto the pavement.

As long as he walked he felt better, he could stave off the panic. He made no eye contact, exchanged no words. Bundles in doorways, huddled down, dogs beside them on charity mats. A woman glanced round at him. 'Light?' He shook his head. Crossed the road and turned up a snicket, where there were houses in which people had once lived, upper storeys overhanging the street and almost meeting. Now, there was no one. He slowed down. No one walked the beat in the old way though there would be pairs of constables still in Leicester Square and Soho and Chinatown. Not here.

A cat leapt from a high wall in front of him and he flinched. Stopped. The street smelled odd, of something sulphurous.

He cut down another side street, came out onto a wharf. Looming apartment blocks were lit up like cruise ships from within, tied up and moored forever. The river gleamed, slick, dark, oily under the moon. A barge. Another. A pleasure boat, dressed in bunting, music floating out into the night air like smoke.

Serrailler stopped and sat on an iron bench. And then, rather than the usual frightening images, the questions came scrolling through his mind like LED messages on a train. Welcome Aboard this Southern Trains service to . . . Next Stop . . . Do I want to be a cop . . . what happens when we die . . . do we stop like a

170

watch do we go on what does dying feel like is drowning a good way to die why didn't I die why did Martha die why was Martha born why . . . He got up and started walking again, along the dark river and then up a street at random and out onto a road down which cabs and cars still sped. He turned into an empty square. On one side were two glass-and-steel office blocks lit up, people-less, blue lights from computer screens. On the others were tower blocks, twenty storeys of little squares. The walkways on each level were half lit, every other bulb blown out. Yellow lights behind thin curtains. It was like a film set from a Japanese art movie. Ten slow minutes in and nothing would have moved, no person would have been glimpsed.

And then, in a sudden swirl of sound and movement, footsteps came running, slapping along the path to the left, one, two, three pairs. White trainers, dark tracksuits, hoods up, identikit figures, one first and then two behind, the two were giving chase, the one was fleeing for his life, dodging sideways, dodging back, yelling something. It was seconds before the two had caught up, jumped the one. There was a brief violent fight, no, not a fight, just an attack, and a terrible cry, scream, yell, of panic and pain and terror and then the two were off, streaking like rats and the one was lying on the path, knees up, head down, and rolling to and fro, and screaming, still screaming.

Serrailler was there, kneeling, seeing the blood pouring from somewhere in the heaving young body, stomach or chest, he could not tell. He managed to get his phone out and call and then lean over, holding the boy's head. 'It's OK, I'm looking after you. I'm a friend. I'm helping you, it's OK, you're going to be OK.'

The body was that of a boy, his terrified eyes, his quivering lips, were a child's. 'Oh man, oh man, oh Jesus man . . .'

'Let me look, move your hand, I need to see.'

He prised an arm loose and saw the blood spouting up, pulsing from the chest. He put his hands one on top of the other and pressed down.

The boy went still. His eyes were glazed over. 'It's all right. You're going to be OK. I'm here, the ambulance will be with you any second. What's your name? Tell me your name. I'm here to look after you.'

The boy opened his mouth and blood bubbled out of it. Simon kept his hands on the knife wound. He could feel the warm blood between his fingers.

'Help, God, help him. Help please.'

The siren came like a banshee, blue light of the ambulance turning fast into the square. Police behind. More.

Simon did not move, just knelt, talking to the boy, pressing his hands down, feeling the blood as it trickled up between his fingers.

Thirty-nine

'DCS Simon Serrailler, Lafferton Police.' He handed his warrant card and the Met sergeant looked at it quickly then back at the man in front of him.

'You all right, sir?'

'Yes, the paramedics insisted on checking me over but I'm fine. This isn't my blood.'

'We'll get you to the washroom, but as you know, they'll need to take some swabs first. You down here on a job?'

'No. And I'm back home tomorrow.'

'Are you staying with anyone?'

'I'm at the Covent Garden Hotel.'

'Bit out of the way late at night, sir?'

'Yes. I'd gone for a walk went a bit further than I'd meant to, and I was trying to find a shortcut through a street I used to know, which doesn't appear to exist any more.'

'Right. Not the best place to be this late and on your own, cop or no cop. Sir.'

'No. Stupid.'

'You told the patrol officers what happened but I'll need a full statement.'

'Of course.'

'Let's get the swabs sorted out and you cleaned up first. And – thanks for your efforts. If you hadn't been there he'd have died by himself. They usually do. Too many of them, too often. It's good you were with him.'

'Any ID?'

'Not yet but chances are his mother will call us when he isn't home by three or four.'

'Or the father.'

'Maybe. Too often there isn't one, too often Dad's left and the mother's on her own working all hours and trying to keep teenage lads at home and out of trouble. What age was he, about fifteen?'

'Not much more. Poor little bugger.'

'Another cup of tea, sir?'

It had been machine tea, hot, double strength, very sweet, and under any other circumstances he wouldn't even have considered it.

'I would, thanks. I guess the coffee's undrinkable.'

'Don't even go there. Soup's the worst.'

The usual interview room. The usual smell. The usual plastic chairs.

When the door closed, Serrailler put his head in his hands, on which the blood had now dried, and wept as he had not wept for thirty years, and the face of the dying boy was before him, the light in the eyes receding and going out as he had looked down into them, as he had talked to him, had tried to stop the blood pumping out of his skinny body. A kid. All right, a kid who might have done the same to another kid, if the tables had been turned, but a kid among kids, running, running, running for his life, not fast enough, so losing it to minutes of terror and unimaginable pain. Another kid. Another stabbing statistic. And the last person his eyes had focused on was a cop. The enemy.

He did not try to stop weeping, it stopped of its own accord, and then he lifted his head.

And immediately he realised something. He felt distress, shock, exhaustion, and those were all perfectly normal, but otherwise, he felt calm, clear-headed and in control. He was not shaking, his heart rate was steady. There were no hallucinatory images running through his head, only the memory of the empty, coldly lit square in front of the tower block, the rush of footsteps, shouts, a scream, a couple of brutal moments and then the racing

174

figures again. The boy, rolling to and fro, knees up, and jerking. The feel of the boy's ribcage, the sight of his cloudy eyes, the wetness of his blood. The second when the life went out of him and he was a bloody mess, still on the concrete pathway, and the sirens came screaming.

He did not stop the ticker tape running on through his mind, did not try to clear the images, did not flinch, he let it go on, repeat itself, rewind. He let it sink in, and he accepted it, as he knew he should have done with his own attack and injury.

He suddenly felt that, somehow, as the boy had died beneath his hands, in his full sight, his own demons were beginning to die too.

The water was clear. For now at least.

He could have lain down on the hard tiles of the interview room, under the strip lighting, and slept for a month.

'Another tea, sir. Then we'll do the swabs. Oh, and the duty sergeant just took a call from a woman asking if we'd seen her son. She lives in the block of flats you were right next to.'

Forty

Agneta crept into the intensive care ward, which was like the control room of a spaceship and intimidated her.

'Hello. Can I help you?' The nurse spoke quietly.

'I've come to see Shenda . . . Shenda Neill,' she whispered. It was like church.

'Bay 4. Are you a relative?'

'No. She's my friend. I work with her.'

'Ah. It's really supposed to be family only in here.'

'I don't think she's got any family. She never . . . I don't think she has anyone.'

'That would figure. We didn't have any ID for her until someone called the police station.'

'That was me. I saw her picture on the news. I was shocked and upset that she looked so awful, but it was Shenda.'

'All right. I'll just pop in first, see if she's up to a visitor, but even if she is you can only stay a few minutes this time.'

Agneta waited. The nurse had been at the bedside of a very old man, his head bandaged, his arm in plaster, one leg raised up on a strap. Opposite her was an empty bed and behind her, another man, young, lying flat on his back, eyes closed, a thick tube held in his mouth with plasters.

She had never been in an ICU before. It scared her. These were people who might die.

'Come in . . . a few minutes, remember, but she's looking brighter. Her readings have improved today.'

Agneta hesitated, then edged round the curtains and into the small space.

Shenda was sitting propped up on pillows. Her face was blotchy. White strips covered cuts and there were bruises on her cheekbones and forehead. Her hair had been shaved in a broad furrow for the dressings, but she looked more like a living young woman, less like the near-corpse pictured on the news.

'Agneta! Oh my God, Agneta!' Her tears brimmed over.

Agneta went to her and tried to hug her gently, kissed her cheek and touched her forehead.

'I am so sorry, I am so sorry.'

'Why? Why are you sorry, Shenda? There is nothing for you to be sorry about.'

Agneta smoothed Shenda's hair on her right side. 'I didn't bring you anything, I just came straight away, and I didn't know what you would be allowed to have, but tomorrow I will come and bring you everything, anything. Oh, Shenda, what happened to you? How are you like this?'

'I only remember some things. Not all of it.'

'Who hurt you? Or did you have an accident on the road?'

'No. I . . . the road was afterwards.'

Agneta pulled up a stool and sat beside her, held her hand. 'But you are alive and here and they are making you well, it's OK.'

'But it isn't. It can't be unless . . . Have you heard anything? Has there been anything on telly or anywhere?'

'About you, yes, they have shown your photo, that's how I am here now. They didn't know who you were, you had nothing on you to tell them, so then I saw the picture and I rang them.'

'I meant . . .' Shenda started to cough, which clearly hurt her.

'Shall I get the nurse? What shall I do?'

Shenda shook her head as she went on coughing violently.

The nurse came, scraping the curtain aside. 'All right, lean forward, Shenda . . . that's it . . . here, sip this, don't gulp it down. You'll be fine.'

It sounded harsh, the rasping in her throat, and she pushed the water aside, trying to control the coughing.

'It hurts your ribs because you've broken five of them. I'll get you some more painkillers, you're due them anyway. Just sip the water, it will help.'

It seemed to take a long time. Agneta stood back, frightened, uncertain if she should go or stay, but in the end, the coughing subsided and Shenda lay back, exhausted, eyes closed.

'I'll get the doctor to listen to your chest again when she comes round. Maybe she'll prescribe something. Try not to talk much.' She looked at Agneta. 'Two minutes.'

A bell sounded somewhere and she dashed out.

'Don't go yet.' Shenda's voice was weak and she faltered over the words. 'I . . . I need to tell you, Ag.'

'Don't make yourself cough again.'

'It's important. Listen, come here.'

Agneta leaned closer, put her hand on Shenda's and pressed it, wanting to reassure her.

'It's . . . I'm scared, Ag, I'm very scared of Jake. He might come here. I have to get away from . . .' She stopped, drawing in her breath with pain. The curtain was pulled back again and there was a young woman with a stethoscope and Agneta said, 'I'll come tomorrow, I promise. I'll look after you, Shenda . . . don't worry, don't worry. It'll be OK.'

But the doctor was bending over her and Shenda didn't reply.

Forty-one

'Take my advice, Aggie, stay out of it. Pass me that meat mallet, will you, girl?'

'I can't stay out of it, she's my friend and something terrible happened to her.'

'Ag, listen, you did a good thing going to see her, you did right, and next time you go, take her something, take her a cake from here, maybe a light sponge, she'll be able to eat that. Get her some flowers, take the money out of the till, only don't get involved. Pass me that paring knife.'

'You need a slave, Wint, and I'm not.'

'Morning.' Lois slipped in through the side door in her usual modest, quiet way, smiling, hanging up her coat, getting her apron, putting her bag in the cupboard, all like a scurrying mouse. But she was not a mouse. She was the one who had thrown out the drunk after he'd been making a nuisance of himself, begging and bothering customers one morning last week. She was the one who had taken her own son to the police station by the scruff of his jacket, after he'd got into trouble bunking off school and shoplifting in the mall, then gone up to the school with him and made him tell the head teacher. Lois took no prisoners when necessary, but in here, she was self-effacing and usually silent, and as Winston said, she cleared and cleaned tables faster than anyone in Lafferton and way beyond.

'We were talking about Shenda,' Agneta said now.

'How was she?'

179

'I told her, don't get involved.'

'And that's where you're wrong. She needs someone, it sounds like that to me, so we should "get involved". And in my book, Winston James, that means helping, being kind, putting someone else first, all of that.' She swung out into the cafe to start laying up. It was half seven, the first breakfasters would be coming in any minute.

'I got no more time for this now, and we need another, how long is Shenda going to be off? Sounds like it's going to be weeks. I need to put an advert out there. Get me the tomatoes, Ag, Veggie Vince was here at six but the bread's late again.'

Then the rush started and there was no chance to talk any more until eleven o'clock when they went quiet, just a couple of coffee and cakers, and Agneta and Lois could have their break.

'Tell me,' Lois said. They ate at the corner table, eggs and beans on toast for both, Agneta coffee, Lois strong tea. Winston was doing the kitchen changeover for lunch service.

'I think she'll be OK. But she might have died, Lois.'

'I don't understand some girls, I don't get how they can't spot a bad egg a mile off. She could have done well for herself.'

'The bad ones have the good looks and they can talk sweetly.'

'And did he?'

Agneta thought back to the ordinary man at the door of the flat. 'He was not so special. But he didn't seem a bad one.'

'Poor Shenda. She'll come back, won't she? Because we can't go on with just us. Look at this morning.'

'Wint says he's putting in an ad.'

'Oh God. Then we'll get a string of useless ones that won't work, don't turn up, all flaky. We've been a good team. Hope she comes back. When she's better of course. You want another coffee?'

The last hour was dead and she left ten minutes early. Lois had already gone. It was a good half an hour by bike to the hospital and it was raining. Twice, she nearly turned back, but she would never have forgiven herself, going home to be safe and well and cheerful, with Shenda ill and frightened, by herself in a dreary hospital.

'You are such a good friend, Ag, thank you.'

'I brought you a big slice of Victoria sponge. You can eat that, can't you? I never thought if they didn't let you have some sort of food.'

Shenda looked better. Her face was less swollen, some of the white strips had been taken off her cuts. But she was still attached to a drip and her head bandage was there.

'Did the doctor see about your cough?'

Shenda shook her head. 'It's nothing. Ag, you said you'd help me.'

'You can come to my place, it'd be OK for a bit.' Though she was not sure if that was right, she hadn't asked her sister and brother-in-law, and they were already crowded.

'No, I have to get right away. I need to go somewhere he can't find me, and he wouldn't guess. I have to, Ag. Next time, he'll kill me.'

'But where can you go, Shenda, and how can you go? You're not well.'

Shenda took hold of her hand and held it tightly. 'Listen, Ag, please, please, you're my real friend, I don't have any others, not any I can trust. Please help me get away. I have that money, it's in the flat, I can tell you where it is and if you get it for me then I'll be fine. I can go a long way with the money I've got.'

'Jake would be there. I can't go.'

'When he's out . . . he's always out in the evening until late.'

Agneta was silent. She could not say that she had been to the flat, seen Jake.

'There's a key under the plant pot outside the door. You go into the bedroom and the money's in a pink make-up bag, it's got flamingos on, it's in my wardrobe on the top shelf. Please, Ag. And I haven't got any clothes, can you bring me a jacket or a coat and some shoes . . . anything?'

Agneta let her go on. She was anxious about doing any of it, but most of all about going to Shenda's flat. Maybe Eric would go with her? Her sister's husband was usually silent and not especially friendly but he was tall and strong and capable. If he was watching the door, she would go. But Shenda wasn't well enough to take off by herself. Anything could happen.

181

'Ag, please, please. He will kill me next time. I mean it. I wish they hadn't put that photo out there because now he knows where I am. Oh God, you're my friend, Ag, please help me.' And then Shenda told her how she'd got the five grand, and what Jake had done.

Forty-two

'Elaine? It's Cat Deerbon.'

'Oh.' The voice was not warm. 'What can I do for you, Cat?'

This did not sound like the Elaine Harper she had known for twenty years. Elaine, the best health visitor she had ever worked with, the one every GP wanted on her team, Elaine who was always up for a joke, some mild gossip, or giving generously to the latest fundraiser. She had retired a couple of years earlier but she and her husband had not left Lafferton, where both their daughters and their families lived. She and Cat had been allies during difficult times with assorted health managers and patients in distress.

'Is this a bad time for me to call you? I can easily ring back. I need your advice. In fact, I was hoping you could spare me ten minutes if I come to see you.'

There was a silence. Cat was baffled at the frostiness coming at her from the other end of the line.

'I'm not sure. Is it a personal thing or what?'

'No, it's professional. It's a family.'

'Then I don't think so. You'll have to find a private agency – if there is such a thing. I wouldn't know.' The penny dropped.

'Elaine? I know you maybe don't approve of Concierge Medical but this is me, I haven't changed.'

'Of course you have. You crossed the Rubicon. Listen, Cat, this isn't personal—'

'It certainly sounds personal.'

'I'm sorry. But the NHS needs you, not a load of spoilt rich people in big houses.'

'That's just ridiculous. If you came out with me for a day you'd see those are not my typical patients at all.'

'And I bet they don't live on the Dulcie estate either.'

Heavens, Cat thought, what was the old rule? Never let politics or religion get in the way of a good friendship. 'I'm sorry you feel like that. It's a pity because it's difficult and I could really use your wisdom and experience, and before you say it, I am not buttering you up. Anyway, Chris would have agreed with you, as I'm sure you know. I'll let you get on, Elaine.'

'No, hang about . . .' A silence, and then a sigh, before the more familiar Elaine came back. 'I'm sorry, Cat. It does rub me up, I don't approve, but we've been friends and colleagues for too long. I don't want to lose that over some political point. I've some cold chicken and bits of salad, Bob is out putting up shelves for Amy, so come and have a quick bite of lunch.'

Elaine lived in what had once been a council house, on a small estate just beyond the Hill. They had bought it thirty years earlier, but Elaine's social conscience had pricked her all the same, believing as she did that council houses should be kept for tenants. But they had not been able to afford anything else.

30 Rossiter Close was one of a pair of semis at the far end of a horseshoe. It had the proud look of a house that had been looked after, maintained, repainted, smartened and re-smartened over two decades. The curtains were new, Cat noted, a soft violet blue, heavy, lined, and unquestionably made by Elaine, who sewed everything, as she also upholstered, painted, quilted and repaired. She had never been without some knitting, crochet, embroidery or mending at any practice meeting, talking sense, being thoroughly informed, joining in the debate, as she plied needles, hooks, threads and pins without pausing a beat. Socks, sweaters, cushions, all grew steadily over the weeks and months. It was in the family. Elaine's mother had been like it, and now both her daughters were the same – one of them taught textiles and design at Bevham College. Cat, in whose hands any needle,

skein or yardage was a foreign body, had admired the skills while never wanting to learn any of them.

Cat and Elaine sat at the kitchen table, watching a party of long-tailed tits at a feeder on the terrace beyond the window. At another, goldfinches pecked at a steel tube of niger seed. Bob, Elaine's husband, was a passionate birder, going away to Norfolk and Wales as well as abroad, to see flocks of migrating geese or terns, or rare little songsters the size of his thumb. Elaine liked those that came to her own garden but had no interest in, as she put it, chasing them round the world.

They caught up on each other's news as they ate and it was only when they took coffee outside and sat in chairs in the fitful sun that Elaine said, 'Right, what's up?'

Her vowels still betrayed her Yorkshire origins though she had lived down south for over forty years.

Where to start? Cat thought. She had gone over the case in as much detail as she could remember, and consulted her own notes the previous night, and now she told it carefully, in what she was pretty sure was the correct order. For years, she had known that, although as a doctor she made her own judgements and acted upon them, she could and should ask for particular expert help if she felt unsure. It did not happen often but she was aware of her own limitations by now.

When she had refilled their cups, Elaine said, 'I can't see them professionally now I'm retired – maybe I could come as your old colleague but you'd have to have a good reason for introducing me and she would have every right to refuse. What was it exactly that made you feel there might actually be something wrong with the baby? Not difficult to see that the mother is not very well. Might you have been hyper-vigilant just because of her own certainty?'

'Seeing what isn't there because I was led to see it, you mean? It's possible. If a mother says she's seen a rash you sort of expect to see it too.'

'And you can hallucinate one, believe me.' She looked across the top of her spectacles at Cat. 'But you didn't, did you?'

'No, I honestly don't think so. But it was all very nebulous. The baby was pale, it was asleep, it was quite still – you know

185

how their eyelids flicker, or their fingers curl, or they give tiny twitches . . . there didn't look to be much of that. But it was breathing fine, and when I held it, it felt . . . no, actually, thinking again – when I held it, I thought it felt slightly floppy. But a newborn sometimes does.'

'Well, there's the normal loose-limbed feel and there's floppy. It's different, isn't it?'

'I asked her a few of the usual questions . . . you know, was she feeding all right, nappies and so on.'

'And?'

'She said yes, but then, she doesn't know what's normal and what isn't.'

'And she was convinced from the start that there was something wrong? I've known that – the sixth sense. I had one woman who was certain her baby was a Down's, though there was absolutely no reason for her to think it – no family history, she was only twenty-seven but she was sure. And she was right. I've always had a healthy respect for intuition.'

Cat sighed. 'Half of me says I should just let it go, to be honest. They haven't called me, I don't have any good reason for accidentally dropping in on them again. I've got enough on my plate without adding this.'

'But your private practice is way less demanding isn't it? No packed surgeries, no stressed-out people who have been waiting two months for an oncology appointment.'

'Come on, Elaine, nobody waits two months for an oncology appointment, they're fast-tracked.'

'Ask Amy. She went to her GP with a tiny breast lump. GP said come back in a month so she did. She's only thirty-four so of course she doesn't get routine mammograms. The oncology department at BG sent her an appointment for eight weeks on. She went. They lost the mammogram results. She had to go for another. Turned out to be negative, it's a benign cyst. But if it hadn't been?'

'Get her to ask for another mammogram in six months' time. She should book it now. Did they do a biopsy?'

'No, an aspiration.'

'Maybe she should get one.'

'You know as well as I do that they won't do a biopsy if they're fairly sure it's benign. And don't tell me she could have one privately.'

'She could.'

'She couldn't afford it, and anyway, she wouldn't, on principle.'

Cat snorted. 'What's more important, your life or your principles?'

'Shall we talk about this baby?'

Cat finished her coffee. 'What's your gut feeling, Elaine?'

'It sounds as if it's worth your paying one more call. I don't think taking me along would be right.'

'Two pairs of eyes.'

'No. This is yours. But talk me through anything you find if you're still worried. For what it's worth, I think you should look at the mother's mental health not the baby's physical. You don't think it's at risk, do you?'

'I doubt it. No.' She got up. 'All the same, I will go again . . . invent some reason.'

'If there had been anything the neonatal guys would have picked it up. They're pretty hot now.'

'I know.'

They stood at the front door.

'You haven't changed, Dr Deerbon.'

'What do you mean?'

'You still fret about your patients.' She gave Cat a hug. 'I'm sorry. All right?'

'Of course. And one day I'll take you through the reasons why Concierge isn't about the elite, how we have a lot of perfectly ordinary patients who wouldn't dream of paying for their doctor if the NHS wasn't in such a mess.'

'If the government wasn't.'

'Whatever.'

Elaine indicated to her to wind down the window as she reversed the car, and when she had, called to her, 'Just don't you change the way you are, Cat.'

Forty-three

The ambulance had just left the house of her last patient of the day, in the farthest village she covered. It was getting on for eight o'clock, she was exhausted, hungry and worried about the woman she had just sent in to Bevham General with a suspected heart attack, a relatively young woman, not yet fifty, whose daughter had called her because her mother had been vomiting and had a pain in her back, not the classic symptoms of an infarct for a man but always suspicious, other things being equal, in a woman. The paramedics had used their defibrillator twice to bring her back and were on a blue light as they drew away from the house.

A text came in.

Just home. Pub supper? Kx

'Hi. Late call?' Kieron was watching the rolling television news, perched on a kitchen stool.

Cat put her arms round his neck and leaned against his back, closing her eyes. 'Bushed. One crisis after the next.'

'Unusual.'

'Hm. Can we not watch people slaughtering one another?'

'And that's only the Middle East. Another stabbing in Bevham this morning.'

'I do not want to know.'

'OK.' He switched off. 'Are you going to have a shower first or shall we just go?'

'Do we have to eat out?'

'Of course not. Just thought you'd like it. I'll cook whatever.'

'Whatever is the problem. No, let's go to the Bell. Give me ten minutes.' Usually she ran up the stairs but tonight, it was a slow climb.

The Bell was a short drive away and the car park was almost full.

'Friday night. If there isn't a table we'll get fish and chips somewhere.'

Kieron took her hand as they walked in. 'There'll be a table.'

'Oh, right, of course. Nothing less for the Chief.'

'We sorted out who had been nicking stuff from their stores, remember.'

'Not you personally.'

Kieron smiled, holding the door open for her.

The bar was packed but Cat spotted that a couple were just leaving and slipped over to bag their table while he went to get drinks. The menu was on a blackboard, not long and rarely the same two days running, depending on the seasonal market and what the fishmonger had brought up that morning from Cornwall.

Cat checked her phone. No messages and she was no longer on call. She let herself relax. Kieron was bringing two glasses of Merlot from the bar when there was a disturbance at a nearby table. Two men were standing up, one waving his arms about, the other banging him on the back. A couple at an adjacent table started to call out.

Cat got up quickly and went over. She moved the back-banger aside. 'Are you choking? Can you breathe?'

The other shook his head. He was panic-stricken, flailing his arms.

'It's all right. Lift your arms. Right, here we go.'

She put her own arms round him, bunched her fists under his breastbone and gave a sharp push upwards. There was a wheezing sound and then the man coughed violently, leaning over the table.

'That's it, you're fine. You're breathing. Don't worry now. Just sit down and recover. Have some water. It's all over.' She sat beside him for a few minutes, as he calmed down. 'Don't struggle for breath, it'll come now . . . your body always takes over. Give yourself time. All right?'

He nodded and clasped her hand.

The room settled down as she went to the bar. 'Do any of you know how to do that? It's called the Heimlich manoeuvre and it never fails. Everyone should learn how to do it but particularly people working in restaurants.'

The barman looked terrified. 'I don't know. I've never done anything like that. Scary or what?'

'Very, but take quick action and it's fine. If you tell the proprietor, I'd happily come over and give you all a lesson any time.'

'I should think he'd jump at that. Thanks a lot, Doc. I remember you. You looked after my gran when she was very poorly. Dolly Venables – Park Road.'

'I remember her! Really well . . . she was a lovely lady. And her house – like a show house even when she was so ill.'

'Oh, Gran will be whiting the steps of heaven and polishing the pearly gates.'

A group came in and Cat returned to her table.

'God I need this,' she said, taking a long drink of her wine.

She looked across the table and suddenly saw Kieron, his face, his steadiness, his calm. Her husband. She put her hand over his. 'Hi.'

'Hello you. Better?'

She nodded.

'I am very proud of you. Do you know that? And don't say, it's all in a day's work.'

'All in a day's work. Just some days . . .'

'Are you worried about a patient or about Sam? Your father? Simon?'

'Sod it. I meant to call Si. He's been in London. How has he seemed lately?'

'Haven't seen him. I've been all over the place. Why?'

She shook her head and turned her attention to the menu. But that head was full of people in trouble. Sam she probably needn't worry about, Hannah was deep in rehearsals, having the time of her young life, yet she was only seventeen and in London, how could she not worry, in spite of the care her theatre school took? And her brother had been a worry for some time. Her father?

Patients she could usually leave at her own front door, as she had trained herself to do over a working lifetime. But once in a while they came with her into the house and stayed there, nudging her.

Like the Pegwells, who had got under her skin because she did not know exactly what was wrong or what she herself could do, if indeed there was anything. A family who might turn out to settle their own problems and live happily ever after. Or not.

Forty-four

Agneta had put some of her own things – jeans, a denim jacket, T-shirt, trainers, a few toiletries – into a carrier bag, and added bananas and biscuits on top, in case the nurses looked in and were suspicious. But when she arrived the cubicle in ITU was empty.

'Hello, you looking for your friend?' The first nurse she had seen.

'She discharged herself this morning. A couple of police came yesterday to talk to her, see if she remembered anything, I suppose. Then this morning, her boyfriend came for her. I wasn't happy but she said she was fine and it's true her stats had improved but really she ought to have been here another forty-eight hours. Still, at least she's going to his family so she'll be well looked after – he said his mother's a nurse in London – Guy's, I think he said – so that's great.'

Agneta stood there, unable to say anything, terrified, unable to think straight. Her mouth was dry.

'You all right?'

She couldn't tell her. It wasn't her fault. If someone wanted to leave hospital they left, they couldn't be imprisoned there.

Images of Shenda, with Jake gripping her arm, pushing her forward, Shenda not daring to say she was not leaving with him, Shenda having to stand and hear the lies, but too afraid to speak out.

'I think . . . I am just . . . quite surprised, that's all.'

'Yes, well, in my view she shouldn't have gone but what can you do? Anyway, she is a lot better and he'll take care of her. I've got to get on.'

She called out as Agneta went towards the doors. 'Don't worry. I'm sure she'll be in touch.'

Forty-five

'I am determined that we will be adventurous in the works we perform. This doesn't mean I want to abandon the *Messiahs* and the *Gerontiuses* and the Brahms *Requiems* which are so loved, all of which fill the cathedral whenever we do them.'

The St Michael's Singers were sitting in the nave, hearing about their fiftieth anniversary celebrations. Two contraltos, a tenor and a baritone had been founding members and sung at the first concert ever given, others had joined over the following years. Cat was marking her own fifteenth anniversary with the choir and other than not singing in the Bach B minor Mass on the night she had given birth to her third child, she had never missed a performance.

'Fifty years is a terrific milestone, and I want us to mark it in a splendiferous way. So we will be giving four concerts, one each season. I hope that doesn't come as a shock to anyone and that you're all up for the extra work next year? Better put your hand up now if you're not. I do understand some of you may just not manage all four, for various reasons – they had just better be good ones. Hands up?'

None.

Jeremy smiled, a little smugly, it seemed to Cat.

'So, we're kicking off with Beethoven's *Missa Solemnis* next January. Our big fiftieth concert is on 16 May which is, by wonderful chance, the date of the first performance St Michael's Singers ever gave, and we will be doing Britten's

194

War Requiem. September, the main item will be Vaughan Williams's *Sancta Civitas*. Magnificent work – dark though, not your English pastoral. Anyone know it? Hm. Shocked to see only two. I assure you it's a great piece and you will love it when you've finally learned to sing it. Our last one will be on Christmas Eve, you'll all be thrilled to hear. We wouldn't usually go so late but it will be a special year. I haven't finalised the programme yet but that's plenty for you to digest. In the meantime, back to this year and the first rehearsal of the Haydn *Creation* which is next week. The scores are in, collect yours from the table by the font as you leave.'

They broke up soon afterwards, although the committee was staying for their own meeting. Cat was conscious that she had not served her turn on it for several years and that now the children were older and her job more predictable, she should put herself up for election again.

She often skipped the usual trip to the pub but Kieron was at home catching up on paperwork and looking after Felix, so she joined the rest as they exited from the cathedral side door. There would be an extensive and vociferous critique of the anniversary programme, so long as Jeremy was not with them, pointed silence about it if he was. She was excited by the familiar and the new and most of all by the prospect of singing the *War Requiem*.

But as she went down the path towards the gate she glanced up as usual, and saw that the lights were on in Simon's apartment. She doubted she was going to be very welcome but it was too good a chance to miss. Once, she would have hesitated because he might well not be alone. Tonight she was pretty sure that he would be.

He was, at his long table with the angel-head drawings spread out in front of him.

'There are twelve so far. I've a way to go but I decided to take some photographs as well.'

'I thought you never worked from photos.'

'I don't but they're a big help in organising and comparing. I don't know how many woodcarvers were employed on these

195

– at least half a dozen probably – and the photographs help me work out those details.'

'Can you really tell the difference?'

'Pretty much. They weren't trying to show off their individual skills – the idea was always to subsume their own talents into the whole, but there are small idiosyncrasies. I've become completely obsessed by them.'

He straightened up and winced. His back had always troubled him.

'Do you want a drink?'

'No, but I'd love a coffee. I'll make it while you do your back exercises. One for you?'

'Yes, Doctor.' Simon lay flat on the floor and drew his knees up to his chest, then began to roll slowly to one side and then the other.

'How's the arm?'

'Good. Fine.'

'Sure? OK, don't look at me like that.'

'I've an appointment at the prosthetics clinic in about six weeks to have everything checked, in case you're fretting.'

Cat held up her hands in surrender.

'Is this just a spontaneous social call?' His tone was sarcastic. 'I mean, always lovely to see you, sis.'

'Stop that. You've been avoiding me.'

'Possibly but I have been working as well. And I've been in London. Let me tell you a story, assuming you have the time.'

She poured them both coffee, and while she drank, he told her about his visit – his panics, his late-night walk. The boy who was stabbed in front of him. Cat listened, aware that he was not holding anything back. She respected him for it.

'It's easy to say a cop gets used to all of that and of course we do, but to watch a kid – a boy of fifteen – being jumped on and stabbed swiftly and, I almost want to say, efficiently, a few yards from you, that is horrible. The professional cop takes over, as always, but it catches up with you and it stays – how could it not? That boy lived in the block right there in front of me; if his mother had been looking out of the window on the ninth floor, she would have seen it all. Jesus Christ, what was it about?

Some gang quarrel and drugs will be at the bottom of it. But these are kids. Kids used to fight it out, a few quick thumps and bloody noses. Now it's stab to death, run away and forget it. I'm pretty sure this kid was known and tracked down – they had a reason – though in London now a lot of the stabbings are random and motiveless.'

He got up and went to the long windows that looked down on the close.

'I could be his mother. I could be looking out to see if he's on his way home, because he's too late and I don't like it. I don't know where he is or who he's with and I'm terrified he's in trouble. And he is.' He turned round. 'The thing she dreads and hopes to God will never happen to her boy has happened and he's on his way to the mortuary. So yes, it was grim. And I waited for it to come back and bite me, but at the same time, I was completely calm and together because I knew it wouldn't. It won't. Something went click. It's gone. Burned itself out. Does that makes sense?'

'Yes, though it's unusual. But it's a bit like people who are alcoholics, maybe for years, and who just stop drinking, like that. They never drink again. That's ultra rare but it happens. I've known it.'

'What, no therapy, no shrinks, no AA meetings?'

'None. I'd just caution you—'

'You can't, that's what I do. What you're saying is, I might be wrong.'

'I suppose all I mean is, be aware.' Cat came over, put her arms round her brother and hugged him tightly. 'Thanks for telling me. Right, back home to the old man.'

'The old man already. How's Sam?'

'He and Rosie are coming to Sunday lunch so we'll see. You too?'

'I'm on duty over the weekend. I'll come if everything's quiet.'

Lights were on all over the ground floor of the farmhouse when she got back but no one was about. Then she heard a muffled snigger from upstairs.

Two iPads were open, one in front of Felix, one on Kieron's knee, as he sat on the bed. Both of them looked sheepish.

'Right, what's going on?'

'Mum, it was Kieron's fault, he wanted to show me a really ace move on my Hounds and Huntsmen game.'

'Have you any idea of the time? Felix, you know perfectly well the iPad is forbidden after eight o'clock and you should have been asleep two hours ago, and as for you . . .' Kieron was sliding his iPad back into its sleeve and not meeting her eye.

'What time did you come up to bed?'

'It's my fault—'

'Well, clearly—'

'I couldn't sleep.'

'He said he just had to check on the school message board about something for tomorrow and when he'd done that he remembered he needed to know this particular way of getting out of the forest.' Kieron stood up. 'Anyway, you're home, that's great, goodnight, Felix, see you in the morning. You really ought to be asleep now.'

He slipped out of the door and downstairs. Felix's face was a picture of self-righteousness and indignation. It was all Cat could do not to burst out laughing at the two of them, but she whisked away her son's iPad, sent him to brush his teeth while she put out his clean shirt and pants for the morning.

He fell asleep as she was tucking him in.

'Let me get you a drink, sweetheart. Gin? Wine?'

'No thanks, I'll have some water and then I'm upstairs with my book.'

'Are we in the doghouse? He really couldn't sleep . . .'

'Come on – he'll wheedle his way into anything and you should know better. Honestly, if he can't get out of bed in the morning it's all—'

'My fault. Oh God. How can I make up for it?'

'You can't.'

She went upstairs, smiling.

Forty-six

Damon Phipps was there first. He was often there an hour or two before anyone else showed up, and that was always the best, when he could unpack his gear, set up his umbrella and get the flask out, and all while it was only just breaking light. He'd never believed the fish were more likely to come to him at this time in the morning, he just relished the peace and quiet and having the riverbank to himself. Those who said men fished to get away from their wives might have a point but he did it not so much to escape from Tina as from the kids. He loved them but Sunday mornings were tribal warfare.

There was a slight mist, there had been some drizzle and the damp might get them to come up and bite. Or not. He poured his tea, opened his box of sausage sandwiches, and settled.

This stretch of the river flowed out of Lafferton gently into the valley beyond the Starlys. On the far side, cows grazed, on this side it was just meadow and the narrowing towpath, which gave out altogether a mile upstream, so that not many people came walking so far. A heron was standing on the opposite bank, prehistoric, predatory. Patient. That made two of them.

He settled into a state that was part attention to the rod and the water, alert to the slightest stirring, and part letting his thoughts break up into fragments and drift. He had nothing on his mind, life went along pleasantly enough. He sipped his tea and thought of 46 Garland Road, maybe still quiet, though not for much longer once Cameron had woken, sprung out of bed

199

and gone over to poke Liam, and their jumping on the beds had sounded through the wall to where their mother would be trying to keep Rhys, the seven-month-old, asleep a bit longer. She was good about the Sunday-morning fishing, knew that he worked in a frenzy of noise and movement all week and never begrudged him these few hours on his own. She was a good woman and he valued her.

The low mist would not clear so long as the air was still but something must have disturbed the heron, which took off, legs dangling, as ungainly in flight as the pterodactyls it descended from. The air settled back again, the surface of the river was unruffled by any movement of fish. And then he saw it. Saw but did not see. Saw, blinked, looked again. Saw. His eyesight was perfect, but it was some distance away, in a curve of the bank. He turned his head away. Turned it back. Looked again. Nothing moved. It did not move. He had to be seeing things.

He got up. Went slowly, cautiously, along to where a clump of willows overhung a kink in the riverbank. Stopped. He didn't look down. He moved a couple of steps closer to the edge. Didn't look down. Took a breath.

Looked down.

Forty-seven

Serrailler squatted down and looked into the face of the dead girl. There was hardly any new damage. A contusion on her right cheekbone and the side of her head which might have come from bumping up against the tree roots, the bank, something below the surface of the water. Or it might have been an injury delivered while she was still alive. He had seen plenty of drowned bodies. She had fallen or been pushed in less than twenty-four hours before.

The lack of disfigurement meant that it was easy to see who she was. The PC first on the scene had already recognised her, so had the DI. So, now, did Simon. Shenda Neill, aged twenty-three, reported missing for the second time by the friend she worked with, who had returned to the station in distress.

'She shouldn't be out of hospital, they said that, she was forced.'

They had taken everything down, reassured her that this would get first priority, given the recent history, put out an alert and the girl's photograph again. Studying her bruises and the strangely blank look that sometimes came over a face after death, Simon knew the pattern. She had upset the boyfriend, who had tried to kill her once already but failed by some rare chance and then found out that she was alive and in hospital because her photograph had been all over the media. Not difficult to work out a way of abducting her in plain sight, and making sure of killing her this time.

He went on looking at the girl, dressed in jeans and a T-shirt which were plastered by the water to her body. At her bare feet. Her face again. This was a human being, a person, the old phrase, 'somebody's mother/daughter/sister/wife'. Young. Hitched up with a bad lot. But why? There was always a reason, not necessarily a good one.

He stood and stretched. Squatting down had not helped his back. The doctor's car had just parked on the path, beside the one containing two forensics who were pulling on their boots and white coveralls. A few yards away, and contained within the crime scene tapes, was the encampment of the lone fisherman who had spotted the body. He was sitting on the ground, staring into the river.

Serrailler beckoned everyone over to him. A team briefing, and then he would have a quick word with the fisherman before heading to the farmhouse for his delayed lunch, during which he would be on duty but, hopefully, not called out again.

Forty-eight

Pauline Mead made the pot of tea, put a large slice of fruit cake and a piece of Wensleydale cheese on a plate and everything on a tray. Declan McDermid was upstairs in his office. She knew he had some papers spread out and his computer open and switched on, and she also knew, having looked round the door twenty minutes earlier, that he would not be doing anything at all with them. He would be sitting staring out of the window at the garden and seeing nothing in it. She came every day now. She cooked, filled the freezer, did his laundry and some cleaning, though there was a firm which came every fortnight to go right through the house. Now, it was hardly worth their while, though they still came. He used his office, his bedroom, the kitchen where he ate, and the den where he pretended to watch television. For the time being, Pauline let him be but that did not mean she was not worried about him. The slow business of taking in and processing everything that had happened had barely begun. His grief was raw and bleeding at the edges and he needed time. But what would time do? Cindy was dead, Cindy had been murdered, and neither time nor anything else could ever undo those facts. She was finding it difficult enough herself. God alone knew what it was like inside his head.

She tapped on the office door.

He was sitting at the desk, as before. 'Thank you, Pauline.' His voice was thick with tears. She set down the tray and did not look at him, but touched his shoulder.

'The gardeners want to know if there's anything special today, otherwise they'll just carry on. The electrician is here doing the fountain lights and he's had to switch everything off at the mains for a bit, but I said I didn't think that would be a problem for you.' She knew he had not set foot in the garden since returning home. It had not been his, he hadn't had any part in the design of it, that had all been Cindy's. He had gone into it, sat there, had tea or a drink out there with her, even walked round, because she had liked that. Not now.

'I've got a chicken casserole on and I'll leave a portion for you tonight, and then freeze the rest. You just need to follow the instructions as usual. I've written it all clearly.'

She turned to go.

'Pauline? There's something I'd like to ask you. I've been thinking. Will you bring yourself a cup and have some tea with me while I explain?'

She had had her own drink half an hour ago but she knew that he wanted to keep her, to talk, to have her company, even for ten minutes. She felt desperate for him. He had not yet recovered from his own injuries but he seemed to be unaware of them. He had said to her once that he should have been killed not his wife, and then that he wished he had been. Mike had told her not to worry, that everything he was feeling and saying was natural, Declan was a strong man, he would be all right in time.

'I'm worried that he won't give himself that. I'm afraid what he might do in that great empty house by himself.'

'He won't. He's got too much sense.'

'I'm not so sure.'

But then Mike had said the one thing that did make sense. 'He'll know it's the very last thing she'd have wanted him to do.'

She brought her cup and some fresh hot water. He had wiped his eyes and was sitting on the easy chair, not at his desk.

'Thank you for everything, Pauline. I couldn't manage without you and I don't just mean your job. You've been a lifeline.'

She looked down into her teacup.

'You know I went off down to Bournemouth and had to come back. Couldn't cope at all.'

'It was far too soon. You'll be able to enjoy your place there one day, but not yet. It'll take time you know, I've said to you, it'll take more time than you think.'

'I can see that now. So, here's what I wanted to ask you. I thought I would perhaps make a visit to where my parents lived when they were first married. I've never been. I expect I should have but somehow, you know, there was work, the business. Then marriage to Cindy.'

'That sounds a very good idea to me. Somewhere new, but with a connection. Somewhere to explore a bit. Somewhere . . .' She stopped herself.

'Cindy never went. Yes.'

'I'm sorry.'

He waved it away.

'So where is this?'

'Norfolk. On the coast. I found a hotel I could stay in very near where they used to live, looks very nice. Very comfortable.'

'Then you should book up and go.'

'Pauline, this is what I want to ask. Would you and Mike come with me? All paid for, of course, and if Mike could drive us in mine then you wouldn't need to take your car. It would be . . . I don't think I'm up to going alone, Pauline.'

She was taken aback and then everything went through her mind, how nice it would be but how awkward, how they wouldn't quite know if they were looking after him or being his guests, if they would do everything together or they would maybe eat separately or . . . no, of course they wouldn't. But it was little things that might make it embarrassing all round. How would Mike feel? Yet, if they turned him down, she knew that Declan would not go, as he had said, he wasn't up to a strange place, a hotel, no one he knew, alone. It would be too hard.

'Of course, you need to talk to Mike. And it's absolutely fine if not. I just thought I'd ask.'

She barely knew what she was doing on her way home, thinking round and round the subject, becoming more and more tangled in her own worries. Mike was cleaning two fillets of plaice when

205

she walked into the kitchen and the vegetables were already prepared and in their pans.

Pauline went to the cupboard and took out a bottle of gin, got tonic, ice, a lemon.

'Has something happened, love?'

'Not exactly happened but I need this. Would you like one? You might when I've told you.'

'All right,' Mike said cautiously. 'Sounds ominous.'

'Put that fish down and come and sit here a minute.'

When she had told him, he was silent. He sat without drinking his gin, though she was halfway down hers and she could tell that he was doing exactly as she had done on the way home, going over it and through it, trying to picture it, seeing all the cons and maybe one or two pros. From next door's garden, a lawnmower started up. There was already one going on the other side – those neighbours were obsessed by slicing the head off every daisy and leaf of clover that dared to raise its head. They set out their bedding plants in regimental rows and trimmed the grass edges with a ruler. The Meads had laughed about it ever since they'd moved in. So did one or two other neighbours.

She glanced at Mike but he wasn't aware of anything but what she had just said. The late-afternoon sun came through into the kitchen and the cat Smokey appeared like a genie out of a lamp to splay himself out in it.

Mike sighed.

'What do you think then?'

'It's a tricky one, P.'

'He'll expect an answer tomorrow. He was keen for me to talk to you straight away.'

'What do you want?'

'I asked you.'

'Come on.'

'I know, you'll do whatever makes me happy, which is what you always say.'

'What's wrong with that?'

'Nothing. Only sometimes it seems like a way of throwing it all onto me so it's my fault if it goes pear-shaped.'

206

Which was true but not entirely.

'Just be honest, P – we can make up a story, both of us, but you need to tell me what you really want.'

'All right . . . I think if we don't go he'll say it's fine, and he'll never go on his own and he doesn't have any friends to take, not so far as I've ever known, just people who work for him and . . . well, like us, I suppose. If we go with him, it's only for a few days and it might do him the world of good. And what will it be? A drive up, a nice hotel, because it's bound to be, and some good food and fresh air and I'm sure we'll get plenty of chances to have a little wander by ourselves. He's not a difficult man, Mike, he's very kind and very generous and he needs us. Only think for a second about what happened. How can we say no to him?'

Forty-nine

'Catherine. I have now left two messages, and you have yet to return my calls. I could well be dying in a ditch for all my welfare seems to concern you. As you are now enjoying the rich pickings and short working hours of private medicine perhaps you might spare your father enough time to ring him.'

She threw the phone onto the sofa, from which it jumped and landed on the stone-slabbed kitchen floor.

Sam dived down and grabbed it. 'Seems to have survived. Lucky.'

'Sorry, but sometimes . . .'

'Let me guess.'

'You shouldn't . . . but you know how often I have to count to ten after hearing from your grandfather. I will call him later but I do get tired of being spoken to like a naughty child. Want a coffee?'

'Tea please. Hospital porters drink tea, well, mostly.'

Rosie was in Cat's office, revising haematology. Felix was hopefully doing homework. Kieron was asleep. Simon had called to say he was tied up.

'Want to go into the den or stay here?'

'Nice and warm here. I can stroke Wookie with one hand and Mephisto with the other. He's gone ever so thin, Ma.'

The old cat was asleep, as ever, in the permanent dent he had made for himself at the end of the sofa. He barely stirred as Sam ran his hand gently over his back, feeling the bones.

'Has he been to the vet?'

'We don't say that word, Sam, you should know that. We have to spell it out: V.E.T. Because he understands.' Felix had come in without being seen or heard.

'Oh, come on, Felix, of course he can't.'

'He understands a lot more than you know, and you'll upset him.'

'OK, OK, whatever you say. Go and get some fresh air.'

'I've got to do my oboe practice.'

'Does it still sound like a duck squawking?'

Felix hurled himself onto his brother who fended him off expertly.

'Oboe,' Cat said. Felix was gone.

'He sounds good actually. The squawking didn't last too long.'

'I'll take your word for it. Anyway, the vet? I refuse point-blank to spell it out.'

'I took him last month. There's nothing much wrong – they did some blood tests. He's just very old. He doesn't eat a lot, he pops out into the garden but he rarely makes it as far as the meadow now, and mice, birds and rabbits are a distant memory of his youth. Have a chocolate?'

'You're not supposed to approve of chocolate. Grateful patient?'

'I'm not suggesting you eat the entire box and yes. Shove up, let me have a bit of sofa and dog.'

They settled with tea and coffee and the chocolates and the kitchen was peaceful, apart from the gentle snoring Mephisto now made in his sleep, like a toy engine.

'I know what I'm going to do,' Sam said.

With her mouth conveniently full of chocolate nougat, Cat could only nod and look interested.

'I gave up on the police idea, you know that, but then it sort of came back, after we were in Scotland. Then it went again. I knew quite soon after I started portering that I wanted to do something in a hospital, only not medicine as such.'

'And obviously not portering, as a career choice.'

'I like portering. I love portering.'

209

'Not a lot of upward progress though, is there? Unless you become a manager and then you're in an office working on shift spreadsheets all day.'

'Thing is, I really didn't have a clue but then I was sent on this job. I had to take a tiny baby from the special care nursery to the mortuary. And I didn't think it was right to just stick it on a trolley so . . . so, I carried it. It was special and I know they're always very respectful whoever you wheel down there, but it's still a bit, you know, check the ID label tied to the foot of the body and then roll it in and close the fridge door after you. But it wasn't like that and I had quite a lot of time to be with it – the baby, the little girl – and I sort of bonded with her. That sounds weird, doesn't it?'

'No. Not at all, Sam.'

'Oh. Well, Rosie said it wasn't either, but then, she's different.'

Cat let that one go. Sam was silent for a minute or two, stroking Wookie, who had turned over to lie on his back.

'Whatever it is, Sam, you haven't rushed into it, you've thought it through and done it while you've put your back into a proper job.'

'Ha – literally put my back into it.'

'Yes. It wouldn't be right if I now turned round and said this, whatever it is, is a bad idea.'

'Thanks.'

'So . . .'

Sam's hand had gone still. Wookie sighed and squirmed until Sam resumed the stroking.

'I want to be a midwife.'

Cat had had no idea at all what might be coming but it was certainly not this. She was astonished.

'I know what you'll say first off – that there aren't many male midwives and that's true. There are a few but they've mostly done general nursing and then moved over. There is actually one in the BG midwifery suite – Max Harper. I did go and talk to him, but he took the sideways route. He was a bit doubtful if they'd look at me, to be honest, but then I talked to one of the midwifery sisters and she said she'd welcome a man, made no difference so long as the patients were cool with it. So?'

'I'm digesting it, Sambo . . . but I think it's a great idea because it's what you want and you've arrived at it the right way – not just gone through a careers book from A to Z and landed somewhere in the middle at M. It's a very rewarding area of medicine – hard work but then, it's all hard work . . . I assume it's Bevham General you're applying to?'

'God no – London. King's is my first choice – where you did your palliative care stuff. It's the best and you can also do an elective year abroad.'

'Would you want to?'

'Sure. Why not? It's got to be a good thing.'

Cat got up and went to the coffee machine. Her son had surprised her, not only with his career choice but by the way he had sorted everything out so efficiently and with such a sense of purpose.

She turned to look at him as he sat teasing Wookie by playing with his ears, which made the dog twitch and sneeze. His face was so familiar, and yet in the last few months the final changes in his bone structure had taken place, so that it was almost fully formed and settled and he was the man he would remain. He was like his father, Chris, but from other angles, even more like her brother. He did not have Simon's height but he had his build and profile, and his hair, although dark, flopped over his forehead in an identical way.

'How will Rosie feel if you go to off London?' Cat did not really know how significant their relationship was, though she liked Rosie who, so far as she could tell, seemed good for Sam, even though she was four years older, an age gap that appeared not to matter to them a jot.

'We'll make it work. She'll be qualified in eighteen months and then she wants to be in London for house jobs. We could both be at King's, who knows? Have to fill in the forms first.' He stood up. 'Got to be in to win it, Ma.'

Fifty

The Hang Seng index was all over the place and he was having to focus intently, and jump in and out fast, but the gains were there to be made, big gains, so long as he didn't blink.

An hour earlier, he had made coffee for himself and lemon tea for Carrie. She had been baking.

'Where is she?'

'In her crib, asleep.'

'Loaf smells good.'

She had nodded, smiled slightly, carried on clearing up. The kitchen was always immaculate, as if cooking never went on there, she was so conscientious about wiping down every surface, putting things away in their proper places, never letting piles of miscellaneous clutter mount up. It troubled her if there was a smear on the windows, inside or out.

In the office, the screens were a turmoil of flashing lights, and excitement surged through him. His job was the closest he had ever got to gambling. He had always expressed a low opinion of those who took chances on the roulette wheel or the racetrack, but deep inside himself, he recognised his affinity with them. Within ten seconds, he was lost to the figures on his screens. Time meant little, partly because of all the different zones he was working in, but an hour later, there was a slight lull in the madness of the day's trading, and he went upstairs to fetch a pullover. The baby was asleep, as usual, the wind had got up outside and was tossing the trees about at the far end of the garden. In the park beyond, branches were swaying and, as he looked, one broke off and went spinning away across the grass. The sash window rattled. The baby did not stir.

Back in the office, there was silence and blackness all round him. He rushed to the kitchen.

'Carrie, have you tripped the switches?'

She was looking out of the window, spoke without looking round. 'It's a power cut. Not surprising.'

'Bloody unstable overhead wires. Time it was all buried underground then this sort of thing couldn't happen. God knows how much I'm missing. We really should have our own generator.'

'So you've said.'

'Yes, well, I'm going to do something about it now.'

'They probably cost an awful lot of money.'

'I've made an awful lot of money today – or rather, I had until it went off. God knows what's happened since.'

'Maybe everyone has a power cut, so you'll all be in the same boat.'

'Do use your intelligence.'

She went to the oven and opened it.

'And I suppose the supper's ruined as well,' he said.

Carrie didn't answer, but went out of the room and upstairs.

The power came back on after only another ten minutes. Colin had sat down at the kitchen table to do some calculations. The sky was pewter, with banked-up clouds, but there was plenty of light coming through the windows. He worked out a simple profit and loss column for the past week without needing access to his screens. It was heavy on the credit side and the half-hour of downtime could not have done a great deal of damage.

He never let emotions in where his job was concerned, but as he headed for the office he felt a quiet relief.

And then he heard Carrie scream.

Fifty-one

'Morning, everyone. Let's get straight in. Shenda Neill, aged twenty-three. She was strangled before her body was put into the river and weighted down – not very expertly because the body came loose and surfaced, got snarled up in tree roots and debris. A fisherman spotted it early morning – he's been questioned but there's no reason to suspect that he had anything to do with it. Because there was nobody else about at that time he has to be on our list, but pretty certainly it is only as a witness. His wife has confirmed what time he left home – some ungodly hour, like all these fishing guys. Let's get rid of him asap because our chief suspect is one Jake Barber, Shenda's live-in boyfriend. He persuaded her to discharge herself from Bevham General and leave with him. In better times there would have been a uniform on guard day and night but Chief has to say no to most of those requests now . . . cuts, staff shortages and all that. Pretty rare for a hospital guard now except to stop murderers from escaping. We need to find this man Jake Barber urgently. There's his photo and you've got it on your screens now. He's originally from Durham but he's been in this area for a good five years. Barber's details are with every force, ports and airports are on alert for him, though I'm inclined to think that he's still holed up on this patch. Let's get him.'

'Guv, message from front desk. The young woman who was Shenda Neill's friend and work colleague came in five minutes ago. Do you want me to talk to her?'

'No, I want you all focusing on Barber. I'll go.'

Agneta Rudkowski was in an interview room. A female officer had brought her a cup of tea and was sitting with her, holding her hand, a box of tissues on the table. The girl was shaking, so that she couldn't hold the drink, crying and pale. She looked up when Serrailler walked in, her eyes full of both pain and alarm.

'Thanks, Mandy. I'll take over.'

'Can I get you anything, guv?'

He hesitated. He rarely drank station brews but he needed to help Agneta relax. 'Would you get me a black coffee, no sugar?' He sat not opposite the girl but beside her. This was not a formal interview, she had come in of her own volition, but he needed her to be calmer and have confidence in him so she would tell him anything vital she might know.

'Agneta, I am so sorry about your friend. I know you've had a tough time dealing with all of this and I know you did your best to stop her from coming to any harm.'

She started to cry again, quietly, in an absorbed, despairing sort of way. The officer brought in Simon's coffee. He waited.

'I am very, very sad for Shenda.' Agneta lifted her head, blew her nose and took a gulp of her tea. 'I am sorry to cry but now I can stop and talk to you. I want to say anything that will help you. I need to speak for my friend, she can't speak for herself now. I need to speak up for her.'

'I respect what you say very much. And I promise we are doing everything we possibly can. We were going to ask you to talk to us but you've bravely come in of your own accord, so just take your time and then tell me anything at all you think would be useful – even if it seems small and trivial. We need to find this man, Jake Barber.' He showed Agneta the photo.

'Oh yes, that's the man, the one who got her into the trouble, I am sure of this. I think she couldn't break away, you know? The thing is, if you met him – he is not very handsome or attractive. But he seemed to have a sort of strong power. I think he made Shenda very anxious to do what he said. She had money. She had five thousand pounds, in cash in a roll in her bag. That

215

is a lot. I was worried for her carrying that around. At first she said she had won a lottery. I didn't believe that. What lottery? Nobody wins five thousand pounds, you win five million or you win nothing. Then in the hospital she told me she got it from what she did for Jake.'

'Did she talk about him much? Where they went, what sort of life they had? Did she tell you she went out?'

'No. She said nothing. Or only, like, we went to see a film. We went for a pizza.'

'Tell me – in the hospital, what else did she say to you? Did she remember what had happened to her?'

He sat back with his coffee while she was quiet for a few minutes, gathering her thoughts in order, trying to remember exactly what Shenda had said about the robbery Jake had got her involved in, before she started to speak.

An hour later, after Agneta had gone back to the cafe on her bike, Serrailler put through a call to the duty judge, applying for a warrant to search Jake and Shenda's flat.

Fifty-two

'Dad, hi, so sorry I didn't get back to you but what with work and the family. I know I haven't seen you for a bit but maybe I could take you out to lunch one day this coming week? Call me back, I'm here now, and we'll arrange something. Lots of love to you.'

Felix had pleaded to spend the evening with Sam and Rosie because, Cat suspected, he adored Rosie almost as much as his brother did, though he would have died rather than say so. She went into the sitting room. It was empty. Peaceful. Quiet. She had Sally Rooney's *Normal People*, her book club's latest choice, to start. As she settled down in her reading chair, first Mephisto and then Wookie pattered in to join her, the cat lifting himself slowly onto her lap, the dog curling up on her feet. She started to think about Sam, but set him aside. She needed to process what he had told her, and for now, all she wanted was an hour by herself with her book without anything else on her mind.

Her phone rang as she was reading the first page but she did not know the number, she was not on call. She ignored it. A few minutes later, it rang again. The same number. She hesitated but something nudged her to answer.

'Is that Catherine? Dr Deerbon?' She did not recognise the woman's voice.

'It is.'

'Oh my dear, thank God you've answered. This is Philippa King, your father's neighbour – we met at his flat.'

Her tone was one Cat recognised as just-controlled panic, familiar to every doctor.

'Of course. What's wrong, Philippa?'

'I'm with your father and the ambulance people. I think he's had a heart attack – I was in my garden when he banged on his window—'

'I'm on my way. I'll go direct to the hospital.'

'I think you should . . . perhaps he will need someone to go with him . . . perhaps I should?'

Cat was adept at getting ready to leave the house while still on the phone.

'It's only that I'm not sure he would want me. We had some words this morning and . . . I feel so bad about it now.'

'Don't. It's better he has someone with him now while the paramedics do their job. Would you mind? I'll see you there, Philippa – thank you. Thank you.'

She called out to Kieron, who came down the stairs two at a time. 'I'll drive you there. Don't argue.'

She didn't.

It was not a patrol car, he had no blue light or siren, but he drove very fast.

'I shouldn't have ignored his messages, but honestly, his tone – he still talks to all of us as if we were recalcitrant teenagers. I was cross.'

'I'm not going to say it isn't your fault because you know it isn't and of course you're now feeling guilty. My mother made me feel guilty from the day I was born, either because of what I did or what I failed to do.'

Kieron rarely mentioned his parents, though he had barely known his father. He and his mother had an uneasy relationship, and as she now lived in Canada with his sister, he only saw her every few years, when he could take time to visit Toronto – she refused to come back to England, so Cat had not yet met her. The only good side to it all was that Kieron had insight into her own fraught parental relationship. But now, she was thinking medically.

'He's not an ounce overweight, he's pretty fit, he's never smoked. His diet isn't bad, he maybe drinks a bit too much but

218

not enough to fret about. He's quite sensible when it comes to looking after himself. He loses his temper easily, he's always had an aggressive attitude to most things, he had that pneumonia and he was pretty stressed last year over the move from France. But he's only seventy-five, he should be able to take all that in his stride.'

'What did his own father die of?'

'Family history? Yes, you're picking this medicine lark up, aren't you? His mother died of pancreatitis and I have a feeling Grandpa did have a stroke but I should check. Altogether he isn't high risk for a coronary but – oh God, he'll be a nightmare patient, he always is, and he'll assume everyone who treats him knows all about him and how important he is . . . or was. Or thinks he was.'

'What will they do?'

'Assuming he's alive, you mean? Sheesh . . .' Cat sucked in her breath as Kieron overtook three container lorries in one move.

'I wish you wouldn't do that.'

'Obviously ECG and a scan. There's a range of things – clot-busting drug, a stent, worst-case scenario a bypass.'

'Presumably he won't be able to go home and look after himself?'

'Not immediately, no . . .'

'Cat, you are my wife and he is your father and if he needs to be with us he will be, it goes without saying, but I won't have him behave like he did the last time, or treat you as he did – let alone me. That's all.'

He accelerated along the bypass and took the roundabout smoothly, but for luck, Cat closed her eyes. They were turning into the hospital entrance before she opened them again. When she did, she said, 'I have to ring Si – before we go in.'

'Not wait till you know a bit more?'

'What do you think?'

'Simon would want information.'

She reached for his hand, as the doors into A&E opened ahead of them.

219

Fifty-three

'It's not a big place but that's all the more reason to leave no pebble unturned, not a square inch ignored – under the carpets and rugs, take the covers off cushions, remove pillowcases, absolutely everything, including inside the lavatory brush holder, if there is such a thing. If there is any item, however small from any of these robberies, and if it's hidden anywhere here, you will find it. If there is anything you think may be faintly incriminating on paper or on a computer or an abandoned phone, you will find it. Go through the recycling, go through the bins – I know you know but I'm reminding you anyway. It will take as long as it takes, and if you need extra help, shout. But too many of us doesn't always make for greater success. Report to DI Grayson initially. I'm around but I'm also heading up the hunt for Jake Barber. Remember, this isn't just about stolen stuff from Ash Farm and the McDermids' place, it is primarily a murder inquiry. Jake Barber probably isn't Mr Big. But he wanted Shenda Neill silenced, or else he was told to silence her. OK, thanks, guys – let's get on with it.' Serrailler thought the chances of their finding anything at all were slim to non-existent, certainly in terms of stolen items, but he hoped there might be at least a lead to some clue about Barber's activities, accomplices, plans – even, just possibly, his present whereabouts. He was conscious that if the flat yielded nothing, he was back in a locked and barred coal hole in the dark. He had the media on his back asking about progress. He had not yet given them a scrap of information other than the initial and formal facts about Shenda Neill's death. He was waiting for the Chief to ask if he was going to hold a press conference and working out how to subdue that line of inquiry.

Finding Jake Barber might be difficult but he was optimistic. He was not especially identifiable but someone would either split on him or spot him, as someone usually did.

He zapped open his car lock as a text message buzzed. *Voicemail. You have one new message.*

'*Si, call me. It's about Dad and it's urgent.*'

Fifty-four

Simon sat in the car park at Bevham General Hospital. There had been no news from the flat search. No news about the whereabouts of Jake Barber. No news. Just the news that his father had been taken ill.

Someone was rapping on the window.

He leaned over to the passenger door, and Cat got in.

'He's had a heart attack. They've done the initial tests and he's in ITU. He may have a stent inserted, but they're discussing whether this will be enough or if they need to do a bypass.'

'What do you think they should do?'

'I'm not a cardiologist.'

'No opinion?'

'Yes, I have an opinion, which is that they should do exactly what they think is best after due assessment and discussion. A bypass is more serious but there's a very good recovery rate now. The stent option is quite straightforward and less risky. I'm like you, bro. I'm waiting to hear. Are you coming up to see him, or are you too busy?'

She got out of the car as she was speaking and walked off towards the hospital entrance.

Simon sat on after she had gone. He needed to calm down before seeing his father, and he realised that he was irrationally angry with them both, Richard for being taken ill, Cat for being so abrupt with him as she had just now. He had to take a deep breath, to prepare for some sort of irritability, blame, complaint on his father's part. Like many doctors, Richard did not cope well with being ill, though he had always put on a great show of struggling to go in to work while suffering from a passing cold.

He sent a message to the team, but a reply came straight back. *Nothing yet, guv.* They might well have to work into the night. The warrant had been late in coming, and once the first searches had been done, he intended to have the floorboards up.

Cat was hovering in the lobby beside the lifts. 'He's in ITU2. We're going to get a coffee and take a walk.'

His father was a bad colour. He had the usual tube and wire attachments to machines and oxygen mask on. The nurse was just leaving him.

'He had a bit of a hiccup with his breathing but it's not serious. He can take it off to talk to you if he wants to.'

'Thanks.' He took the chair by the bed. Richard looked at him but didn't touch the mask.

'Cat's gone to get a coffee and stretch her legs. I'm sorry I didn't get here sooner.'

He looked smaller, somehow, though he was well propped up. He had never looked his age but now he seemed like a much older man, the flesh on his face had fallen in.

'Can I get you anything?'

A small head movement.

'Any pain?'

Another.

'I gather they're deciding what to do . . . you know more about it than them, but whatever, it'll be state of the art. They owe you that and they're probably aware of it.'

Richard reached up and pulled the mask to one side. 'I doubt it.'

'Of course they do.'

'I didn't expect this. Does anyone? But I haven't been a cardiac risk. Brings you up short.'

'I'm sure. Even if people are, do they really think it's going to happen to them? Like the proverbial bus – who expects to be run over?'

He was babbling about nothing because he had no idea what else to do, what to say. He was only used to his father's sarcasm

223

and disapproval, his competitive need to be ahead and to be right, always. The last time Simon had seen him ill, he had known that it was temporary, a nasty bout of pneumonia, dangerous but unlikely to prove fatal – or at least that was how it seemed to him looking back. This was different. He had no idea how serious the coronary had been, how much at risk he still was.

He wanted to say the right thing for fear that he might miss the chance. But what was that "right thing"?

'I imagine Cat has been in touch with Ivo. The time difference is always difficult.'

'He can't be expected to care.'

'Why ever not? Of course he cares, Dad, we all do.'

'Really.'

No, he could never accept that. Was it because he didn't want it? How much had he cared, did he care, for them? His grandchildren seemed to be of far greater concern to him than his children had ever been. Was that really so? What did he feel, deep down? He had never given the slightest indication.

'I wonder if Sam's on duty. He'll come to see you when he has a spare minute. They don't have much slack in that job.'

Richard looked away. Hospital porters were necessary, but he would never in a millennium have expected to see his grandson as one.

'He won't do it forever, you know, Dad, but until he's sure about his future, it's better to do this than wander round the world taking selfies in dangerous places.'

Simon got up and stretched. His back had improved but sitting badly on a hospital chair made him aware of it again.

He had nothing more to say but he couldn't leave, at least not until Cat returned.

'Can I have a drink of your water?'

He poured it into the plastic cup and drank. Lukewarm.

'Would you like some?'

He did not know if his father couldn't be bothered to reply, didn't want to speak to him, or even was unable to nod or shake his head because he was in pain.

Help me out here, he thought. But when had Richard ever done that?

Fifty-five

'My, I haven't walked like that for I can't think how long,' Declan said. They had set off in the morning, found their way to the beach and then walked beside the sea as far as Salthouse, before turning onto the marsh paths, meeting birders draped with cameras and binoculars, shouldering telescopes, energetic couples with Labradors and terriers, striding out, stopping now and then to look up at a bird, or out to sea, the white wind-farm posts like modern sculpture installations against a brilliant blue sky. It was cold but very still, they were not pushing against a wind. They did not speak much, conserving their energy for walking and because there was no need to chat. Companionable, Pauline Mead thought. She looked at Declan's back and shoulders as he went ahead. Even after a couple of days, he was better, everything about him seemed more alert, less despondent. This had been a good idea.

They tired and agreed that they should turn round just in time to see the bus that ran along the coast between villages, and reached the stop as it pulled in.

'It was a bit of a hike back,' Mike said, gazing at the tide flowing in fast between the banks opposite their hotel. 'Bus was a godsend.'

They looked at one another, feeling pleased.

'I think maybe a light lunch and a bit of a rest? How does that sound?'

'Perfect.'

But Declan did not move for a moment, just stared at the water and the sky and the boats moored, the masts of a training ship tied up at the quay.

'She'd have loved this,' he said quietly. 'I wonder why we never came here. She'd have revelled in it.'

They did not know what to say, so said nothing. Pauline touched his arm.

'Soup,' Declan said. 'A good soup and a toasted sandwich is what speaks to me.' He led the way in briskly.

They had a corner of the lounge overlooking the water.

'It's so nice here. So very nice. Thank you, Declan.' He had persuaded Mike to use his first name. It made a difference. They were friends now.

'Can I ask you both something? Just because I don't know if I'm making something out of nothing, I probably am, but it's been niggling away at the back of my mind.'

He chewed his toasted sandwich for some time, looking out of the window.

'The police . . . I don't want to say anything against them, you understand. I have every respect for them. If I didn't I wouldn't have given them the bobby van, I wouldn't have been so involved. I know they have a difficult job, everyone expects them to sort things out overnight, and they can't. It's not just a question of money and numbers, I know that. Some criminals are not only vicious and ruthless, they're bloody clever.'

'Some of them are professionals,' Mike said.

'Exactly. The ones who targeted us . . . who . . . they're not breaking a back window and stealing a few quid and the telly. Anyway, as I say, the cops have got their work cut out and I'd never criticise the way they do it. Only, they do make mistakes. They're bound to.'

'What do you think they've done, Declan? What have they got wrong?' Pauline asked.

He shook his head. 'Maybe I'm barking up the wrong tree. But . . . it was something the family liaison officer said . . . let something slip, really . . . and I can't get it out of my head. You see, I thought, well, I assumed, that what happened in our case was a one-off. They'd checked us out, you remember, they'd seen what we had in the way of valuables, and they had a plan. That's what I mean by being professional. This was worked out carefully in advance. But according to this young woman . . . she said that there had been another robbery of a similar kind – valuable artworks and antiques – in Lafferton, a few weeks before they got us. No one was hurt, there wasn't anyone at home.'

'But they hadn't expected you to be at home, had they? You got back early. They had it in their heads that the coast would be clear and it should have been. You panicked them. But are you sure this is exactly what she said? I always watch the local news and we get the *Gazette* and I don't remember it – and I would have done after yours, it would have rung a bell, don't you think so, Mike?'

'Not sure. If nobody was hurt or even at home then it was just another burglary and how many of those are there every week?'

'Not ones that are so professional, where the people know what they're after. Don't tell me that happens every day.'

'Exactly, Pauline, that's just my point. Anyway, there was this other one and the reason it doesn't ring any bells with you is simple. They deliberately kept it out of the press. They kept it quiet.'

'Why did they do that?'

'I was still a bit shocked, you know, but the way I understood it was that the men who did it would think, if there was no mention of it anywhere, they'd got away with it so well that they'd have another go straight away.'

'Perhaps those people had stuff they didn't want anyone to know about.'

'If you ask me,' Mike said, 'the police got it wrong. If you'd read about the other one you'd have been more careful, wouldn't you? Everybody would, with valuables and that round their houses, they'd have been a bit more suspicious of strangers hanging about.'

'That's not fair at all,' Pauline said. 'Declan and Cindy were always careful about the alarms and everything.'

'Maybe. But too trusting.'

'And better for it. I hate people who are always suspicious, always sure someone's about to do the dirty on them.' Pauline glared at him, and turned to Declan. 'I think you've every right to be annoyed – more than annoyed, no matter how great you think the police are. I'd put in a complaint.'

'No, no . . . I wouldn't dream of that. But . . . well, I do think that with hindsight they might have done it differently. I do.' He stood up. His eyes had filled with tears and his face had fallen into the deep lines of despair again. 'I think I'm going to have a nap. You do whatever you fancy and shall we meet up for a drink before dinner? That'd be nice. Yes.'

Fifty-six

'All right, Dr Serrailler, it's twenty past seven, you're first on
the list and here's your ride, nice and early.'

'Morning, Grandpa.'

Richard stared at the young man wearing a hospital porter's
uniform of blue short-sleeved T-shirt and trousers.

'I'm your transport down to theatre. How are you feeling?'

In answer, Richard reached out a hand. Sam took it and held
it firmly. It was steady but he could feel a fast pulse.

'This is a stroke of luck.'

'Not exactly. I rearranged my shift. Wanted to get you down
safely.'

'You mean you chose to take me?'

'Yup. Now if you're comfortable, I'll put the bed sides up
and we'll get going. Anything you need?'

The nurse came to check the bed and his chart. 'Fine. Good
to go. See you soon, Doctor. You'll be in resus immediately after
your operation but then back up here with us before you know
it. It'll be fine.'

'Thank you, but I am well aware that I may not be so perhaps
we should say goodbye.'

'I'll do no such thing. All right, Sam, thank you. Off you go.'

His grandfather was silent on the way, along the corridors,
in the lift, through the doors into the anaesthetics room,
giving no sign of how he felt, whether he was concerned or
sanguine.

'Is it true that doctors make bad patients?' Sam asked after he had checked him in.

'Many do. I myself am a model. Thank you, Sam. Good of you but don't stay chatting to me, you have to get on with your important job.'

'Place couldn't run without me. Good luck, Grandpa.'

Richard reached out his hand again. He is as worried as anyone could be, Sam thought, because he knows the score. His grandfather was a poor colour, his eyes were slightly sunken. He looked old.

Still holding his hand, Sam bent over the trolley, kissed his cheek, and did his best to hug him, at an awkward angle.

'Thank you, Sam.' The anaesthetist waved a hand.

'You know him?' Richard said.

'Oh, we all know Sam. He's one of the good ones – goes the extra mile to help us out.'

He was tapping the back of Richard's wrist, to raise a vein.

'I'm very pleased to hear it. He is my grandson.'

'Really? Then I guess he won't be staying on too much longer as a porter – waiting to go to med school, I suppose?'

Richard watched the needle, poised over his now prominent blue vein. He longed for the coming oblivion, to spare him more anxiety.

'What Sam's future career will be,' he said, as the cold liquid started to run through his hand and the swirl down into unconsciousness took him over, 'is anybody's guess.'

Fifty-seven

The flat once lived in by Jake and Shenda looked as if it had been gutted by builders before some sort of revamp. The floor-boards had been taken up and every wall cupboard taken down, the ceiling lights, bathroom fittings, kitchen cabinets taken apart. Cushions, mattress, tins and jars and boxes had been opened and investigated.

'How're you doing?' Simon asked.

One of the PCs straightened up. 'Nothing,' he said. 'Not even anything to identify either of them in the flat. Just got to look through all the copies of the free sheets and the cornflakes boxes.'

'No mail? Old envelopes?'

'Not so far. Circulars, catalogues but most of those are addressed to other people – previous tenants presumably.'

'Guv.'

Simon turned.

'Not sure if it's anything, but I was checking the bedroom again and I found this.'

The screw of paper had been rolled and scrumpled, probably in the pocket from which it had fallen.

'Expect it's nothing.' The PC was a rookie, fresh-faced and anxious. 'Sorry, guv.'

GROVE INDUSTRIAL AND COMMERCIAL PROPERTY
44 Arthur Road
Bevham

PAYMENT REMINDER

For rental of lock-up premises: Unit 7, Simms Business Park,
Bevham
Quarter ending 31 March: £250

If we do not receive your overdue payment within 7 days
from the date of this letter we will enter the premises and
remove any goods etc to the value and your rental will
terminate.

Signed (scribbled initials)
For Grove Industrial and Commercial Property

The paper was dated two months previously.

Fifty-eight

'Catherine . . . oh. I hope this isn't bad news. But come in, please.'

Philippa King was dressed properly. She wore a pale blue cashmere jumper, darker blue beads, a tweed skirt and tights, was made-up and groomed. Her only concession to informality were backless slippers.

'Can I offer you a cup of tea? Coffee?'

'No, thank you. I can only stay a moment. But I thought I ought to let you know what's been happening to Dad.'

A slight frown. A clouding of her features. Cat could not read the other woman's expression. Did she want to read it?

'Of course. It was very alarming.' But she sounded collected.

'Dad had a heart attack, as you probably realised.'

'Yes, the paramedics were working on him for some time before they went off. How safe one is in an ambulance nowadays – sometimes safer than in the hospital itself, I often think. I was a theatre sister, by the way – perhaps you knew?'

'Oh, I'm so sorry – then of course you knew what was going on.'

'Retired ten years ago, but yes, I had a pretty good idea. So, how is your father?'

Cat noted how she referred to him and her tone was concerned but politely so.

'He was in pretty poor shape last night. He had an ECG and a scan which showed three blocked arteries, one partially, the others more so.'

'A bypass then.'

'Yes, triple. He had it this morning and it was successful, but as you will know, the risk period isn't over. He's doing all right but I'll be happier if he improves considerably over the next twenty-four hours or so.'

'That sounds likely, doesn't it? Your father seems a fit man, a non-smoker.'

'There's a bit of a family history, but you know, after all my years as a GP, and unless there is a very obvious direct cause, I tend to say "these things happen". I've seen many coronaries where the reason was by no means clear, just as I have seen more cases of lung cancer in people who have never smoked than in those who have. Not that smoking is a good idea.'

'No.'

Philippa was quiet and thoughtful and Cat sensed that she was trying to decide whether to say something or not.

'Do you know, if that cup of tea is still on offer . . .'

'Of course it is. Good. I want one myself.' She jumped up and went briskly into the kitchen. Her apartment had the same layout as Richard's but the opposite way round, and her garden was on a slight slope, longer and narrower than his. There was the same small area of terrace, with a padded swing-seat to one side, and large, flower-filled pots. She obviously spent time in it. The flat itself was immaculate, without any clutter. Even the few books on the table and a sheaf of magazines on the window ledge were neatly arranged, edge to edge. Cat could imagine the perfect hospital corners on every bed she had ever made.

She brought leaf tea in a pot, on a tray with a pristine white cloth. Biscuits on a matching plate.

'I feel I should have spoken to you before. Today is perhaps not the time but when is ever "the right moment"?'

'I'm a doctor. I'm used to hearing anything, whenever – as you may imagine – so please don't worry.'

'Professional matters. But this is . . . more personal.'

Cat set down her cup. She had to trust Philippa, trust her to be honest and straightforward. She seemed to be both those things but Cat was always wary, always waited. She also had to judge whether she herself could speak frankly. Her own intuition told her that she could and should but she had no facts or knowledge to back that up.

'What do you know about my father, Philippa? If you're happy to tell me?'

'I know that he was a well-regarded consultant, and something of an academic at the same time. I know that your mother died what, five or six years ago?'

'Nine.'

'And that he spent some time living in France and . . . well, he implied that he had a companion out there. I know that he adores his grandchildren, and perhaps has a somewhat tricky relationship with you and your brothers.'

'He talks about us?'

'Not a lot. I confess to having read between the lines.'

'Did he mention Martha – our younger sister?'

'No. I had no idea that there was another.'

'That doesn't surprise me. Perhaps he will tell you one day. Perhaps I will. For now, I don't think our conversation is going to relate to her. You'll correct me if I'm wrong. Has he talked much about Judith?'

'Is that another sister? I don't remember hearing her name either.'

'Right. Philippa, I know you want to say something to me so perhaps you should do that. Martha and Judith aren't – well, I can't say they're not important, they both are and were, very. But you don't need to know about them now. I suppose it depends entirely on your relationship, whatever it is, with Dad.'

'I have no relationship with him, Catherine, and I'm afraid I would prefer to keep it that way. I am a neighbour. Of course I came to help him when he was taken ill, as I would have done with anyone.'

'Thank you.'

She shook her head. 'Your father was outgoing when we both moved in and that was very pleasant. I have made friends with one or two other people here. Not intimate friends, but we are people with similar interests who enjoy each other's company occasionally. For example, we play bridge, four of us, we have a book group . . . It's a sociable community but you can join in or not, just as you choose. That suits me very well. But what happened . . . well, your father seemed to be trying to appropriate me – it was as if he had decided we were to be friends and anyone else – anything else – should either take a back seat or even be abandoned. I liked him, I enjoyed our conversations, but that was all. Then –' She stopped, and looked down at her empty tea cup, staring into it as if it would provide her with the words she wanted. 'I am trying not to appear . . . I am trying not to make something out of nothing, Catherine. I'm not a teenager, I think I have a measured approach to most things.'

'It's all right. I'm sure you are not someone who easily gets anything out of proportion.'

'I really don't think I am. Perhaps rather the opposite. My son always tells me I shouldn't make light of things. I have a son and two daughters, by the way, and I see a good deal of them. Would you like some more tea?'

'No. I would like you to tell me what happened.'

'Yes. What happened was that your father propositioned me – that seems a pompous way of putting it but I'm not sure how else I can put it. I was taken aback and then I was really quite angry, because I thought I must have hinted at something, or misled him. I am sure I did not.'

'I am sure you didn't as well. There will be nothing in this for which you can possibly, remotely, blame yourself, I promise you.'

Cat could feel her own anger growing, like a balloon being blown up very fast.

'Philippa, do you mind my asking – how did he take your rejection?'

To her surprise, the other woman smiled. 'I think he was rather taken aback. Perhaps he isn't used to having his overtures turned down. I wonder if his pride was hurt. But do you know, I can't say I care very much what he thought. But, Catherine, you don't seem entirely shocked or surprised.'

'Surprised – no. Shocked – yes. My father continues to shock me about many things. There is one thing I think you should know – you have every right to and I have no idea why he chose to conceal it. A couple of years after my mother died, he remarried – the widow of an old hospital colleague. Judith. She was perfect – perfect for him and perfect for us and we loved her. And he treated her very badly. She left him and they divorced. She went to live near her daughter but she and I do keep in touch – I am very fond of her and I feel guilty about her. So we're quits – two of us feeling guilty when we are not. Typical. That's how my father – and a lot of men like him, come to that – manipulates people, women especially. Philippa, I know it isn't my fault, but I still have to say that I am so sorry. I'm ashamed of him and for him. I hope you believe me.'

'Of course and thank you. Don't run away with the idea that I have suffered anything over this, Catherine. I'm a strong woman and I have had a very great deal worse things happen to me in my lifetime. I have brushed it aside. But when he comes home, I intend to make myself scarce. Anything other than politeness is out of the question, and that's a pity because I liked your father's company. We had plenty to talk about, and not only because we both had medical careers. But something has to be sacrificed, I'm afraid.'

'My father is his own worst enemy and if he ends up a lonely, embittered old man it will be no one's fault but his own. I'm sorry if that sounds harsh.' She stood up. 'So now, he's in a life-threatening condition and I feel guilty on top of everything else.'

Fifty-nine

'I want three of you. This takes priority over anything else unless you've urgent appointments directly connected to the murder of Shenda Neill. Right, thanks . . . Andy, I want you there too. Half a dozen uniform are meeting us there, plus a dog handler. I don't see any need for armed response but I've given them a heads-up in case. You just never know. Now, let me take you through.'

Serrailler clicked on the screen. 'This is the area. There's an entry road here and that's the exit road as well but we can also gain access in 4x4s and heavy vehicles if we need to, by coming across this scrubland from the back. There are three blocks of storage units, two of garages. Nothing else for a hundred yards or so, just derelict land, some old fencing. This area is not much used, the buildings are old and it's not a convenient site for anyone wanting to use their unit daily, you have to go via the level crossing and the facilities are basic – there's electricity and water and that's about it. Here's the unit we're interested in – at the end of the first block. Dave did a quick recce. It's well secured – bolts, locks, bars . . . not going to be turn the key and in we go. Questions?'

'Is there likely to be anybody on the premises?'

'Probably not. Patrols have been round at random but frequently in the last forty-eight hours and there's been no sign of either people or vehicles. A couple of the garages had cars taken out and away, one of them was returned at the end of the day. Nothing else.'

'What are we looking for?'

'Our first priority is finding Jake Barber but he's pretty unlikely to be at the unit. It's stolen goods – valuables, antiques, works of art, all sorts. I've got the inventory from the two robberies and some photos, but there could be stuff from other jobs. Just don't know.'

'Any other names?'

'No.'

'Needle in a haystack then.'

'So our job is to take apart the haystacks, straw by straw. Right, eleven o'clock at the units. Thank you, everyone.'

As Fern Monroe was getting ready to drive off she saw Kelly coming out in a group of uniform, and tooted at her. 'You on this lock-up job? Get in.'

'Thanks for that,' Kelly said, fastening her seat belt as they headed out of the gates, 'You spared me going with the two Matts – don't mind them but they're Melton Town supporters and they'll take the piss the entire way.'

Bevham had lost comprehensively to underdogs Melton in the semi-final of the league.

'So, how's it going? I haven't seen you, but then I was off for a week, and then you were away.'

'Yes, my gran's funeral. Cut me up, actually. I was very close to her and I wish I'd gone to see her when she was first ill, only honestly, I didn't know it was that serious. Always do it, Fern, always say it or go there or do it. Been a lesson to me. You?'

'Grim.'

'How's the dreamboat?'

'What dreamboat?'

'Come on. Any more cosy dinners à deux?'

'No. Don't suppose there will be either. Didn't mean anything. The Super's struggling, if you ask me.'

'What, with a woman?'

'The job. There's something not right, only I can't quite put my finger on it.'

'Maybe he's still in pain from the arm?'

'Not that sort of thing. I dunno – ignore me.'

'You still fancy him though, don't you?'

'Not so much.'

'Come on.'

'How's the swotting?'

Kelly was working for her sergeant's exams.

'Don't ask.'

'That's a deal. You don't ask, I don't ask.'

Fern switched on the radio. Ed Sheeran's was the only voice in the car for the next five miles.

'Where have you brought us to, guv? Like the back of the bloody moon.'

The industrial units seemed to have been dropped down from nowhere and left stranded for years. Scrubland, waste ground, concrete tracks leading nowhere, the foundations of long-demolished buildings, a couple of burned-out trucks, a Nissen hut. The storage units and garages were set at right angles to one another.

'Can we claim for new tyres?'

'You can.'

The land did not have potholes so much as craters, as well as a few rusting iron posts cut off at the foot to leave stumps which were invisible until the moment just before a car went over them.

Everyone had tried and failed to find a parking spot on level ground. Now, they were lined up on more broken-up concrete and paving, outside Unit 7.

'They call this a *business park*, you said, guv?'

Serrailler was clearly in no mood for joking. Kelly gave Fern Monroe a nudge. 'He's got that pompous look.'

'It's a murder inquiry.'

'You know what I mean.'

'When I have your attention?'

But her friend had a point and Fern knew it. Pompous. Stuffed. Whatever, he was still the best-looking man in the county and she still wanted him.

'Listen up. When we get in, however we do it, everyone stand back. I doubt if anyone is inside waiting for us with a machine gun or a machete but still. We are looking for the proceeds of at least two robberies – antique items, china, paintings, jewellery, clocks and so on. We're also looking for Jake Barber – it's unlikely that he'll be here but take nothing for granted. Otherwise, anything at all – anything incriminating, anything likely to lead us to him or an associate. If you ask me what, I don't know, could be paperwork, could be – well, anything. Careful search, gloves on, if there are packing cases and other containers to be opened, we do it by the book, with extreme care – I don't want any claims for priceless Ming vases dropped on the floor and smashed. Dog handler's on the way, he'll go in and sniff for the usual – explosives, blood, drugs, though I'm not expecting those. Right, guys, just give a bash and a shout before you start – in case our man's having a kip in there.'

The others watched.

'Police. Anyone inside? Anyone in there, identify yourself.'

No one did.

Work started on the locks, bolts, chains, steel bars. After twenty minutes nothing had yielded an inch.

'This is a fire brigade job, guv, no way are we going to get in with the equipment we've got on hand. They knew what they were doing when they locked up and left.'

The two women were leaning on the bonnet of Fern's car.

'Wonder he didn't have them here to start with.'

'Probably didn't realise the extent of the security.'

'Yeah, right. I could tell from one look at those crossbars.'

'I'm amazed you're still a constable.'

The fire service arrived more than an hour later, by which time everyone was seething. There was no cafe or shop to get refreshments and a ban on people leaving the site to recce for one. Serrailler spent the time on his phone in the car, working through emails. Cat reported his father 'stable, holding up nicely'. The chief of restoration at the cathedral wanted to know how much longer he might be working up in the roof. The rest was routine signing off on jobs. He glanced up once or twice, to look round at the disgruntled faces of his team, in their own cars, leaning on the bonnets or marching round the perimeter of the waste ground in a depressed and half-hearted attempt at exercise.

It took the firemen five minutes to cut their way into the unit.

'At last,' Serrailler said. 'Here's hoping.'

The unit was large, with an open second floor reached by metal stairs. Boots clanged as they ran up. There were four shallow alcoves in the brick sides of the main space.

The entire unit was empty. There were no remains of packing materials, no debris, no oil marks, the floors had been swept clean. There were no marks of any kind in such little dust as remained.

'Eat your dinner off it,' someone said.

Sixty

Lois and Agneta had stayed after cafe closing, to help Wint do the once-a-week fridge and freezer full clear-out and swab down. It took time, and there were always items to check for date and either dispose of or share between them.

Everything had been done and they had a carrier bag each of stuff to take home. Wint had left to go to his silver band practice.

'Take the weight of your feet, Lois, I'll make us a coffee.'

'You're a hero. How are you feeling now, anyway?'

'I'm all right. But . . . I think of her often, I wonder, I ask if she suffered a lot, I miss her. I had a Mass said and I always have her in my prayers. What else can I do?'

'I wish they'd find the bastard. I wish I could get my hands on him.'

'I know. I think they never will find him, Lois, he is gone. Escaped. He's in some other country now.'

'Never. He's holing up somewhere. Maybe still in Lafferton.'

'How could anyone do that? How could anyone kill a lovely person like Shenda?'

'How can anyone kill anyone is what I ask myself. Robbing's one thing—'

'You couldn't even rob, Lois, you're a good woman.'

'I could rob for my kids, if they were starving. I could do a lot of things for them, but killing's different. Oh dear lord, what a thing to be talking about.'

243

Ten minutes later, they had locked up the cafe. Agneta wheeled her bike to the end of the passageway. She heard nothing. Saw no one. An arm came round her throat, her bike crashed to the floor and she was pulled very fast into a backed-up delivery van which was waiting, doors open. The van overtook Lois's car as the traffic lights went from red to amber.

Sixty-one

Simon had gone straight home from the units, changed into running gear and driven to Starly. If he could have gone up the motorway a few hundred miles, to the Peak District, and done a hard cross-country run there he would have felt better, but a local ten miles would have to do. He could run off his anger and frustration, which the team had been able to see and hear clearly enough as he did a swift debrief and sent them back. What he hoped to God they did not guess was his feeling of humiliation. He had used a sledge-hammer and there had not even been a seed to crack let alone a pea.

The day was cool and dry, perfect for running, and he ran hard and thought about nothing. He was long practised at letting his mind go blank. Only the rhythm of his legs, the pounding of his feet and the sound of them on the beaten path and of his own breathing, only the sensation of air flowing across his limbs, pushing his hair back.

He had told no one where he was going and left his phone in the car. As he was still on duty, he could be reprimanded for both those things. All the same, he just ran. A buzzard was above him, resting on a thermal, wide wings outspread. Sheep bleated in the distance. He climbed up and stopped for breath and half the county was spread below him, blue-brown and green, the contours blurring together in the bland light.

He ran on.

In the glove compartment, his phone recorded two messages and received half a dozen emails and texts.

'*Urgent, guv, can you come in? Reports of a girl being seen bundled into the back of a van and driven off. Call when you get this.*'

'*Si, give me a ring, need to talk about Dad. He's OK post-op, being discharged on Friday. It's not that.*'

He ran on. Got into a rhythm that felt perfect. Hypnotic. This was how it should be and why he ran, other than for fitness. He couldn't stand gyms, the atmosphere, the smell, the soullessness of them depressed him. Swimming was always good but only wild swimming, never in echoing, chlorinated baths, but running was better and now he ran beyond his planned ten miles, to twelve, thirteen . . . and had to stop, his legs almost folding under him, his chest aching. He was on the flat again and he could only get back to the car by climbing up another hill.

He sat down, then lay down, stretched his back, rolled to and fro, bicycled his legs. After that, he lay still. He would be fine. He closed his eyes. After a few moments he heard a voice, and then felt something cool and damp on his face, as an eager young Labrador licked and licked it.

'Sorry, sorry. Bert, come here! Here now.'

'You OK?'

'Thanks, just resting.'

'Sorry about the dog.' The man hesitated. 'Don't I know you?'

'Yes.' Simon stood up. 'I came to your house with one of our DCs. Simon Serrailler, and you're Dr . . . ?'

'Tim – Tim Letts.'

'Did you have the dog when you were burgled?'

'It isn't our dog, it belongs to a colleague. I borrow him for long walks. You should try it. They're great company.'

Bert the Labrador was now sitting down, a model of patience.

'I don't suppose there's any news?'

'Yes and no. I'm satisfied we've identified at least one of the criminals involved but at the moment he's evading us. We'll get him.'

'Is he anything to do with Cindy McDermid's death – can we call it murder? It certainly looked like it.'

'It's unlikely they went in there planning to kill her, or harm either of them. They were expecting the house to be empty.'

'So – we were lucky? Because of course we might have decided not to use the opera tickets.'

Simon nodded, then bent to make a fuss of the dog. He wanted to get moving again, not only because he didn't want to get cold but because he was feeling uncomfortable with the conversation. They were further away from both catching Jake Barber and finding the stolen goods, though since the murder of Shenda, the latter were now low down on the list of priorities.

He started to jog on the spot. Tim nodded. 'Keep us in the loop.'

Sixty-two

Slower. Slow. Stop. She heard him swear through the panel behind the driver's compartment.

It was quiet for a few minutes, and then she heard cars passing to one side. A temporary traffic light then. Judging by how long it had been, she thought she knew where they were. If she was right, the lights were three-way, and slow.

He had grabbed her, pushed her into the van, closed the doors and moved off, fast, scarcely looking at her, not checking anything.

Checking whether she had her phone.

She prayed for them to be stopped here long enough. There were two bars. Then one. Then two again. She'd stored the number the police had given her while she was still at the station. Just in case.

In small grey van. Melton Lane roadworks? We move. Help me. Agneta

Did it go? There was no swoosh. But still two bars. Still a signal. Still moving.

Jake took me from outside cafe. He killed Shenda. He will kill me. Help me. Grey van. Agneta

The message went. They were speeding now. Turning corners fast. She had lost sense of where they were. Held on to a spare tyre to save herself sliding and crashing into the metal side.

Strangely, she was calm. Something in her knew. She had said prayers over and over again. She would be all right but what would happen first?

The van slewed round another bend and she clutched the tyre and closed her eyes and went on praying.

Sixty-three

It had been a quiet morning. All the requests for calls had been from patients who were not emergencies and not seriously ill, but who needed attention for what Cat always called 'talking problems'. One had insomnia, one was worried that she was in the early stages of dementia, and wasn't, one was still coming to terms with a sudden bereavement. The last had a sinus infection. She headed home to get some lunch for herself and for Rosie, who also had a talking problem, about her future career in medicine. She bought some salad stuff and eggs and cheese from a new farm shop, where she also got coffee and a home-made cinnamon bun, picked up messages and then simply sat, in a patch of sun, feeling the warmth on her face but, even while she enjoyed it, worrying about her father. Her feelings about him were as confused as they had ever been. She was angry with him, after her conversation with Philippa, angry and also ashamed and embarrassed. In recent years, she had found herself looking back into the past and wondering if he had behaved badly when they were all young and still living at home with him and their mother. People did not usually start behaving as he did later in life, the pattern had been formed over many years. Had Meriel known? Had she simply ignored his behaviour and carried on? There was no way of telling, and going back to it all over and over again was like picking at a scab.

She had also deliberately turned aside from the more immediate question of where Richard would go on his discharge from
hospital. As if there were any choice.

She got a second coffee and had a chat with the owner of the
shop, bought a bar of chocolate and a brownie for Felix and was
given a sourdough loaf, because they hadn't baked any before
and she was to be the first tester. The sun was fitful but she still
sat outside, enjoying time to herself without any pressure to do
this, go there, write up that. She told herself not to spoil it.

On the way back, she passed the end of the lane that led to the
Pegwell house. After her visit to Elaine she had gone over the
case in detail with Luke and voiced her concerns. He had agreed
with her but cautioned her not to put any backs up.

'I think you were right to talk to your friend Elaine and she
was right not to agree to visit. She's retired, but even if she
weren't, it wouldn't be ethical, Cat. Getting her take on it for
yourself is different and if at any time you get the faintest sense
that the child is at risk – well, you know what to do. Did you
feel that?'

'I'm just not sure. It's nebulous . . . but then, sometimes it is.
I've seen families where I've been sure there was abuse going
on but I was wrong and I have also known families where I
would never have suspected a thing – one where I was prepared
to give evidence on their behalf   but I was even more wrong
there. It still haunts me The Pegwells? I think she's depressed
and that he bullies her in a sort of passive-aggressive way. I
don't think either of them have bonded with the baby. I am
pretty sure neither wanted to have one at all. They more or less
told me so.

'What do you think you should do, Cat? It's your case.'

'Not much I can do really, unless they call me.'

They had not called her. Nevertheless, she turned left, parked
at the gateway, and walked up to the house. The sun had
gone in.

Cat rang the doorbell. After waiting a few minutes, she rang
again.

251

There was no sound from inside. Clearly the Pegwells were out but something in her felt a frisson of unease. There was more than the usual absence of activity when people had left a place for a few hours. She sensed a strange and absolute stillness.

She went to the side and looked in, but that window only faced the hallway and all she could see were two closed doors.

There was a high gate over which honeysuckle scrambled and sprawled, tangled up with ivy and Russian vine. She went through into a rectangle of grass which needed cutting, and at the end of it, flower beds and what looked like a vegetable patch which someone had begun to dig over, then abandoned. Beyond, the parkland and its great, graceful trees spread away towards the big house.

The silence and stillness were uncanny. There was no breath of wind. No birdsong. No soft movement of the grass made by some small creature. Cat stood, listening, looking. The place had an oddly abandoned air, probably because the Pegwells had never done anything to their outside space and had spent little time in it. They had never struck her as outdoor people, and she was surprised they had ever come to live here. But the house belonged to the estate, she knew, as did many in the adjacent village, so they would be renting it, while they found somewhere of their own.

The sun came out again but that did not affect the desolate air of the place. Cat went back and rang the bell for a last time, and when there was still no reply, cupped her hands and peered through a window into the sitting room. It was empty. The house was lifeless. The Pegwells had gone.

Sixty-four

Agneta's message was received at three minutes past seven. At five minutes past a call had gone out to all patrols.

'Small van, grey, no make, no number. Believed heading south or west out of Lafferton. Driver, IC1 male, thirties. Believed young woman, Agneta Rudkowski, held in rear. Stop vehicle and hold driver. Repeat STOP vehicle.'

Coming out of the service station with two beakers of tea and assorted snack bars, PC Lee Combes heard his partner yelling at him from the car and collided with a woman, who took the force of the hot liquid.

'JeezUS!' PC Danny Brocklebank jumped out of the car.

'Shit, sorry, sorry . . .'

'Lee, give that to me. Get in the car. Madam, are you hurt? Scalded or otherwise injured? Good. Call or go to Lafferton police station and explain. Here's an incident number, 5240 – quote that.' He scribbled on a note. 'We'll have your clothing dry-cleaned or whatever. Sorry to rush off but we're on a blue light call.'

She had barely time to register what had happened, what he had said, take the note, before both men were in the patrol car and speeding away.

'Feckin' clumsy idiot.'

'I don't think it actually scalded her, come on.'

'No, but now I haven't got my tea.'

'What's it all about anyway? Steady on.'

'Small grey van with a girl held in the back speeding out of town in a southerly direction. What did we just see, going like the clappers with the exhaust belching out and you said "Leave it, someone else'll give him the ticket." We're due our break.'

The van they had seen, small, grey and belching out exhaust fumes, was three miles away and the tyres were burning up. More by luck than judgement, PCs Combes and Brocklebank took the right direction off the bypass and a second patrol car caught sight of the same van as it sped ever more recklessly towards the motorway junction, swerved away at the last minute from taking the slip road, and went back on itself.

'Hold on,' Molly Duncan said, putting her foot down.

'He's not going to get far, look at that rear tyre. Bloody hell . . .'

The van hit the kerb, managed to stay upright, and took off across a field that led towards a building site, the developer's flags waving at the entrance by the show home. There was a single strip of tarmac down the centre but otherwise there were no roads, only temporary tracks surrounded by mud and wire fencing. The van careered down, both patrols some way behind but making progress.

'If this is it and there really is someone in the back, God help her.'

The end came quickly. The van spun round, the tyres smoking, the exhaust fumes now black, and came to a halt beside the foundations of a house. The driver was out and running very fast and smoke had started rising out of the bonnet.

The patrol cars came up behind, and Lee Combes was out and giving chase before they had stopped.

'Get the back doors open, get them out, get them out, but watch yourselves, this is going to go up.'

It went up seconds later. Danny had reached the back doors of the van, pulled them open. The girl stumbled out, almost falling. 'Run. Get away!' He had her by the wrist, hauled her up and they were on the far side of the building as the vehicle burst into flames.

'Fire and ambulance units required, J. T. Wilkins new housing development, Woodlands Drive. Vehicle on fire. One passenger possible injuries and shock.'

Agneta sat on the grass verge with her head between her knees then leaned sideways to be violently sick.

'You OK?' Danny Brocklebank was bending down to her as Molly touched his arm.

'Fine thanks.'

'Close.'

'Too close.'

Agneta sat up. 'Thank you,' she said, 'thank you so much,' and burst into tears. Molly took off her jacket and put it round the girl's shoulders. From a distance, the sirens, the blue lights, the engines roaring up.

It was more than fifteen minutes later when Lee Combes limped over the site towards them, blood on his hands and shirt. It took him time to get his breath before he could say, 'I'm all right. Bloody barbed-wire fence.'

Danny looked at him hard. 'And?'

'I lost him,' Lee said.

Sixty-five

The house felt cold, not in temperature but in atmosphere. Cold and lifeless and empty. The Meads made tea and took his bags upstairs and then left him, though they would have stayed, Pauline had said so and meant it, she would have cooked him supper, kept him company. But he had to face it straight away, he had to feel what it was like to come back to this house without Cindy in it. Without Cindy in it ever again.

'It's been lovely,' they had both said. 'A very special break. We've so enjoyed it. Thank you. Thank you. Thank you.'

And again and again and he saw how much they meant it, and yes, they had enjoyed it, had had a lovely break. He had too. He had missed Cindy but in a different way, because he had company and because he was in a place she had never visited, so there were no memories, no trapdoors waiting for him.

But he had to be on his own now. He heard the Meads' car drive away and then the house settled back into silence again.

He sorted through the post, which was mainly catalogues Cindy had sent for, and one or two last condolence cards from people who had only just heard.

He put the paper rubbish in the basket and went to stand at the window. There was a little sunshine but it would not last.

'Cindy,' he said aloud.

And then without warning, or any expectation, he had a sudden overwhelming sense of her presence, there, beside him,

256

so strong, so unmistakable that it almost knocked him off his feet. He sat down at the kitchen table. She sat opposite him where she had always sat. He saw nothing, heard nothing, but she was there as surely as he was there himself. He had never known such a powerful sensation.

'Cindy,' he said again. 'Cindy, what am I going to do?'

He did not know what he had expected. A voice? A nudge? But there was nothing. In the end, he went upstairs to unpack. He heard nothing, felt nothing. Of course not. And Cindy was no longer there. He did not know how he could be so sure but it was very clear to him that she had been there and now she wasn't.

But as he opened the laundry bin to drop in his washing, something did happen. It came back to him, like a coin dropping inside his head. He had talked to the Meads about the other robbery, and they had urged him to complain to the police about there having been no publicity. If the news and local papers had been full of reports, the criminals would have thought twice about doing another job so soon, or ever, in the same area. Cindy might still be alive. The stuff taken wasn't important, his own injuries did not matter. He had been lucky. It was Cindy.

He stood with two shirts in his hand, going over what he would do, and then he realised that it was what she wanted him to do. He did not want to make a formal complaint but he did want to ask questions and to let the police know he felt they had made a serious mistake. Nothing to be done about it, of course, it was far too late, but if lessons could be learned that would be something.

He finished unpacking quickly, and went straight to his office.

Sixty-six

'Hi. I've been trying to get you.'

'I went for a run. Clear my head.'

'You OK?'

'Better for a run, yes.'

'Right. It's about Dad.'

'Course it is.'

'It's all very well—'

'—for me, yes I know and I know the lot always falls on you but I can't have him to convalesce, can I?'

'No, but it's about that. Because honestly, I can't cope with him again and nor can Kieron. So I'm not sure what to do.'

'Have you talked to him?'

'No. I've been avoiding it. He's OK – I rang the ward earlier. He'll be out in a couple of days but that doesn't mean he'll be fit and well.'

'So what will he be like? Bedbound?'

'No, he shouldn't be, but he will be exhausted. It's a big thing, a cardiac bypass, and it means weeks of recovery – he'll need to take short gentle walks and eat properly but he'll sleep a lot too.'

'Sounds right up his street.'

'That's unfair. He won't take kindly to lots of rest.'

'Can't the place he lives in provide him with meals? I thought they had a dining room or restaurant or whatever they call it. For the inmates.'

'Simon . . .'

'All right, I know. But seriously . . .'

'He just ought not to be alone all the time. Ideally, he could do with some sort of convalescent home for a week or two.'

'You must know of one.'

'Not so easy. They've mostly either closed or been turned into long-stay care homes. Private hospitals aren't for recuperation.'

'I've got to ring off, sis. Call coming in. All sorts going on. Speak to you later. Andy, what's happening?'

The DS told him in half a dozen words.

'Oh for God's sake. So, what are they doing now? Barber's on foot, he won't have got far.'

'No sign, as yet, guv.'

'What are uniform mucking about at? They should have the dog handlers, the chopper if we can get it, as many feet on the ground as we can manage and then some. Jake Barber has got to be in our hands by the end of this shift, do you hear me? He's on his own, he probably isn't armed, he likely doesn't know the area all that well, on foot at least. He'll be hiding out and easy prey. What the hell happened? "Lost him." Can't the plod run?'

The DS had rarely heard Serrailler rage. He was generally calm and measured, steely when he needed to be rather than explosive. Something on his mind then.

'Put a bomb behind them.'

'Guv.'

Another call came in.

'Serrailler.'

'Chief Superintendent, it's Razia.' She was Kieron's terrifyingly efficient and delightfully pretty secretary. Simon's bad temper evaporated.

'Hi, how are you? If he's working you too hard, tell me, I'll sort it. I have a private line.'

But he did not detect much of a smile in her voice.

'He'd like to see you tomorrow afternoon. Can you come in around five thirty?'

'What's happened?'

'Shall I tell him you'll be with him then?'

'All right. Yes, of course. Thanks, Razia. I'll be there.'

He guessed what it was, as he went down the corridor to the CID room. Kieron wanted him onside if there was any prospect at all of Richard's coming to convalesce at the farmhouse. He had put up with him after his bout of pneumonia the previous winter, and he was sending out warning shots that it wasn't going to happen again.

Simon did not blame him for a second.

Sixty-seven

'Hi, Grandpa – great to see you up.'

'My dear Sam, they dragged me to my feet and propelled me down the corridor when I was still under the influence of anaesthetic. They're exercise fiends.'

Richard came slowly into the room and sat down on the bedside chair. He looked tired and his face was drawn, but Sam knew that was normal.

'Do you want me to help you back into bed?'

'No, I'm fine here. It will be lunch any minute. Are you at work?'

'Yes, but lunch break. I had mine.'

'Canteen? The food is not very good. Or at least it never was in my day.'

'I don't go there, Rosie packs us both a lunch.'

'Ah, Rosie. Time I met Rosie, isn't it?'

'That's actually one reason I've come by. When are they discharging you?'

'Friday, all being well. You won't see me blocking a bed.'

'Are you going to Mum's? Because I maybe have a better idea.'

'Better in what way, exactly? I think I will get back into bed, if you'd give me a hand, Sam. Ridiculous how walking at snail's pace down a corridor can exhaust one.'

'Sure. Take your time, lean on me however's best.'

As Richard prepared to sit on the bed and lift his legs up, his pyjama jacket flopped open, to reveal the dressings covering the stitches that ran in a line across his chest. A long line.

261

It took some minutes for him to settle against the backrest and get his breath and colour back.

'What we wondered was this . . . maybe I'm wrong but it does seem to me you'd probably be happier going straight back home to your own place, your own bed and everything . . . and no stairs there either.'

A shadow of anxiety passed across Richard's face.

'I know what you're going to say and of course you can't look after yourself there but what if Rosie and I were to come and live in with you for a couple of weeks? I have nine days' leave coming up and Rosie has time off preparing for her exams. She wouldn't be around all the time but she would sometimes and so would I. We can cook and clean and generally look after you and take you for your walks and keep you company if you want and get out of your hair when you don't. What do you say?'

Sam refrained from telling his grandfather that the idea had not been his but Rosie's, who had sensed that Cat and Kieron were dreading the thought of Richard staying at the farmhouse again.

But Sam knew that she was right, was happy to agree, and besides, his grandfather's place was a good deal more comfortable than their flat. A couple of weeks looking after Richard would be no hardship.

'I would like to give it some thought,' he said now. 'But only on a practical level. It's extremely good of you and Rosie. I'm touched. May I let you know tomorrow? Would that give you time to organise things? I haven't had my discharge day finally confirmed anyway.'

'No problem. I hope you'll say yes. We'd really like to help. Oops, I've got to go. Are you OK right now, Grandpa?'

'I am indeed, Sam. And thank you again.'

Sixty-eight

Razia made a slight face as he reached the outer office, a face he would normally have interpreted as 'watch out'. She picked up the phone. 'Chief Superintendent Serrailler is here, sir . . . Yes, I will.'

She looked at him but now there was nothing to read into her expression. 'He says will you wait a minute. Have a seat?'

'No, I'm fine. How are you, Razia?'

'Good thanks. Excuse me, I've got to finish this before I go. I'm sure he won't be a moment.'

The offices at the top of the building were quiet, away from the almost non-stop clatter of footsteps on the concrete stairs and the swing and bump of doors opening and closing. The top landing had carpet and doors that hushed together. Otherwise, though, there was no air of luxury about anything in this station, for the Chief or for anyone. Perhaps Kieron's chair was better padded and swung round more smoothly. Perhaps his desk was a bit bigger. Perhaps not.

Razia's phone buzzed and she nodded at Serrailler to go in.

The sun was shining through the windows behind Kieron, who was standing up, behind his desk. He waited until the door was closed, and then before Simon could greet him said, 'I'm afraid this is going to be a formal conversation, Superintendent, and I've asked the ACC to come in on it. She'll be here any minute.'

'What on earth's wrong?'

'Ah . . .'

The door opened on the Assistant Chief Constable of under a year, Caroline Bugler, a woman Simon had found difficult, mainly because she clearly had no time for him, which didn't trouble him at all, but she had put obstacles in his way and made his life tricky on several occasions. He had picked up on gossip that she had not approved of his coming back to the job after his attack. He was not the only one in CID who had had run-ins with her. Now, she barely glanced at him. Kieron was in shirtsleeves, as usual in the overheated station, but she had on her jacket, buttoned, the pips on her shoulders glinting in the sunlight.

'Please sit down, ma'am. As this is a formal but not an official and minuted meeting, would you like to sit too, Superintendent?'

Taken aback, though still not worried, Simon sat on an upright chair by the desk. The ACC took the one next to it. Kieron sat down.

'I would like to say straight away that the ACC is here as a witness and an observer. I have looked into the circumstances and I have been fully briefed on the case throughout. As you know, a robbery was committed at Ash Farm. It was an expert job and well planned, and as intended, the householders were out when it took place. You, as the SIO, and after your investigation, took the decision to put a full news blackout on the incident. I wonder if you would explain your reasons for this now.'

It was so far from what he was expecting to hear – if indeed, he had expected anything – that Serrailler was caught unprepared and for several moments was silent, trying to marshal his thoughts.

'After visiting the house where the robbery took place and hearing from the owners, I took the view that this was a robbery that had been extremely successful, from the point of view of the criminals, and that as a result, they were likely to use the same MO to target another property, probably, though of course not necessarily, on our patch. If the incident was reported in detail in the media – extensively in the local media and perhaps in brief nationally – then they would go to ground and either move away completely and or lie low for some time before trying again. I know that these are highly professional operators and they are rarely careless, and certainly they are not opportunists. If the public and more particularly the residents of large properties which are either isolated or at least set apart, and with high-value contents, were alerted, they would take precautionary measures, tighten security and, above all, not fall victim to the pre-planned visits by the criminals, sussing them out. Those guys would know this and move off our police area, we would have no chance of catching them or of clearing up this case. On the other hand, media blackout would cause them to believe they had got away with it. Silence would make them feel safe, and try their luck again, perhaps straight away. There would also be far less chance of any copycat robberies. In other words, we would have a greater chance of apprehending them. With intelligence, preparedness – and a measure of luck.'

'Luck. Right. Do you think you made the right decision in the light of subsequent events, Superintendent?'

'Policing is so often a matter of balancing risks, of making choices – like medicine.' He looked at Kieron, who chose not to pick up on the underlying reference.

'As a result of the media blackout, the criminals – almost certainly the same ones – prepared another robbery of the same type, during which they were surprised by the householders – Mr and Mrs Declan McDermid – returning home early. In order to complete the job, they became violent, Declan McDermid was seriously injured and his wife was killed. As a result of the media blackout you ordered, Superintendent. Do you agree?'

'Not entirely . . . it was shocking and of course I deeply regret what happened but I don't agree that it would not have happened if details of the first robbery had been made public.'

'You are contradicting yourself, Superintendent.' The ACC clearly did not believe that she was obliged to remain silent and act as a witness to the conversation only. Simon waited for the Chief to remind her. He did not.

Neither did he wait for a comment.

'The reason you are here is because yesterday I received a complaint. It states that a decision you made resulted in a woman's death. Now, although you are not being accused of her death – that is, charged with manslaughter – and I believe that there are other factors involved and that the CPS would judge there not to be sufficient strength for a case to be brought against you, I am in no doubt that you made a serious error of judgement. Do you agree that you did not think through carefully the possible consequences of your decision?'

'No, sir, I don't. I had what I deemed very good reasons for making it and I would argue that it is not right to query the judgement with the benefit of hindsight, after other things happened. Yes, it may be that if I had made the opposite decision, the consequences would have been different. Or not. How can we know? You can't, I can't. I'm sorry if there has been a complaint – may I ask who made it?'

'I am unable to tell you that, I'm afraid.'

'You were sworn to secrecy?'

'That's a rather dramatic way of putting it. As I said, I am not at liberty to give you a name. That is by the by. Other things have gone wrong recently. You made the decision to have an industrial unit opened up because, presumably, you thought you had good reason to believe that the proceeds of one or both of these robberies were stored there, and possibly from other robberies we know nothing about.'

'I did have reason, sir, and I am fully prepared to defend myself against any charges on that score.'

'Yes, but don't you think you deployed far too many officers, both from uniform and CID, plus a dog handler? You then called on the fire service. An expensive operation, with zero results. This case is an example of one damn thing going wrong after another. And we've lost the prime suspect.'

'With respect, sir, that has nothing to do with me, that was purely down to the incompetence of uniform.'

'I would ask you not to raise your voice, Superintendent.'

'I'm sorry, sir, but—'

'But you're correct and I was voicing my own frustration not blaming you. Still, I'm not overly concerned about that – we'll pick him up, no doubt. He is without resources, wearing light clothing, he is almost certainly unarmed and he's definitely without a vehicle, he's trying to dodge and hide and he won't succeed for long. Let's leave that side of things. Having thought about you, the decision you made and the consequences of it, I believe an official reprimand is in order, and I intend to put that in writing. I do not think there are grounds for a formal disciplinary hearing, and I do not think it would serve any purpose to suspend you. But I do order you to take one calendar month's leave, on full pay, and that during this period you do not come into this station or contact your team or in any other way participate in police work. I think you should go away somewhere and recharge your batteries. Switch off. Do some drawing. And have a long, retrospective think about whether you might still benefit from talking to a therapist about the aftermath of the attack. Time doesn't always heal by itself and the longer you go on avoiding this, the more you are at risk of a serious challenge to your mental health and therefore to your work and your subsequent career. Is there anything you want to say to me?'

Simon felt a head of steam building up inside him, could almost see it, pressure about to explode out of his head into the room. He knew what he wanted to shout. 'You've been talking to my bloody sister and finding out things from her that are nothing to do with you. You have overstepped the mark as one of my family and used private information against –' He took a deep breath. Held it. Released it slowly.

'No, sir. When am I to start my leave?'

'At the end of your shift. That should give you time to hand over and tie up urgent business. You don't need to make excuses, you are not being disciplined and no one is entitled to an explanation. You say what you like, or you say nothing. Say more work has to be done on your arm, if you like . . . perfectly plausible.'

'Sir.'

'Thank you.'

Kieron stood up.

267

'You can't even meet my eye, can you?' But Simon did not say it, he simply left the room, wondering what the two Chiefs were going to say about him now that his back was turned.

Razia gave him a sympathetic smile. And why, Simon thought, would she do that if she didn't know most of it too?

Sixty-nine

'*Mummy, I think Kieron was meant to be here but he isn't.*'

'*Mummy, he still isn't here.*'

'*Mummy, Archie's mum says she'll bring me home but I don't know because shouldn't I wait for Kieron?*'

Cat listened to her messages as she left the meeting. Felix was sensible, if he had had to wait until whoever he was expecting turned up, he would simply go back into the music room. Kieron did most of the morning runs and rarely picked his stepson up, but on those rare occasions he had never failed to arrive on time. Cat had been to a meeting with Luke, Holly, the new partner in Concierge Medical, and the Healthcare Commission, and Kieron had said he wanted to get home early for once and picking up Felix would be a good reason to leave the station promptly. It would take a major emergency for him to forget. She did not know whether to be anxious or angry.

'Felix? Hi, can you hear me?'

'Hi, Mum, it's OK now.'

'Are you in Melanie's car?'

'Yes, and we're going to their house first, I was going to text you, I'm having tea there and doing my practice and she'll drop me home later. Hang on . . .'

'Cat? Mel here. I'm on speaker. Is that all right with you? They made a plan between them but I can easily bring Felix straight home if you want me to.'

'No, it's fine, if you're happy to have him. Thanks so much, Mel, you've saved my life.'

'Not a problem. Archie, will you STOP that?'

The phone cut off.

There was a bar of chocolate in the glove compartment. Lunch had been a salad but they had been too busy talking for her to eat much of it and now she had a hunger pain, but as she put the first squares into her mouth, her phone rang. The line was poor, the voice at the other end fading in and out.

'Is that . . . huuuuuuhshshshshsh . . . it's . . . shhhhhhhhhu-ubbbaaa . . .'

'Hello? I can barely hear you. Can you speak up?'

The crackling and hissing continued and the voice tried to find a way through but then it was clear enough for her to hear 'Is that the doctor?'

'Yes, Dr Cat Deerbon. Who is this?'

'It's . . . please listen, I can't speak for long, he's coming back. I need to tell you . . . shhhhshshshshsh . . . hsssssss.'

'Who is this? I'll call you back and we might get a better line.'

'Cshhhhhh . . . Carshhhhhh rie . . .'

'Did you say Carrie? Is this Carrie Pegwell?'

'Hello . . .'

'I can hear you. Carrie?'

'Yes, I can't be long, I need to tell you . . .'

'Go on . . . where are you, Carrie?'

'Shhhhhhhhhhhcrrrrwhhhhhhhhhhh.'

'Carrie?'

'It . . . it wasn't my fault.'

'What wasn't your fault?'

'He'll come back in a minute, we're in a motorway cafe place . . . he said it was the best thing.'

'What was, Carrie?'

'Shhhhhhhhhhhhhhhhssssssss . . . he didn't know I'd done that.'

'Done what? What's happened, Carrie? And which motorway are you on?'

'. . . wanted her to be . . . not that. Can you—'

'I can hardly hear you. Can you move so you're clearer?'

'Not . . . sorry, I know you . . .'

'You're so faint, this is an awful line. What motorway, Carrie? Just say the number. M what?'

Silence.

Cat waited until she was sure the line was dead, then called back but there was no connection. She tried again. Still nothing.

She hesitated, partly in case Carrie called her back, partly to think it through. She had checked with the Concierge office after she had found the Pegwells' house empty, to see if they had left a forwarding address but they had not even let them know they were leaving.

She could go back to the house but she wouldn't be able to find out anything more by peering in through the windows. They had rented from the estate so perhaps they would have some information, a forwarding address. Anything. She called the estate office.

'Mr and Mrs Pegwell left last week. They actually went before the end of their tenancy but he said they were going abroad. Something to do with his work but I didn't ask any more. They didn't leave an address with us, sorry.'

She did not know what to do. Was there a way to locate the call? Simon would know. Or Kieron. Was it a waste of their time? She tried the number again but there was still no connection and no voicemail message.

The traffic raced by on the main road behind her, but here a wooden gate led into a meadow and a party of long-tailed tits swooped down onto the hedge, swooped off again.

She drove onto the bypass. She wasn't going to find the answer at home and if she went to the station maybe Simon could put someone onto tracking Carrie's phone number. She might also have a word with her husband.

Simon came out of the building as she drove up, his face set and angry. Cat pipped her horn and he glanced across but then went on, walking fast to his own car, which he reversed without looking in her direction. He had seen her, she was certain. Something was on, then, some urgent job, which meant half a dozen others would come pouring out any second and no one would be able to stop and deal with her phone issue.

271

Unless it was a major incident, Kieron would not be going. Now she was here, she might as well try his office, but it looked as if he might have had a good excuse for forgetting to pick up Felix.

The reception area was empty, the rest of the building seemed quiet but otherwise much as usual. She met no one on her way to the top floor.

'Oh, hello, Mrs – Dr Deerbon. Does he know you're coming in?'

'No, but is he even here?'

'He is and there's no one with him. It's fine for you to go in.'

It seemed to Cat that Razia was looking at her with some meaning she couldn't quite pick up on. Then she turned back to her keyboard and Kieron came out of his office. He looked puzzled for a split second before realisation washed over his face.

'Oh my God – Felix!'

'It's OK, don't worry, Mel picked him up and he's gone home with them. What's the big panic – or maybe you can't tell me?'

Glancing sideways, Cat saw that Razia was still concentrating fiercely on her screen.

'Come in here.' Kieron hugged her. 'Do you want a cup of tea? Raz will oblige.'

'I'd love one actually, I haven't had anything to drink since lunch.'

'I cannot believe I forgot Felix. Darling, I am *so* sorry.'

'Don't worry, tea will make up for it, and I know you wouldn't forget if it hadn't been something very important. I won't go on asking.'

He opened the door and asked Razia for tea, closed it again, then hesitated before turning back to Cat. 'It's lovely to see you, goes without saying, but . . .'

'Why am I here. Yes.' She took out her phone, put it on his desk, and began to tell him the story from the moment Carrie Pegwell had first called her. It didn't take long and she had finished just as Razia brought in the tea.

'Tea on a tray with biscuits – perk of the job?'

'About the only one. Let me look at your call record.'

Cat poured their tea as he scrolled, clicked and tapped proficiently before saying it needed an expert.

'I can't do without my phone.'

'How vital is this?'

'Before that call I'd have said not very, I've just had this hunch about them all along – something not right – but now I think it's urgent.'

'I can get someone downstairs to see if they can find out where the call came from, but they may say it will take a while, or have to go to the techs at Bevham. What precisely is worrying you?'

She went over the whole case.

'When I saw her with the baby, she worried me, she hadn't bonded with it at all, almost didn't seem to know what to do with it, how to hold it – you know how some people are when they're given a baby and they've never held one before.'

'Can't say I do actually but I'll take your word for it. Do you think they've just gone away somewhere? Because there's no reason why they shouldn't.'

'I know. I don't know what I think – not exactly. I can't put it into words.'

'Try.'

She looked him in the eye. 'All right. I'm worried it might come to harm.'

'That one or both of them might have been abusing it?'

'I honestly don't know. Look, forget it. She'll hopefully ring me again and I'm probably making a drama out of it. Other than that, everything's fine – Felix is sensible, he rang me and he asked the school office if there'd been a message. But it's so unlike you, Mr Reliable – what was going on?'

If she could have put a word to it, Cat would have said that for a moment Kieron looked shifty, or at least embarrassed.

He sighed. 'I had to call Simon in and give him an official warning, with the ACC present.'

'Good God, what's he done?'

'Made a bad call which had dire consequences. Really, he took his eye off the ball. I can't say more.'

'No wonder he went past me with a face like thunder. I thought he was on an emergency job.'

'He was heading off on what is euphemistically called "sick leave" – I ordered him to take a month out and to see a therapist, either a police-appointed one or any other. He's got to deal with all this now, Cat.'

'All what?'

'Everything you talked to me about – his panic attacks, the feeling of apprehension, physical symptoms. It's clouded his focus, and that is in no way his fault, but it is his fault that he's failed to address it.'

'You told him this? You told him you knew things I had said to you in absolute confidence?'

'Well, I didn't actually put it so bluntly.'

'Either you did or you didn't, Kieron, and if you did, I'm absolutely furious with you because you betrayed me and him and you've landed me right in it and he won't come round any time soon. He trusts me and you've just blown that.'

'Of course I haven't. I'm sorry, but this has had work consequences, and that overrides everything else.'

'Your loyalty to me? Your relationship with your brother-in-law?'

'You know what the rule is, Cat, I made it clear to him and to you from the start. Family and everything that word means has nothing to do with and must never impinge on police matters. At home, he's my brother-in-law – in here, he is the DCS.'

She sat trying to take in what had happened and what now would. She felt angry and hurt, but the question staring her in the face was who mattered the most. Who came first with her? She got up quickly. 'Can I have my phone? I'll see you at home later.'

'We're not leaving this room until we sort out any misunderstanding about this. More than anything, you and I should not be angry with one another just because things aren't clear.'

'They're clear to me. I—'

There was a knock on the door and Razia put her head round. 'Call from DI Grayson, sir, thought you'd want to know, they've apprehended Jake Barber. Bringing him in now.'

'Excellent. At last.'

As Cat went to the door, her phone rang. It was still on Kieron's desk and he handed it to her.

'Could it be your Mrs Pegwell?'

The line was still not very good but she could now make out Carrie's voice.

'Dr Deerbon? I have to be quick. Please—'

'Carrie, listen, just tell me what's happened and where you are.'

'France. We're driving down France.'

'Are you all right? Are you in any danger?'

'No. I'm . . . but he won't want me to talk to you.'

'Why not? I'm here to help you, Carrie.'

'Yes . . . yes.'

'And you must know that or you wouldn't have rung. Why did you leave?'

'It was . . . something, something . . . Oh God.'

'It's all right. Just tell me, whatever it is, as simply as you can. Are you unwell or is your husband threatening you?'

'No, but . . . I can't say anything else.'

'Yes, you can, you know you can and you should. Carrie, is the baby all right? Carrie?'

'The . . . she isn't here, she isn't here. I have to go.'

Kieron was watching her intently.

'What is it?'

'I think we need to go to the Pegwells' house.'

Seventy

After he had gone home and changed into jeans and T-shirt, he went to the cathedral. The nave was empty but the restorers were working on the scaffolding high above. If he had been a praying man he would have knelt down in a pew and asked for help, an explanation, forgiveness, solace – what did his sister pray for? She was here almost every Sunday, and she popped in during the working day sometimes, just to kneel, just to have holy space around her. Simon was not an unbeliever – he did not know exactly what he was but he recognised a need within himself for something. Someone.

He wandered down the side aisles, looking up, at the roof, the pillars, the carvings, the angels, the wall painting towards the chancel, revealed only in the last few years and not complete. It showed saints ascending, ladders, devils, part of a wall, a cross, and a portion of azure sky, faded but still breathtaking, with gold stars looking as if caught in a fine net.

He had expected the rage and frustration to stay with him, to want to roar and lash out, to justify himself, make excuses, but all he felt was tiredness, and a sort of half-resolution. The Chief had been right. He would defend his reasons for making the decision he had, but he knew he was still affected by the attack and its aftermath, and knew that he had blithely assumed he was a hundred per cent better when he was only perhaps half that.

He shied away from thinking about a therapist, for now.

Meanwhile, he had four full weeks free, in which to do what he liked, with a view to restoring his mental health and getting back on track. He could go away but he had no idea where and he needed to finish the drawings here, then work on them quietly at home. There might be a long weekend in the Yorkshire Dales, or by the sea. No rush.

The face of the medieval head he was working on was familiar to anyone who had known any of the old residents of Lafferton, those who had been born and brought up in the terraced houses in the Apostles and perhaps lived there all their lives. There were few of them left, even fewer with the local accent, but this face belonged among them, though he had lived here seven centuries ago. Simon sat down and studied him. He liked the face. Over the next few days, he would come to know it as well as his own. He was soon absorbed in his work, delicately sketching in the frown lines on the face, the furrows down the sides of his nose. The carvers had taken pride in their detail.

He was startled out of intense concentration by the sound of the cathedral bells ringing the hour. They would be locking up and he had no desire to spend the night in the building. He packed up quickly, wondering what it would be like, how alarming, how uncomfortable. Felix would ask, how spooky, but he had no sense at all of that. For some obscure reason, his only concern, as he climbed carefully down the ladders, was how would it be if he went to sleep and woke to find the cathedral on fire.

Seventy-one

The estate had given permission and handed over the keys to the Pegwell house.

Three uniform. Three CID. Dog and handler. Kieron, observing. Cat.

Inside, it had the usual atmosphere of a place that had been emptied of everything personal, as well as of people. Tidy. Clean. Lifeless.

Cat did not want to get in the way, but she went into the study, the kitchen, the sitting room. Nothing. No trace. The Pegwells might never have been here.

'Clear.'

Footsteps on the stairs. The team gathered in the hall. The sniffer dog sat beside his handler. Obedient. Quivering.

'Garden. Sheds, outbuildings, garage.'

'There isn't a garage.'

'Go.'

It didn't take long. 'Over here.'

The bins were emptied out onto a plastic sheet. Baby clothes. Vests, T-shirts, bodysuits, tiny socks. Bottles. Teats. A steriliser. Nappies.

The handler put the dog to sniff a bundle, then released him with 'Go, Buster'.

They watched it dash about purposefully, first into the house, round every room, in, out, in, out, until there were a couple of barks from upstairs.

'He's found something,' Des, the handler, said.

The dog was standing in the main bedroom, beside the cot, tail wagging, barking again.

'Good boy, well done!'

'Right, it's the cot of course, because the baby was in it not long ago, but we'll get someone to sheet it up.'

Now the dog was racing down the stairs again and outside. Cat and Kieron watched as he made straight past the shed, over the terrace, then across the grass to the farthest corner where the garden ended in a ha-ha, beyond which was the park.

'They're unbelievable. How do they pick up a fragment of a scent?'

'Dogs smell molecularly. He doesn't need much.'

Buster began to bark insistently.

'Over here!'

Two of the men began to dig with extreme care, at the spot where Buster was standing, quivering again, giving out small yelping barks. After a few minutes, they set aside their spades and knelt, to begin shifting the soil by hand.

Cat had hers together over her nose and mouth. Kieron was close to the digging, looking down. Everyone was quite still.

'Something here.'

'The earth is loose, not been turned over long.'

Between them they lifted out a blue heavy-duty plastic sack, sealed at the top with tape, and set it on the grass.

'Chief?'

'Forensics have to take over now. I'll wait until they get here. You two, stay where you are, but nothing and nobody else is to go anywhere near. The rest of you can go. Thanks. Good work.'

He and Cat went back into the house.

'Poor little thing. Assuming . . .'

'It looks likely. Come into the kitchen, we can sit down here. You know that if it is the baby, you may well have to give evidence, don't you?'

'That's all right. Chances are there won't be much I can say, but so far as I was concerned, it wasn't the baby I was chiefly worried about. Perhaps I should have been but I was far more worried about Carrie's emotional and psychological state. It wasn't postnatal depression, or not only that, because she was mentally unwell when she was pregnant.'

'You said she was sure there was something wrong with the baby.'

'She had a feeling, a hunch. It's something many pregnant women wonder about, but once they have the first scan, which generally shows up any problems, they stop because they're reassured. But Carrie was convinced. Though of course she didn't have her antenatal scans anyway.'

'What about him?'

'Cold fish. I couldn't really make him out.'

'Would either of them have been likely to kill it?'

'Either of them *could* have done. But would they? It's impossible to answer that, Kieron. I don't think I'd be totally surprised at anything.'

He reached for her hand. 'Thanks. And about Simon . . .'

'No. It's all right. But he's been put on gardening leave – that's a big deal. How's he going to be?'

'It isn't like being suspended. That's a real blow to everything, pride, sense of status. You no longer have your authority as a member of the police force. You're barred from your station, your team look at you sideways, you become paranoid that everyone is talking about you behind your back, which of course they are. It's lonely, being under suspension.'

'How do you know?'

'Happened to me once, as a sarge. I made a wrongful arrest because I made too hasty a judgement and there was a complaint. It was sorted within three days but those were the longest three days of my police life. It's horrible, and ever since then I have hated suspending anyone in my force – no, actually, once I was delighted to do it, because she'd been passing on info to the press and it resulted in a colleague being in serious trouble. In my book, talking out of turn to the media is a hanging offence. Simon was unlucky . . . an understandable error of judgement led to someone's death. The chances are one in a million.'

'I should go and see him.'

'Yes, I think you should. But only you know how best to do that.'

'I'm an old hand.'

'You're a very good sister. And wife. Thanks for being onside with all this.'

'I'd say it's my job – however you want to interpret that. I think that's a van arriving.'

'It is. Are you all right to be there?'

'Kieron, I'm a doctor. Is there anything I haven't seen?'

It took little time for two forensics to set up the usual white tent inside which they were going to work. Cat and Kieron stood just inside it watching, as they cut open the blue plastic sack and out of it brought a small wicker basket, with a leather fastening, the sort of basket that might well have been meant for a cat. But it was not a cat which lay inside, wrapped in a white nightdress and a white shawl. White mittens. White bootees. A white crocheted bonnet with satin strings.

Cat let out a faint murmur. It was not possible to tell at this point if the Pegwell baby had been harmed but her face was unmarked. Candle-coloured, eyelids, faintly violet, closed over her eyes.

Another wait. No one felt like talking. Cat went for a slow walk around the garden, going over every visit, every conversation with both of the Pegwells, every detail of the way the baby had looked, smelled, felt.

The pathologist arrived, photographer close behind. She knew the doctor, Phoebe Donato, well. They had trained together, gone their separate ways, and met again here a few years ago.

'Cat. This one of your patients?'

Cat filled her in.

'Good. I will need your take, but I'll do my job first.'

The sun had come out, it was warm inside the tent, and strangely peaceful, as the pale translucent light shone on the baby.

'Beautiful,' Phoebe said. 'So beautiful.' She touched her finger to the baby's face.

It was all over an hour later. The garden and house were cordoned off with SOC tape, the tent was left *in situ*, the earth piled up in its neat mound, the burial site uncovered. The ambulance had taken the body, Phoebe following it, the photographer on the way to his next job.

'I'll go to the mortuary,' Cat said to Kieron. 'I must. You may be home before me.'

'Andy is liaising with the French in search of the Pegwells – might take some time. There's nothing else we can do right away. We'll need cause of death as soon as she can give it to us. I'm handing over now. I'm at Hendon tomorrow, then in London for a Home Office meeting.'

He put his arm round her as they walked to the cars.

'Never gets any easier,' Cat said. 'A child.'

'Nor should it.'

'No. I'd better check my messages before I go. I heard a couple ping in.'

One of the couple was from Sam. *Got update about Grandpa. Home tomorrow. Ring me.*

She read it out and noticed Kieron try to conceal his reaction.

'Knowing the hospital, they'll have sent him out a day early and he'll be on the doorstep as we speak.'

But Sam, between bringing up patients from theatre, told her the plan he and Rosie had made.

'It's all sorted, Mum, he's said he'd like it, so there's nothing for you to do, nothing for you to worry about. Gotta go, sorry.'

Seventy-two

Fern, I've got a day or so off. Late notice I know but how about dinner? Hope so. SS

   Hi Simon. Thanks, I'd love to! What time/where? x Fern

She deleted the x before pressing 'Send'.

Great. Do you know the Burleigh? In the bar there, 8? S

She picked up her phone and rang Kelly but it went straight to voicemail. 'Hi, it's me. I'm having dinner with SS at the Burleigh tonight. Only saying . . . catch up later.'

Shoes. Shoes. She had so many shoes and not one pair right.

It was only going to be dinner. He liked her, she was good company, and she definitely liked him. He just needed a change of scene, to get away from his drawing board. Above all, he didn't want to be alone in the flat, thinking. He had thought quite enough. A month's enforced leave was light punishment, and he knew he was lucky.

He showered, changed into a cream linen jacket and dark blue trousers, new, open-neck shirt and as he drove out of the close, he was sure of one thing. They were not going to talk about work.

'Hi! You got my message. I'm just waiting for my cab.'

   'Fern, you haven't heard, have you?'

   'What?'

   'Serrailler's been suspended.'

   'Don't be daft. Who've you been talking to?'

'Andy, but everyone knows.'

'Bollocks, Andy's got it wrong.'

'No, he was called in to the Chief earlier and word is he's definitely been suspended. The whole station's talking about it.'

'I bet they bloody are. But how can he have been, Kelly, you only get suspended when it's serious.'

'It was . . . remember the McDermids – she died.'

'Well, he hardly killed her, did he? Listen, the cab'll be here any second.'

'Fern, you can't go out with him now! Haven't you heard what I just said?'

'Listen, if you ask me, I think everyone must have got this wrong, but whatever, what's it got to do with me going out to dinner with him?'

'If you're seen to be on his side and consorting with him—'

'Consorting!'

'You're climbing the ladder, so a fat lot of good being his girlfriend will do you.'

'I'm not his girlfriend.'

'Your choice. But just think about it before you land yourself in a mess you can't get out of.'

Seventy-three

Carric got up again. Opened the windows, letting in river-smelling air.

'Close those or we'll have mosquitoes in here eating us alive. Come back to bed and try to settle down. What's the matter with you?'

'It's so hot. If I close the windows it will be even more stifling.'

'You don't want to be bitten and nor do I. All right, keep the window open but close the shutters, that will help.'

'It doesn't.'

But she did as he suggested, as usual, and then went back to her bed.

'Now for heaven's sake try to sleep.'

'I can't sleep. How long are we staying here? I don't like this hotel very much.'

'We'll move on tomorrow. Better not to stay in one place long. Brantome is about a hundred miles from here. Do you know it? Pretty little town.'

'I don't care where we go.'

She did not. It made no difference to her feelings and her thoughts. To what had happened.

'Did you do it, Colin? Just tell me.'

Colin sat up. 'Will you stop this? You cannot go through the rest of our lives asking me that, looking at me as you do.'

'You have to tell me.'

'There is nothing to tell, and I need to sleep.'

She waited. He went to sleep quickly but she had to let him go deep down before she dared move again. Her phone was in her bag by the dressing table.

He had done it. The baby had apparently been all right, and then he had gone upstairs and when she herself went back up to the nursery, she had been dead.

He had said it was a cot death but that they shouldn't call anyone, not the doctor, ambulance, anyone, he had said there would be too much fuss, too many people intruding, asking questions, too many official forms and police and doctors coming to the house. None of it was necessary when they both knew what had happened. What use would an investigation do? It wouldn't bring her back. He had seemed calm about it and to know exactly what he was doing, so she had agreed, because of course she had not wanted any of that. Yet when he had first told her the details of what they were going to do she had been horrified and frightened, she had said she would have no part in it, he would have to manage it by himself. She had sat at the kitchen table and waited.

He began to snore slightly. Another ten minutes by her watch and then she crept across the room to get her phone. She could not risk talking on it again, and in any case it was very late, but she could send a text.

Colin was not asleep, he was just good at acting as if he was. He had done it often enough and always convinced her. He could sense where she was in the room by the sound of her delving into her bag, retrieving her phone, tapping in the message and sending. He didn't know who she was texting and it really didn't matter. No one knew where they were and he planned to keep moving on for several weeks.

He knew what she had done and he felt deeply sorry for her, and yet he was without emotion himself. She had gone upstairs after he had, smothered the baby, and then after a moment or two, screamed for him to come. He had persuaded her that the child had died of cot death and of course she had agreed, as she had agreed that they would tell no one, that it was better to deal with it themselves. What good would the police and the doctors and a post-mortem and a coroner's report and possibly an arrest and charge, what possible good to anyone would all of those things do, most of all to the baby? It had not been difficult to deal with it and he had been careful, tender even, respectful. Thorough. And then they had packed up over a couple of days, and left.

He heard her slide the phone back, come quietly across the soft carpet in her bare feet. Get back into her bed. He waited. Carrie lay very still, as she always did. She was a silent and almost unmoving sleeper.

In ten minutes, he knew that he could relax and sleep himself. He was not angry with her, not at all, because he understood. She had believed that there was something wrong with the baby and she had not been able to bond with it or care properly about or for it, though she had seemed dutiful. But she had not been able to live with it or love it and so she had done what had seemed best.

Colin Pegwell slept.

Seventy-four

The lounge and bar of the Burleigh were pleasantly busy but there was always space, always the feeling of quiet relaxation, together with the first-class, attentive service. Simon had booked a table but arranged to meet Fern in the bar, where there were groups of low tables, sofas, comfortable chairs, as well as stools up at the counter. He ordered a glass of Sancerre, and found a table before a curved sofa and two softly shaded lamps. Voices were quiet, so was the ambient jazz. He ate two olives, took a sip, and leaned back. He felt better just for being here, he was looking forward to dinner and Fern's company. His meeting with Kieron seemed a world away, its outcome of no importance. A month's paid leave was a month's paid leave, enforced or not.

He finished his drink and ordered a tomato juice. Looked at the dinner menu. Saw two couples arrive, and a few people leave. Knew no one. He asked for more olives.

Waited.

The music went pleasantly, unmemorably on. Scribble music, he had always thought jazz, though he did not dislike it.

The barman glanced at him once or twice. The waiter replaced the olives.

After almost forty minutes, he checked his phone again in case he had somehow missed a call. Nothing. He rang her but it went straight to voicemail.

Had she had an accident? Possible but unlikely.

Then, as he walked across the bar, a text did come through.

So sorry, can't make it after all. F

He understood. The station gossip mill had been working overtime and the news had reached her – that he had been suspended, dismissed, taken down to the cells in manacles, that he was guilty of gross misconduct, that the Chief had wiped the floor with him . . . he had seen rumour expand and balloon out as it travelled round a station too many times, and he knew that the reaction was always the same. Keep out of it. Don't ask. Stay away. Better not to take sides. Better not to stick too closely, not be too good a friend, not be a loyal colleague. Mud sticks. Tar defiles. There is such a thing as guilt by association.

He was furious and yet he understood. She was young and climbing the career ladder, she had listened to them. 'You've got to watch out for yourself, Fern.'

The waiter gave him a sideways look as he went and the look said it all.

He was not going to eat dinner on his own, he would pick up a takeaway.

The lounge was busier, people were being led into dinner, others were just arriving. He went towards the door, stepping aside for a woman coming in.

'Simon?'

He stopped dead. Rachel was wearing a sapphire-blue silky dress. Very high heels.

She looked the same.

'I'm meeting a friend . . . are you just leaving?'

'Yes . . . I . . . I had a call. I have to get back.'

'Ah, work.'

'Yes.'

'I heard you had some sort of accident? Injury? I'm sorry, I can't remember exactly what, or who told me. Maybe it wasn't even true.'

'It was true.'

'Oh, I'm . . .'

'Rache, hi, hi, sorry I'm late.'

Another woman, smart, black suit, blonde hair. Red handbag.

'It's fine. Helen, this is Simon. Simon, Helen . . . she's a very old friend and we just reconnected by wonderful chance.'

'Yes, so loads to catch up on. Nice to meet you, Simon.' And she steered Rachel towards the bar, clearly assuming he was a passing acquaintance, to be got away from. Rachel did not protest.

He sprinted to his car. Seeing her again had been a shock. He did not know what he felt or thought, how she had seemed, other than generally friendly, apparently pleased to see him but no more.

Rachel. Yes. It had been good. He looked back on his time with her fondly.

Meanwhile, Fern Monroe had stood him up and he was hungry but he no longer felt like eating a takeaway alone in the flat.

He drove off, in the direction of the farmhouse.

Seventy-five

'Cat, it's Phoebe. Have you got a couple of minutes?'

'Hi. I have indeed. I'm lounging here with a gin and tonic and a good book. Been a bugger of a week.'

'And I'm not helping, dragging your mind back into it, but I'm sending my full report on the Pegwell baby tomorrow and I thought you'd appreciate a heads-up first.'

'I certainly would. You're a star.'

Cat's stomach tightened. The baby had been smothered? The baby had been abused? She should have spotted . . .

'The baby died of a bleed into the brain, but not as a result of trauma. She had an inherited coagulopathy.'

'Christ Almighty. That is something I could never have detected.'

'Nobody could, Cat. There were no symptoms, though she was possibly quite a sleepy baby.'

'She was. I told you, the mother had said she knew something was wrong, right from early in the pregnancy, but she had no antenatal.'

'This wouldn't have shown up anyway. So, that's my conclusion in a nutshell.'

'I can't tell you how grateful I am – not to mention extremely relieved.'

'There is one other thing – either one or both of the parents are carriers. There's a fifty/fifty chance of any child of theirs inheriting it, higher if they both have it, but that's very rare.'

'But symptomless, right?'

'Yes. What's happening with them?'

'They've vanished. It's thought they're in France – there's an urgent callout. They're facing charges – or they were until we knew the real cause of death. In any case, they have to come home.'

'But not for murder.'

'Thank God. I'll sleep tonight.'

'Lucky you. I have a suspected poisoning coming in. Let's catch up one day?'

'Please. And let's mean it.'

They always meant but somehow never managed it. Work pushed itself into first place, family second. Friendships suffered.

She heard the car but Kieron was in London tonight. Simon?

Simon. 'Hi.' He looked hesitant, as if unsure of his welcome.

'Hey, bro. Well met.'

He gave her a hug, meaning he wanted to forget his day.

'It's just me and Felix and we've eaten but you're welcome to forage. You look cool.'

'Thanks. I was meeting someone but they had to cancel.'

'Bloody work.'

'Indeed. I'll make a coffee – you?'

Cat shook her head. 'I've got a gin. Might be warm enough to have these doors open actually. Come in here when you've got what you like. There's some cold roast beef in the fridge if you want to make a sandwich.'

But the garden was in shadow and a breeze had sprung up. Cat closed the doors and settled back with Sally Rooney. Simon made his beef sandwich and coffee, put them on a small tray, using kitchen paper as a cloth and went out, stroking Mephisto on the way.

'Is it all right if I bring my food in here?'

Cat looked over her reading glasses. 'Well, you don't usually ask.'

He sat down and realised how hungry he was as he bit into the mustardy meat and fresh bread.

'So, what's been going on? Sorry, I was in a rush at the station.' He looked at her but for the moment Cat had decided that she was letting that whole subject lie.

'I had a phone call before you got here just now that took a weight off my mind – I hadn't quite realised how heavy a weight, to be honest.'

He nodded, mouth full, and she told him.

'I really would never have diagnosed that. Some things go right under everyone's radar until either they cause a catastrophic incident, or death, as in this case. There was no foul play, and nothing at all anyone could have done.'

'But you said the mother knew something was wrong.'

'Pregnant women do get intuitions like that. We've all been afraid in case something was wrong, that's normal, but a few not only have a very strong hunch but they're proven right. Carrie Pegwell was one of them. I couldn't have known about it but maybe I could have taken more time to have the baby checked again in hospital, because she went on being so sure, even when she had given birth and the hospital and I said it was fine.'

'We both deal with this same thing, you know. I should have thought through what the consequences might be of putting a media blackout on that first robbery but I didn't. Doctors, coppers – we make decisions all the time, we make judgement calls. Sometimes we're wrong, sometimes we're right, sometimes we just get away with it and sometimes we don't. Come on, you know all this. Neither of us is to blame – or, no, maybe we are, actually. Whatever. Who told us we were going to be one hundred per cent right for the whole of our careers? Did we think we were perfect just because we qualified?'

He put the last chunk of beef and bread in his mouth and picked up his coffee.

Upstairs, Felix had finished his homework, finished his chapter of *Harry Potter and the Prisoner of Azkaban*, but not finished his hot chocolate and it was now cool. He put on his slippers, went downstairs and slipped into the kitchen. He had heard his uncle's car drive up, then his voice, and now, his voice again, together with his mother's, from the sitting room. He put the mug of chocolate into the microwave, timed it and went over to sit on the sofa.

Felix put his hand out and started to stroke Mephisto. He stroked him for a few moments, then stopped. Stroked again. Touched the cat's head. His tail. Mephisto hated his tail being touched and always twitched it, even in sleep. But now, he didn't. Felix held his hand just under the cat's nose. Touched the tail again.

Then he jumped up and made for the sitting room. The microwave timer pinged.

'Felix!' Her son stood before her, white-faced, his eyes strange.

'Felix?'

'I think . . . Mummy, I think you should come and look at Mephisto.'

'Mephisto's fine, I gave him a stroke as I came out of the kitchen, not long ago.'

Felix turned to Simon, two points of pink flaring on his otherwise chalk-white face. 'Well, he isn't fine now. He's dead.'

Later, when they had sat with Mephisto, stroking him and talking to him, saying goodbye, Cat held Felix as he lay in bed sobbing, letting him do it, saying nothing. Understanding. He had never known his life or this house without Mephisto, who was older than Sam. He had even won over Chris, who had never liked cats but had gone from disapproval to acceptance, to affection.

In a while, Felix stopped crying, and blew his nose on the tissue she handed to him, but then lay on his back, sniffing, holding her hand tightly, eyes still full of tears.

'I know,' she said, 'I do know. He was a very special cat and we loved him.'

'I loved him.' Simon had come into the room quietly. 'I was going to head off, but if you'd rather I stayed . . .'

'No, it's OK.'

'No, it's not OK,' said Felix, 'I want you to stay. I want you to be here when we have his funeral in the morning.'

Cat looked at her brother.

'Then of course I will. It will have to be early though, Felix, you've still got choir and then school.'

'Sam and Hannah ought to be here.'

'Darling boy, I don't think either of them could make it but I will ring them both and tell them and I know they'll think of him.'

'They will be very upset and they'll probably cry. Even Sam will cry and I expect Rosie will too.'

'Yes. They will.'

'We'll find the right place for his grave and we'll have prayers and a hymn.'

'Maybe just prayers.'

'I am a *chorister*,' Felix said. Then he turned over and pulled the duvet up to his chin.

Seventy-six

At seven o'clock, Cat carried out Mephisto, who weighed very little now, wrapped in the fleece he had slept on, and as they went, Sam's motorbike roared up the drive and he and Rosie came to join them, walking to the far end of the garden and the lilac tree, close to which Simon had dug a small grave.

Cat placed the cat's body gently into it.

'Thank you, dear Mephisto, for being our family friend and companion for almost twenty years. Goodbye and happy hunting.'

Simon covered the place with earth. The minute they had got up that morning, Felix had found two pieces of plywood cut from an old apple crate, and once they were tied together as a cross, Cat had written Mephisto's name and the day's date and planted it at the head of his small mound.

There was a silence. Sam coughed and was about to move away, but then Felix took a couple of steps forward and, with complete composure, began to sing in his crystal-clear treble.

> Morning has broken
> Like the first morning,
> Blackbird has spoken
> Like the first bird.
> Praise for the singing
> Praise for the morning
> Praise for them springing
> Fresh from the word.

He stepped back again and bent his head and they all five stood in the early sunshine. Cat saw that Felix was dry-eyed now and that it was Sam whose tears flowed, to match her own, and that Simon was only just holding his back, and she thought of the affection that had surrounded one black cat all his life and now in death, and of the baby who had lived, died and been lovelessly buried in the soil of another garden.

But how did she know? They had seemed not to have cared for their infant daughter, but could she be sure of that? They had been opaque. She had not been able to read their hearts. Perhaps they had not even be able to do so themselves.

They walked back to the house, and she put one arm round Felix and the other round Sam. Mephisto did not need prayers and so Cat said hers silently, for the baby's parents who were desperately trying to escape but, in every important sense, never would.

Inside the house, Sam and Rosie hugged her hard and went. Felix ran upstairs to get his blazer, school bag and oboe.

'I'll take him in,' Simon said. 'I'd like that. I don't get much time with him now.'

She was about to say something when his phone buzzed, and instead she went to check on Felix and his gear.

Simon wandered back outside, looking down at his phone screen on which was a short message.

Sorry it was all a rush. So good to see you. Maybe meet up some-time? Rachel x